PENGUIN · SHORT · FICTION

"Not that the story need be long, but it will take a long while to make it short."

— Henry David Thoreau

# Champagne Barn

Norman Levine was born in 1923 and grew up in Ottawa. He flew with the RCAF during the Second World War, then returned to Canada to study at McGill. On graduation, in 1949, he went back to England with the manuscript of his first novel. For the next thirty-one years he lived in England, mostly in St Ives, Cornwall. He returned to Canada in 1980 and now lives in Toronto.

Levine had published two books of verse and a novel before he established his reputation with *Canada Made Me* in 1958. His other books include *One Way Ticket* (1961), *From a Seaside Town* (1970), *I Don't Want to Know Anyone Too Well* (1971), *Selected Stories* (1975), *Thin Ice* (1979), and *Why Do You Live So Far Away?* (1984).

# CHAMPAGNE BARN

## Norman Levine

Edited by Wayne Grady

Penguin Books

Penguin Books Canada Ltd., 2801 John Street, Markham, Ontario, L3R 1B4, Canada
Penguin Books Ltd., Harmondsworth, Middlesex, England
Penguin Books, 40 West 23rd Street, New York, New York, 10010, USA
Penguin Books Australia Ltd., Ringwood, Victoria, Australia
Penguin Books (N.Z.) Ltd., Private Bag, Takapuna, Auckland 9, New Zealand

Published in Penguin Books, 1984
Reprinted 1985
Copyright © Norman Levine, 1984
All rights reserved

Manufactured in Canada by Webcom Limited
Typesetting by Jay Tee Graphics Ltd.
Series design by David Wyman

**Canadian Cataloguing in Publication Data**

Levine, Norman, 1923-
Champagne Barn

(Penguin short fiction)
ISBN 0-14-007255-1

I. Title. II. Series.

PS8523.E85C52 1984          C813'.54          C84-098290-9
PR9199.3.L468C52 1984

For my daughters
Cassie, Kate, and Rachel

# Acknowledgements

The stories in this volume were selected from the following collections.

*One Way Ticket* © Norman Levine, 1961 (Secker & Warburg).

*I Don't Want To Know Anyone Too Well* © Norman Levine, 1971 (Macmillan, 1971; Deneau, 1982).

*Selected Stories* © Norman Levine, 1975 (Oberon).

*Thin Ice* © Norman Levine, 1979 (Deneau & Greenberg, 1979; Wildwood, 1980).

*Why Do You Live So Far Away?* © Norman Levine, 1984 (Deneau).

Eighteen of the stories have been broadcast on the CBC radio series *Anthology*. Most were written as commissions.

# CHAMPAGNE
# BARN

# Contents

# Introduction

In the spring of 1979 I was in Leipzig. My East German publisher had arranged a reading of my stories. It was to take place in a large bookstore. I was invited to sit, at the front, facing a well-dressed audience. On one side was an actor from Berlin. On the other an actress from Leipzig. They would read alternate stories. But before they began I was asked, unexpectedly, by the publisher to say a few words in English. I stood up and nervously said.

'I have been to Leipzig once before — but then I was above it.'

In the silence that followed I remembered my West German publisher coming to see me in Cornwall in late July 1970. He had flown from Hamburg. The first words he said to me as we shook hands.

'My brother was in the SS.'

This need to come clean (or not to) is only one of the things that happen when the present, unexpectedly, confronts the past.

It happened, somewhat differently, on a visit to Ottawa in the summer of 1972, when, obsessively, day after day I walked through the streets where I grew up. Something had come to an end. The houses were gone, the streets were being changed. And, of course, the people I knew were not there. I went away and wrote 'In Lower Town'.

Six years earlier, on another visit to Ottawa, I went to see my father. He was in a nursing home. When I left him before, I left an active man. Now he was dying. I went away and wrote 'A Father'.

I wasn't aware, when writing these stories, that I had stumbled on a way of getting at my material. That these confrontations would be brought about by simply making a journey. But, looking back, it now seems inevitable from the sort of life that I lived.

Because I wanted to be a writer, I left Canada for England in 1949. And for the next thirty-one years I lived in London . . . Brighton . . . Sussex . . . Devon . . . but mostly in St Ives, Cornwall. During that time I made visits back to Canada. And people from Canada came to see us in England. These journeys, across the Atlantic, are behind the stories: 'A Visit', 'Class of 1949', 'Grace & Faigel', 'Why Do You Live So Far Away?', and 'Champagne Barn'.

There are also domestic stories (by this time I was married, had a growing family) where the confrontations came from everyday life. And to cope with these pressures the journeys had to become imaginative: as in 'Ringa Ringa Rosie' and 'I'll Bring You Back Something Nice'.

At other times it was more complicated. As in the story 'By a Frozen River'.

This came to be written because I had read a short piece in the Penzance weekly, *The Cornishman*, of July 16, 1964. Of how the town's dis-used Jewish cemetery was opened for the first time in fifty years and a Jew from Redruth 'was laid to his last rest'.

Penzance does not have a Jewish community. But there was one, thriving and articulate from what I have read, that went back to the mid-eighteenth century. Over the years it gradually died until 'By the beginning of this century only Mr Morris Bischofswerder, son of the former minister, remained and at the High Festivals he would open the synagogue and recite the prayers in melancholy solitude. In 1913 he too left the town.'

As soon as I read that I saw a series of pictures — of a man leaving his house, walking along Morrab Road, to the small synagogue near Market Jew Street, opening the doors, staying inside to say his prayers, then locking the doors behind him, and walking home . . .

A year later (in 1965-1966) I was in Fredericton as the first resident writer at the University of New Brunswick. I stayed in a run-down hotel where I came across an unhappy marriage.

When I returned to England, I forgot about Morris Bischofswerder or the unhappy pair. I wrote a novel, *From a Seaside Town* (1970). Then a book of stories, *I Don't Want To Know Anyone Too Well* (1971). I had a few odd stories that I left out of the book. I sent these to Robert Weaver for his CBC radio series *Anthology*. He didn't want them. Instead he commissioned me to write a new story which became 'We All Begin in a Little Magazine'. After he read it he commissioned another new story. Wondering what to write about I remembered Morris Bischofswerder. And those pictures came back of a man walking alone through the streets of Penzance to go to an empty synagogue. At the same time I remembered this unhappy married couple I met in the run-down Fredericton hotel. Instinctively I felt there was a connection between these two, apparently, unconnected human situations. But I didn't know what it was. So I wrote the story . . .

Altogether the stories form a kind of autobiography. But, as in 'By a Frozen River', it is autobiography written as fiction.


November 11, 1983.                    Norman Levine

# Part One

# In Lower Town

When I was a kid we lived in Lower Town, Ottawa. The first house was on Guigues Street. It was a brick house on a corner. On one side was King Edward Avenue with its boulevard of tall elms, their roots above the ground. And on the other, our neighbour, Nadolny. Mr Nadolny, a nice-looking man in glasses, had been something different in Europe. Here in Ottawa he was, like my father, a fruit peddler. The rest of Guigues Street was French Canadian.

It was a large three-storey house and to help things out my mother took in boarders. All of them were recent immigrants from Europe.

There was Isaac and his wife Ethel. He looked like a professor with his monocle, and worked in a jewellery store, uptown, doing watch repairs. She stayed home as she was pregnant. She looked a bit scatty with her blonde fuzzy hair that she had difficulty in combing and her large pale eyes. She also couldn't speak English. When she started to have labour pains, she called out to me.

'*Me hoits. Me hoits.*'

They soon left Ottawa for California.

And there was Bobeh and Zaydeh Saslove. They were
brought over by their sons when they were in their late sixties.
He was short and quiet and had a long beard and not much to
do except go to the synagogue. In Poland, when he was
younger, he was something in wood. Here he would go to the
market and buy, in summer, the wood we needed for the
winter. I'd see him come back with the horse and wagon and
blocks of wood piled high in the back. He made several trips.
Then he spent days building the blocks of wood carefully
together along the back fence near where the wild cucumbers
were growing. He took care and had the wood meshed evenly
— like I tried to do on the table with matches. After he had
stacked the couple of cords he would ask us to come out and see
how it looked. We all said it looked very nice. A couple of days
later he would knock it all down flat. And then start to build it
up again, very neatly.

Both he and his wife spoke in whispers. And they ate their
meals together out of the same bowl.

My father only knew a few words of English and a few words of
French. When I was twelve — and we moved from Guigues to
Murray Street where just about everyone was either a fruit or a
rag peddler — I decided to help my father with the peddling.
When school finished at the end of June, I left the house early
in the morning and walked to the market and helped him load
the wagon with the fruit and vegetables that he bought from the
farmers and the wholesale stores. Then we went out — the
white horse pulling the high red wagon, over Rideau, along
Nicholas Street, by the jail, over Laurier Bridge and across the
Rideau Canal, to the first street with my father's customers —
Gloucester.

It was a quiet street with lots of trees and squirrels on the
grass lawns and wooden houses with verandahs painted green
or brown. In the middle of the block there was a greystone convent where someone was always practising the piano.

It was a humid day and our shirts were damp when my
father asked me to come along to his first customer — to help
break me in.

We walked around to the back of the house to the kitchen. He knocked on the screen door. A pretty woman in a black slip appeared. She was in her thirties. She began to ask questions as to the price of the corn, bananas, tomatoes, cucumbers, potatoes — and she started to squeeze the peach I had, as a sample, in my wicker basket.

'*Kvetch. Kvetch.*' My father began to talk in Yiddish. 'I bet you know how to squeeze in bed.'

I looked at the woman's face trying to pretend I didn't hear what my father was saying.

'How much are the spring onions,' she asked.

'Three bunches for twenty cents,' I said.

'Look at the prostitute,' my father said in Yiddish. (The word he used was *curveh* which is much more evocative.) 'You can see she's got nothing on underneath.'

'How much are the cherries?' the woman asked with a nice smile.

'Twenty-five cents a box,' I said looking at her brown eyes, the dark hair cut short, the even teeth.

I tried to keep a straight face while she gave me her order and my father went on in Yiddish about her likely performance in bed.

As we walked back to the wagon to get her order made up, I felt embarrassed and pleased. I had never heard my father say anything like this before. Without turning my head, I glanced at his face. He was grinning like a kid.

That evening, after he had put the horse in the stable and had his supper, he came outside to sit with my mother and sister on the verandah. He was the same self I had known before, in his chair, in the corner, by the hanging Morning Glory, drinking *Kik*. And looking at the families sitting outside on the other verandahs doing much the same.

I thought it was only my father who behaved differently away from Lower Town until I happened to be in one of the wealthier West End streets a couple of days later. By now I knew the route as well as the horse. And I used to go well ahead of the horse and wagon so I could sit on a verandah, in the shade, and rest a bit, while my father served his customers.

I was sitting like this when I saw old man Pleet — our neighbour on one side in Murray Street. He had a broken-down horse pulling a shabby wagon with old mattresses, old bedsprings, bottles, and sacks. But instead of calling out, 'rags, rags for sale', which he did in Lower Town; here he was saying, in a slight sing-song, the evening service of the synagogue. He didn't see me. As the horse and wagon went by I looked at his face. Mr Pleet was miles and miles away.

Another time, also in a wealthier street, in Rockcliffe, I saw Mr Slack, another rag peddler from Murray Street. He too was going through with his horse and wagon, very slowly, on this hot summer's day. Junk piled behind him. And calling out sadly in Yiddish.

'Thieves. Thieves. Nothing but a bunch of thieves live here.'

I guess they knew that once away from Lower Town they might as well have been in a foreign country. And they also knew that they could never become part of it.

But I would.

At school I not only played with the other Lower Town kids but also with kids whose parents only spoke English. Had nice jobs in the government. Some of these kids asked me back to their houses. (It was a very democratic place.) Large houses with maids and with trees and bushes and lots of grass. I remember being asked back by a classmate whose father was an aide-de-camp to the Governor General. And when I arrived there was a garden party on the lawn. Another time a doctor's son asked me. And after we had nice things to eat in a large gloomy house we went in their white boat along the Rideau Canal. Another time a blonde girl in the class asked me back for her birthday party — it was to a large house off the Driveway. We had to take our shoes off because the floors were new.

I couldn't invite them back to the house in Murray Street. They had made me ashamed of where I lived, of the house that smelled of the stable, and of parents who couldn't speak English.

I used to go to school day-dreaming that I had other parents, pretending I lived somewhere else. And wondering when I could get away from here.

I did get away when I was eighteen-and-a-half. The war was on. I joined up, went overseas. And after the war I went away to university in Montreal. Then moved over to England and thought I had put all this very far behind me.

But what happened.

Now that most of the fruit and rag peddlers are dead and Lower Town has changed — I find I am unable to stay away from it. It's become like a magnet. Whenever I can, I return.

The last time was this summer. I was supposed to go to Montreal and Toronto. But I only spent a short time in those places. I wanted to be in Ottawa. And though I stayed in a hotel with everything modern and neat, I kept on walking through the streets of Lower Town.

On Rideau, I went into Nate's delicatessen. And saw some of the kids I grew up with — children of those men who used to go out with a horse and wagon.

'You've really made it,' Moe Slack said, shaking my hand. 'Both *The Citizen* and *The Journal* gave you a full page. My wife bought your last book when it came out. I tried to read it but gave up halfway. Why don't you write dirty books? That's what people want to read.'

Harvey Reinhardt came in. He was the same size as me but had put on more weight.

'How are you?' I asked after he sat down.

'I'm impotent,' he said.

(Except he pronounced it important.)

'Ten years ago I had five dames going at the same time —'

'What do you mean?'

'I had five mistresses,' he said. 'My mother caught me with one at home. She said if you don't get that woman out of the house, I'll cut my throat right here. Do me a favour, I said, go out on the lawn. You'll spoil the carpet. I was a real bastard,' he said with a grin.

We were sitting around a table in the back of Nate's. Moe Slack and I were having smoked meat sandwiches and coffee and there was a blown-up informal photograph of Trudeau on the wall. We were now about the same age as those fruit and rag peddlers.

Harvey Reinhardt ordered a kipper.

'I like an English breakfast,' he said. 'The English girls — do they like to screw? What is it?' he asked me.

'It must be the damp climate,' I said.

'You think so.'

The kipper came.

'Have you ever gone to these group things?' Harvey Reinhardt said.

'No,' I said eager to hear more.

'Very high-class people,' said Harvey. 'They only let you come with your wife or your girl-friend. It starts off like a real party. They give you a drink. Then you start dancing. And you go off to a room. I had this beautiful twenty-five-year-old. And I couldn't do a thing.'

'Didn't she know what to do, to help things along?' I asked.

'She knew what to do,' Harvey said. 'But it was no good. She said she worked at some agricultural place with boars. And when some boars overdid it they were no good after that. I think this has happened to me. Later I saw her go off with some other fellow into a bedroom. I don't think I'll go again. There's no fun in it for me.'

'You're a millionaire — I hear,' Moe said to Harvey.

Harvey takes out a cigar and winces. 'Who knows,' he said.

I left them at Nate's, remembering when they were younger and I was younger, remembering their mothers and fathers, their sisters and brothers. And crossed into Lower Town.

The streets were being altered, the wooden houses demolished and other houses had doors and windows boarded up waiting to be pulled down.

I walked along York, Clarence, Murray, St Patrick, Rose, McGee —

Here my father's horse got loose from the stable and came out into the street one summer evening. And then the whole street came out to watch the men coax him back.

In this courtyard I saw a wedding where the young red-haired bridegroom broke the glass on the ground under the held canopy. And the white bits of fluff from the dandelions, or the trees, were blown across by the summer wind so that it looked like falling snow.

Here in winter we hired two horses and a long sleigh without sides. About ten boys and ten girls. We rode at night to the sound of bells on the harness. The overhead street light showed the hard-packed snow. And in the shadows, on either side, the wooden houses moved slowly by. We pushed one another into the snowbanks, then ran to get back on to the sleigh . . .

I came to the small park at the end of King Edward Avenue, sat on a green bench, and felt strangely timeless. The white Minto bridges across the hardly moving Rideau River, the swans, the blackbird in the tall grass seemed — like the streets — to be frozen like a photograph. And in an extraordinary stillness.

I went to see my mother.

'Where have you been?' she asked.

'I walked along Murray Street and St Patrick Street and down to King Edward Park.'

'I haven't been there for over ten years,' she said.

'They're knocking the wooden houses down,' I said. 'And changing the streets. Soon there will be nothing left of the place the way it was.'

'You'll see how nice they'll make it,' she said. 'All those wooden houses — that's past. We need high-rises, motorways. It will be a lot better. You can write about that,' she said. 'Tell how nice everything is here. Look at that high-rise across the park. At night, when the apartments put on their lights, it looks like a ship . . . You won't write any more about fruit and rag peddlers?'

'No,' I said.

'That's the old life — it's finished.'

She fussed over me, giving me things to eat. And as soon as I finished something on a plate she quickly took the plate away and I could hear her washing it up in the kitchen. Her whole flat was spotless, everything in place. After a while, all this neatness was getting me down. Until I went to look in the drawer of a dresser in the living room for the old photographs. And saw, to my relief, that the neatness, everything in its place, was only on the surface. That in the drawers, in the dresser, things were still jumbled up.

I looked at the faces of people in the Lower Town of not so long ago. There was a photograph of my mother in her early twenties with two friends . . . my father on the verandah . . . a family picture in front of the house . . . a photograph of my sister and me by a large elm on King Edward Avenue when I was five and she was three . . . a gathering at someone's wedding . . .

My mother watched me. 'When I'm gone,' she said, indicating the photographs with her hand and then sweeping her hand downwards. '*In* the garbage! *All* in the garbage. You'll see.'

She said it almost defiantly.

On the day I arrived for this visit men in yellow machines were busy knocking down the large convent on Rideau Street. I asked Harvey Reinhardt why were they knocking down a perfectly good convent?

'You can't make a buck out of a convent on Rideau Street,' he said.

A few weeks later all that was still standing was part of the chapel. I could see a large painting painted on one wall of the chapel. It showed a young nun in a black and sky-blue habit. And coming down from the top left of the picture, down to the upturned eyes of the nun, was a wide ray of sunshine. Several cherubim were in this ray of the sun. They had curly blond hair and wings.

On the day I left Ottawa the chapel had also been knocked down, the rubble cleared. It was all very tidy. Nothing to show that there ever had been a convent there at all.

# A Father

There is a picture of my father that is still around the house in Ottawa. It shows a youngish, handsome man with a magnificent moustache, waxed ends; a fine head with black wavy hair, and eyes that I know to be brown. That picture was taken in Warsaw. And to it belong the anecdotes: 'Man about Town', 'Friend of writers and painters' ('Yes, I knew writers. I used to buy them meals'), 'Owner of a shoe concern' ('You can always tell if the leather's good by the way it creases'). And 'Smuggler' — I'd like to think it was of diamonds.

I never knew that man.

The person I got to know in Ottawa was in his early forties, a fruit peddler. Slightly built, bald, with a sardonic face. And very emotional.

He was five-foot-four yet he had the highest wagon of all the Ottawa peddlers. It was painted a bright red. And it had, on its sides, wooden steps and iron rungs to help him get up to the driver's seat and to the wooden boxes where he kept the fruit and vegetables. Over the years the red wagon was pulled by a succession of second-hand horses — discards from the local bakeries and dairies. Yet even these nags could place him in

difficulties. The one that was around the longest was called
Jim. A heavy white horse with nicotine-coloured tufts, and a
delicate slow walk. My father jerked the reins. He said,
'Gid-yup.' He shouted, 'C'mon Jim.' He even used the whip.
But the horse ignored them all, until it was time to go home.
Then he would gallop — the wagon swayed as it went through
red lights, took corners flat out: father pulling back on the
reins, standing up, fists against his chest, red in the face —
until he turned into Murray Street.

Mother watching on the verandah took this running as a sign
that the wagon was empty and father had a good day.

Saturday was a fruit peddler's busiest day. And being
twelve, and not having to go to school, I'd go peddling with my
father. I'd walk along Murray Street (our lunch in brown
paper bags that mother made up), past the houses of sleeping
friends. Up King Edward Boulevard. Between the large elms
where I skated and skied in winter. Crossed the streetcar tracks
at Dalhousie. Hung around the Francais, looked at all the
stills. By the time I arrived in the Market the clock in the Peace
Tower showed after eight. And my father had bought the load
and loaded it on the wagon himself. He had left the yard,
behind the house, in the dark, before five.

When we came back that night he put the horse in the stable,
gave him oats, hay, water. And by the time he had unloaded,
washed, eaten, counted his takings, it was nearly eleven. Then
he joined the others outside. A whole street sat on the wooden
verandahs, in rocking-chairs, on the verandah steps, in the
shade of the hanging Morning Glory.

In winter, Saturday nights were spent in the kitchen around
the linoleum-covered table playing cards. The players came
from different parts of Ottawa. How much of these sessions
was due to gambling fever, I don't know. But some of it, I'm
sure, was just to get together with their own kind. They played
from Saturday night right through Sunday and usually Sunday
night as well.

The games they played were twenty-one and poker. And for
holding the game in our house mother collected ten cents from
each pot.

I'd watch. Standing behind the players' chairs, so I could see their hole cards. If they were winning they wanted me to stay behind them. They said I gave them good luck. If they lost, they said I was making them nervous, and I moved on.

Around ten I'd be sent to bed — school tomorrow. Upstairs, in the dark, I listened to the sounds of the game that came through the floor-boards and wondered when we would be raided by the police.

Nearly all the players were born in Europe and had come to Ottawa just before or after the first world war. There was Shalevsky — he used to deliver bread for a Lower Town bakery (he gave me rides on his sleigh) before he went into real estate. There was Joe — the youngest player (he was born in Ottawa) — he drove for the same bakery after Shalevsky left. Then worked as a porter at the Lord Elgin and told me marvellous stories of what went on in the hotel. He was killed delivering a new car from Toronto. There was Harry, our silent roomer, who worked for his cousin in a paper factory — he sorted the rags the rag peddlers brought in. He died of lung cancer. There was Mr Nadolny and Soloway, also fruit peddlers. And Sam Shainbaum who had a fruit store uptown then went into real estate. And I hear he's made a bit of money too. The only woman among the men was my mother. She won fairly consistently. My father always lost.

He made costly mistakes. He thought the ace of clubs was the ace of spades — in a flush hand. He mistook numbers. He took twice as long as anyone else to decide whether to call, pass, or make a bet. They always had to wait for him. And when he ran out of money he reached over for a couple of dollars from my mother's winnings — a habit she didn't like. After a while of his inept card-playing, Sam Shainbaum said.

'Why don't you give up, Moyshe?'

'You're spoiling the game,' Soloway said.

'Why do you have to think so long when you've got nothing,' my mother said.

'Just one more hand,' he pleaded with her having gone through five dollars of her winnings.

'You'll only lose it.'

'Just Nadolny's deal.'

He tried this time. He had a pair of tens showing, but he didn't raise. When the five cards were dealt my father passed to Soloway who had four hearts showing. Soloway bet a dollar and my father, who didn't have a dollar to call, folded up his cards.

Soloway began to rake in the money.

'I wasn't bluffing, Moyshe,' he said. 'I've got the flush.'

He turned up his hole card — a seven of hearts.

No one spoke.

'I didn't have to show it to him,' Soloway said angrily to the others.

On the next deal they missed him out. He watched the cards go to either side of him for a couple more deals. Then he got up and stood behind my mother. After that he didn't play any more.

Instead, he went on errands for the players. He went to Dain's on the corner and came back with a brown paper bag of soft drinks. He opened up the bottles, handed them around. In below zero he walked to the Smoke Bar on Rideau Street and came back with corn-beef, smoked meat, rye bread, that he made into untidy sandwiches, gave them to the players, and to me as well. And apart from a quiet game of casino, during the weekdays with his cronies who dropped in for a social call, no one played cards seriously with him any more.

In February 1944, I was on the last day of embarkation leave. I was sitting in the living-room with my parents, in a brand new pilot officer's uniform, waiting for a taxi to come to take me to the Union Station. Mother had cried earlier. She was sure I wouldn't come back. And as we waited she sat in the chesterfield chair staring in my direction. Her anxiety unnerved me as well and I remained in the chair not knowing what to do or say.

'You know this town called Chelm,' father said. 'A town of halfwits?'

I nodded, wondering what he was getting at.

'They were having trouble with a cat. They decided to get rid of it.' He got up from the chair and stood in front of mother and me. 'They went to the beadle and convinced him that it would be a blessing for him if he put the cat in a sack and went with the sack to the bottom of the river.'

My father paused.

'— the beadle drowned. The cat managed to get out and scrambled ashore.'

My father came over and touched me on the shoulder. 'The wise men had another council. They decided to tell the people to bring pieces of furniture. And the people of Chelm came back with brooms, tables, beds, chairs. Piled the stuff in a heap in the shul. Put the cat inside. Set fire to the wood. Locked the doors.'

My father grinned.

'The shul burned down. The cat feeling the heat leapt through the window . . . Then the wise men had another meeting. They decided to approach their hero, Abrasha — he killed twenty Cossacks in one pogrom. They told Abrasha to take the cat up their highest building, the old people's home, and jump.'

My father was speaking with eloquent gestures.

'Abrasha said a weeping goodbye to his wife and children. He took the cat in his arms. All of Chelm came to watch. He climbed to the top of the old people's home. The band played the National Anthem. When they finished, Abrasha jumped. Abrasha was killed. The cat, on the way down, wriggled loose and landed safe.'

My father was laughing. And I laughed because he was. And we both glanced to where mother sat. And though she didn't join us she had visibly relaxed. And suddenly I felt immensely proud of my father — who cared about those cards.

'Two liars met in the street,' my father said with growing confidence. 'And one liar said to the other: *Guess what I saw today —?*'

But the doorbell went. It was the taxi. We embraced and kissed and said goodbye.

I was riding away to war in a taxi. Along the streets I had walked and played as a child. Murray Street looked drab, empty, frozen. Solemn boxes with wooden verandas. Brown double doors and double windows. Not a soul was outside. On King Edward the snow heaped in the centre had a frozen crust. It glittered underneath the street lights. And the houses, on either side, in shadow, appeared even more boarded up, as if you would have to go through several layers before you found something living.

# By the Richelieu

Until I was eighteen I spent my summer holidays at the family cottage on the banks of the Richelieu south of Montreal and six miles north of the American border. Two miles away is the French Canadian village of Ile Aux Noix. There is an island in the river, opposite the village, with a decaying fort and a moat with shallow water. Water lilies and a thin green scum cover the surface. During the last war the fort was used as an internment camp for aliens.

I imagine that until the road was built, during prohibition, the river was busy. But though the channel is still occasionally dredged and the red and black buoys that mark its passage are sometimes re-painted, I have seen few riverboats go by. The only traffic now comes from the small hired boats with the sport fishermen. For alongside the channel the weeds are thick — so thick that sometimes I have been stopped, as the keel or the propeller became entangled.

The countryside is not exciting to look at. Even from the water. It is flat with a few isolated trees and farm fences. The farmers have small fields. They are all French Canadian. They grow wheat, corn, potatoes. Some have chickens and pigs. The two hotels along the bank shut in winter. They are there for the American businessmen who come down in the summer and fall to play cards, drink, and fish. For this part of the Richelieu has some of the best fishing I know. I've anchored by the red buoy, opposite the Grand Hotel, for muskellunge; trolled along the banks for pike; caught carp at night using a light and spearing them as they rose to the surface a few yards from the shore. There are also fine black bass and perch.

When I first knew the place it still hadn't been discovered by the tourists, although the signs were there — a cluster of stilt-cottages along the bank, nearer Montreal. And every spring afterwards, when I came down, the cluster of stilts grew and spread downwards to the border.

Until the arrival of the stilts the people by the river's bank lived in a few proud old cottages. The one my parents had was built by a priest — so village rumour said — who came from Rimouski to retire after he won a lottery. It was made out of wood: dark green with white trimmings, and a wide verandah went right around. The main highway was a quarter of a mile away. Between highway and cottage were empty, gently sloping fields. And between cottage and river there was a raised walk of rough planks. In spring the water came up the cottage steps so that I could take out the dinghy, the canoe, or the rowboat from the shed and push it down a few yards to float it. In summer I had to push the boats through mud. By the time I reached the deep water the bottom and sides of my feet were covered with mud and bloodsuckers.

Two miles down from the cottage, towards the border, the river had taken a small bite out of the land and left a cove. The banks of this cove are lined with magnificent elms. Whenever I was fishing or sailing near here I could see the hulk of a great house almost completely hidden by the trees. It was the largest house not only along the river but, I imagine, between Montreal and Montpelier. Sometimes I caught a glimpse of rough greystone, large windows, the wood a shiny black. I knew, as did everyone else around here, that the house belonged to the Dobells.

Like individual people I sometimes think that families also have a zenith to their lives. So many generations have to be sacrificed in the climb upwards for another to have that bright interval at the top. After which there are others to take the decline down. From what I have read, and what my parents told me, I would say the Dobells were at their peak in the early 1920s. Arthur Dobell, who now had the house, was of the fifth generation. He rarely occupied it. Usually he was photographed at his place in Bermuda, or in Palm Beach, or somewhere on the Riviera.

My first meeting with him was accidental. It was a hot August afternoon. I had taken out the sailboat with the drop-keel — which was a present for my sixteenth birthday from my father — and combined sailing across the river while at the same time trolling for pike. I let the line out, tied it to my big toe, and felt the pleasurable vibration of the spoon travelling through the water. Not far from the island I felt the bite. Then I saw him drift alongside. He looked like some seaweed with the sun shining on it. I had a spinner with three hooks. One of the hooks had got inside the edge of his jaw, through the flesh, and come out again. I could see the blue end of the hook clearly. I landed him and clubbed him to death. I didn't know how much he weighed. But when I held him, he stretched from the bottom of the boat up to my hip. Then the storm came. I had to tack several times to make any progress back. When the rain began I decided to shelter in the cove in front of the Dobell house.

He must have watched me for he came running out. Helped me tie up, dismantle the mast, and brought me inside where I rang my parents. Then we stood by the large windows and watched the lightning over the river and the rain. It didn't look like easing up so he suggested that I spend the night there.

I had changed my clothes. Wrapped myself up in one of his expensive dressing-gowns that had a silken Miami-Florida label sewn inside with his name. And sat in front of the fireplace. He had lit the set-logs and quickly they were blazing away. It was the most impressive fireplace I had seen. A cement roof and sides came out from the wall like a canopy and leaned into the room.

'My great-grandfather built it from pebbles in the cove,' he said quietly.

Thousands of small round bluish-green stones were set in the cement.

The butler came with hot cocoa. I sat there drying out, feeling warm, and looked around the room. At the heavy curtains; the large oil paintings on the wall of the dead Dobells; the heads of stuffed animals, all with the same brown sad eyes.

'How heavy was the fish?'

'I dunno. But it's the biggest pike I've ever caught. Do you want it?'

'No thanks.' And he smiled, a shy, understanding smile.

I was disappointed when I first saw him. He looked much smaller than his photographs, about five foot seven, slightly built. And his appearance was entirely commonplace. Yet I felt a curious sense of detachment about him. Though I knew he was in his late thirties, he looked amazingly young. Money, I thought, had preserved him, like it did this house.

'Do you like music?'

'I can play the trumpet,' I said, 'not well.'

He went to the gramophone by the wall, lifted the lid until it locked in its hinges, took out a collapsible steel handle, wound it several times, then put on a record.

'Are you going to college?'

> *In the morning*
> *In the evening*
> *Aint we got fun?*

'No. Not till next year.'

'What will you study?'

'Medicine.'

> *The rent's unpaid, dear,*
> *We haven't a sou.*

*But life was made, dear,*
*For me and for you.*

'Isn't that Sir Nicholas Dobell —?'

I indicated the second-last oil on the wall. It was a rhetorical question — the Kipling face, the weak eyes looking through glasses, the high white collar — were familiar to me from photographs. Nicholas Dobell had, along with Charlie Conacher and Sweeney Schriner, been one of my schoolboy heroes. I knew he had lectured in surgery at McGill, then went on to a chair in Cambridge, and was knighted just before he died.

The record stopped.

'When you graduate,' he said. 'I hope you'll go and see something of this world. I don't think these boys did. Not until it was too late. It's not the same after thirty. You begin to look at things differently. And things begin to flatten out . . .'

And again I felt that curious feeling of tenderness emanate from him and with it the sense that it was impersonal. It was the kind that one usually gets from a doctor.

For the rest of that summer I was often in this house. I went sailing in his yacht up and down the river. Sometimes we swam out to the white raft anchored in the middle of the cove and lay there and got brown. And sometimes I was with him for meals when the butler brought the food to one of the wicker tables under the large striped beach umbrellas which were stuck like mushrooms on the lawns. He introduced me to various dishes. He taught me how to make a passable omelette. He taught me what little I know about wines. There was always a phonograph handy, portable ones on the yacht and in the house, which he would take out on to the lawns and keep playing records — they were only records of the twenties. It was in his library that I first came across Hemingway, Fitzgerald, and Faulkner. He taught me to drive his Plymouth coupé with the white tires and we raced along the highway flashing by the empty fields, the slow river, the signs showing how many more miles it was to *Morgan's*. On week-ends he took me into Montreal or Ottawa — and bought me a small present, usually a book — and then to one of his favourite restaurants, or to a country place by the Lakeshore. Meals with him were always an event.

I guess all of us have a favourite period in our lives. That summer was mine. It was one of those times that now, looking back, I realise how much it influenced my life. What I sometimes tend to forget was just how easy it was to live it, without much thought. Although I did sometimes wonder — especially at dusk when I saw him on the lawns against the large house, a solitary figure watching the sun set over the river behind the trees — why someone as likeable and with so much money had no visitors. I had the feeling that he only used Ile Aux Noix in the sense of a retreat. That away from it he was quite a different person. Certainly the impression of an irresponsible playboy created by the papers and gossip did not bear out in what I knew of him.

The next summer he was away. I received a post-card from Antibes in June. A month later another card from St Tropez. In the fall I went to McGill and began my pre-med. Then the war came. I joined the RCAF and went overseas. And I heard no more of Dobell. When the war ended I went back to McGill, got my degree, then took six months off and visited parts of Europe and Africa that Dobell had told me about.

I intended to practise in the east — but things didn't work out that way. And after a few stopping-off places in Northern Ontario, I found myself in Vancouver, which was very pleasant. For ten years now I have built up a fairly successful practice, married, have a son and daughter, friends, and a fair amount of cash to do the things I wanted to do. Then last summer something curious happened.

I became homesick for the east. At thirty-four, with youth definitely over and middle age relentlessly approaching, I found myself turning more and more to my roots and the friendships those bred. And though I have very close friends on the west coast I felt that I wanted to go back to the places and the people with whom I had the formative experiences of my youth. I seemed to have reached a point where I wanted to take a look backwards and sum up an epoch in my life, so as better to go forward. I felt a curious lack of completion. The momentum of youth was dying down without regenerating a new passion. And although I'm interested in medicine, I cannot say that it grips me totally.

So I flew back. Spent the first three days in Montreal. Montreal was a reassurance. It had not changed too much. Not along the parts of Sherbrooke Street I knew or walking along St Catherine . . .

The water still dripped from the gargoyles of Christ Church Cathedral and at noon the carillon at St James's played its tinpenny tunes. At the corner of University the man who sold *The Star* and *Gazette* (under the turning clock of the Bank of Montreal) looked, with age, even more like Ernest Hemingway. In Phillips Square the pigeons pecked at soaked bits of bread and in the pools of water the sharp reflections of Birks and Morgans, the statue of Edward VII, and the taxis on either side; while a Jehovah's Witness stood with a copy of *Awake* in his hand. At night, the gay neon of the restaurants, the films, the delicatessens, the grey buses. And above them the three sweeping searchlights probing aimlessly through the low clouds. While at the end of each intersection the black shape of Mount Royal with the lit stubby cross on top.

. . . Except it was a different person now seeing this. And though I kept bumping into acquaintances, and bits and pieces of my past, there was the inevitable disappointment. I suddenly wanted to go back to Ile Aux Noix.

My father had sold the cottage just after mother died and had come out to Victoria. There was really only Dobell. I sent him a telegram on the off-chance that he might be there. When I returned to the Mount Royal that evening there was one waiting: LET ME KNOW WHEN ARRIVING CHAUFFEUR WILL MEET TRAIN — ARTHUR

The chauffeur who met me at St Johns was new and had nothing of the servant about him. Although he wore the traditional dark double-breasted suit and chauffeur's cap — on him it looked a masquerade. He was stout, short, and slightly bowlegged. The face, although clean shaven, was swarthy. He looked like a well fed peasant. We talked on the drive in. I said he was new. 'A little over a year — You have pleasant journey — You are tired at end of day —'

His English was full of copybook phrases and he volunteered on his own that he was Hungarian. Outside. A few lights of farmhouses and lights by the river and patches of water in the fields lit up by the moon. I asked after Dobell. He appeared non-committal. 'He has waited to see you.'

He was waiting in that room with the oil paintings and the stuffed animal heads on the walls. I was prepared for the usual signs of old age, but not what appeared a different person. He was thinner, and this made him even smaller. His face was long and sallow, empty of any kind of expression. He rose to meet me, and his legs, bent at the knees, dragged across the floor. His hands hung near his chest like a pair of lifeless claws, and they shook. The left hand more than the other. When we grasped hands, there was no pressure in his. He said.

'It is good to see you.'

But there was no emotion in his face. All vitality seemed to be drained out of him. I must have talked to cover up my embarrassment. But he stopped me.

'I imagine this is a shock to you.'

The left hand began to tremble more than the other, and the right hand went over to steady it.

He still spoke quietly but the voice was coarse and less distinct. And looking at him I wondered if the brain was still active in the man and was only imprisoned by this shell of a body. I had, professionally, diagnosed as soon as I entered that Dobell had Parkinson's disease.

At supper, the chauffeur was also the butler; but Dobell hardly touched the food.

'Tell me what happened to you. I saw in the paper that you did graduate.'

I told him of the west, marriage, the family, wartime flying. He listened. But there were many silences. And there was an unhappy quality about the silences.

The cook was also the maid. She was also new. A German girl who spoke a shy English, in her twenties, pretty, with prominent cheekbones and high breasts.

I waited for him to tell me his story. But he didn't. Sometimes while I was talking the trembling hands forgetting to hold on to each other would creep up to the chest, and then he would remember and bring them down again.

The room hadn't changed. Except that his portrait was added to the others on the wall. It was painted the way I remembered him.

He appeared to be exhausted quickly, and we went to bed early. I had the same room as that first time. There were dried pussy-willows in the small ornamental brass vase on the dresser, and a picture of himself, as he used to look, on his yacht, with me beside him. In one corner were several of the portable phonographs, and stacks of old records.

I don't know what time it was when I woke up. My light was still on and the wind was blowing the curtain from the window. I heard a cock crowing. I looked at the window — it was dark outside — and saw my face in the glass. I waited, and heard it crow again. Only instead of coming from the ouside it seemed to come from somewhere in the house.

I put on my dressing-gown and went out. There was a small night light on in the hall and I could see from the landing straight down to the large room with the paintings and stuffed animal heads. The room was in shadows except for a wedge of light from the door to the kitchen which was open. Then I saw the chauffeur come out of the shadow of a corner, in his bare feet and long winter underwear. He was shuffling in front of the cook, who also had her clothes disarranged, her hair loose, and who kept making furtive little gestures of trying to escape, while the chauffeur kept following. He continued to stalk, shuffling his legs, and holding his hands lifelessly up in front of his chest in a cruel parody of Dobell. Then suddenly he leapt up, arms and legs flung out, and gave a crow of a cock.

Finally he cornered her — gave one more pathetic shuffle, then a vigorous crow — and hugging her to him like a bear, he lifted her off the ground. She immediately threw her arms around his neck, her legs fastened around his buttocks. Then he carried her inside the lighted door of the kitchen. I returned to my room, went back to bed, and listened as the clock in the house struck two.

In the morning I was awakened by a cock crowing not far from the window. It was the real thing this time, it sounded asthmatic. Then it was answered by another cock, some distance away. I dressed and went outside.

The morning had a fresh clean smell. The air cool. In front of the house leading to the elms and cove, the lawn was beautifully kept — the slugs moved like pieces of slow rubber across the cut grass — but where I remembered similar lawns on the sides and behind the house, there were chickens.

I watched the birds come running — heads forward, flapping wings, sometimes leaving the ground — as the chauffeur brought pails of food to the small, rough, wooden houses. While the roosters stood on the roofs of the houses, stretched up their necks magnificently, and crowed.

From the kitchen a nice smell of coffee and the cook greeted me shyly and asked if I would like three or four eggs with the bacon. Then the chauffeur returned.

'You like my hens? I ask Mister Dobell if I can have them. He say to me OK. In the back. We start in the back but soon they need more room. Now we have the sides.'

The cook said something in German to the chauffeur.

'You like a drive, sir. Mister Dobell never wake until midday?'

I suggested we drive down the river to where the cottage was.

There were stilts on either side of it, all deserted. The old road had not been mended and the car climbed and heeled and swung sideways as it went in and out of the large holes. I went down the gravel path. My parents' cottage looked shabby compared to the stilts. Two planks were missing in the raised walk. The grass had overgrown. The flagpole was no longer on the lawn by the mountain ash. I looked around and for a while it brought back sadly the happy time I had here. I peered inside one of the windows. Whatever furniture was there was draped in white sheets.

The chauffeur watched me.

'I used to live here,' I said.

'Once upon a time ago?'

'Yes.'

'You now come back?'

'No. I don't think I could, even if I wanted to.'

We drove back in silence. Passed the low fields. A few horses were grazing. A child stood on a hay-wagon. The wind lifted her skirt above her head. She waved in our direction. I waved back.

Back to the house, and a chicken squawked as it ran in front of the car. Dobell was sitting in a large chair on the flat stone porch looking out to the elms and the river. He was bundled up in a black winter coat, hands in a muff. From the kitchen I could hear the chauffeur and the cook talking in German. They had a radio on, and a girl with a husky voice sang about 'Real Love'.

The chickens were supposedly kept behind the wire fences, but some had come through holes, or over the top, and were invading the front lawn and the approaches to the river. I watched a honey-brown rooster head off a couple of hens then, as they settled down to peck at the earth, he nervously lifted his neck and crowed. And he was immediately answered from the other side of the house. And then another crowed even further away; before he replied.

Dobell sat there motionless.

A duck waded in the shallows. And across the river swallows became thick like carboned dust from a sharpened pencil. While in the marshes splashes of red flew slowly by, then settled black on the reeds.

Occasionally we spoke, but it was only small talk. Our thoughts remained and we had nothing to say, because there was nothing for either of us to discover in each other. I knew I would leave soon. And I also knew that I would not come back, except as a tourist.

# Part Two

# In Quebec City

In the winter of 1944 when I was twenty and in the RCAF I was stationed for seven weeks in Quebec City. Fifty newly-commissioned pilot officers were billeted in an old building right opposite a cigarette factory. It used to be a children's school. The wooden steps were wide and worn in the middle but they rose only a few inches at a time.

We were sent here to kill time and to learn how to behave like officers. Some of the earlier Canadian Air Force officers who were sent to England lacked the social graces. So they had us play games. We took turns pretending we were orderly officers, putting men on charge; being entertainment officers, providing the escort for a military funeral. We were instructed how to use knives and forks. How to make a toast. How to eat and drink properly. It was like going to a finishing school.

To keep fit we were taken on early morning route marches. We walked and ran through frozen side-streets then across a bridge to Lévis. And came back tired but with rosy cheeks. Evenings and weekends were free. We would get into taxis and drive to the top to the restaurants, have a steak and French fries, see a movie. On Sunday we behaved like tourists. Took pictures of Champlain, Bishop Laval, The Golden Dog, the Château Frontenac, the wall around the city, the steps to Lower Town. There was not much else to do.

On the Monday of the second week Gordie Greenway, who was make-believe orderly officer for the day, came up to me during lunch.

'Someone rang asking for you.'

'Who?' I asked. I didn't know anyone in Quebec.

'They didn't give their name,' he said and continued his tour of inspection.

Next morning I received this letter.

> Quebec, 15 January.
>
> Dear Pilot Officer Jimmy Ross,
>
> We would be honoured if you could come to dinner this Friday. It would give me and my wife much pleasure to meet you. If I don't hear from you I'll take it that we'll see you on Friday at 8.
>
> Yours sincerely,
> Mendel Rubin.

Out of curiosity I decided to go. The taxi driver drove to the most expensive part, just off Grande Allée, and stopped at the base of a horseshoe drive in front of a square stone building with large windows set in the stone.

I rang the bell.

A maid in black and white uniform opened the door. She said with a French accent, 'Come in, sir.'

I came inside. A short man in a grey suit came quickly up to me, hand outstretched. He wore rimless glasses and had neat waves in his dark hair.

'I'm so glad you could come,' he said smiling. 'My name is Mendel Rubin. Let me have your coat and hat. You didn't have any trouble getting here?'

'No,' I said.

He led me into the living-room. And introduced his wife, Frieda. She was taller than he was, an attractive dark-haired woman. Then to their daughter, Constance. She was around seventeen or eighteen, like her mother, but not as pretty.

'It's nice of you to ask me over,' I said.

'Our pleasure,' Mendel said. 'Now, what will you drink. Gin? Scotch? Sherry?'

'Gin is fine,' I said.

He went to a cupboard at the far end of the room.

'Where are you from?' Frieda asked.

'Ottawa.'

'I've been there a few times,' she said. 'But I don't know it well. Mendel knows it better.'

He came back with drinks on a tray.

'Do you know the Raports?' he asked. 'The Coopers? The Sugarmans?'

'I went to school with some of the kids,' I said.

'Where do you live?'

'On Chapel Street — in Sandy Hill.'

'It's a part of Ottawa I don't know too well,' he said. 'What does your father do?'

'He's a teacher.'

The maid came in to announce that dinner was ready. And we walked towards the dining-room.

'I bet it's a while since you have had a Jewish meal,' he said.

'Yes,' I said, 'it is.'

'Every time a new draft comes in I find out if there are any Jewish officers. Then we have them up. It's nice to be with your own kind — you can take certain things for granted. Come, sit down here.' And he put me in a chair opposite Constance.

While Mendel talked I had a chance to glance around the room. The walls were covered with some kind of creeper. The green leaves, like ivy leaves, clung to the walls on trellis-work and to the frames of oil paintings. The paintings looked amateurish, as if they had been painted by numbers.

'Do you like the pictures?' Mendel asked. 'My wife painted them.'

'They're very good,' I said.

Mendel did most of the talking during the meal. He said they were a tiny community. They had to get their rye bread, their kosher meat, flown in from Montreal.

'We're so few that the butcher is only a butcher in the back of the shop. In the front he sells antiques.'

After the meal we returned to the other room. It was dimly lit. The chandelier looked pretty but did not give much light and there were small lights underneath more of Frieda's pictures on the walls. The far wall was one large slab of glass. It had now become a mirror. And I could see ourselves in this room, in the dark glass, as something remote.

Mendel went to a cupboard and brought back vodka, brandy, whisky, liqueurs. He gave me a large cigar.

'You know what I feel like after a meal like that? How about we all go to the theatre?'

'But it's half past nine,' Constance said.

'How time goes when you're enjoying yourself,' Mendel said. Then he glanced at his wrist. 'I think we'll still catch it.'

He walked to the far cupboard and turned on a radio. A Strauss waltz was being played. It stopped. And a commercial came on. A sepulchral voice boomed *Rubins*. And then *bins* . . . *bins* . . . echoed down long corridors. Then another voice spoke rapidly in French. And again *Rubins* and the echoing *bins* . . .

He switched the radio off.

'I have a store in Lower Town. We carry quality goods and some cheap lines. Sometime I'll show you around, Jimmy. But what can we do *now*?'

'Mummy can play the piano,' Constance said. 'She plays very well.'

'I don't,' Frieda protested.

'Play us something,' Mendel said.

Frieda went to the piano and played 'Für Elise,' some Chopin, while we drank brandy and coffee and smoked cigars.

At eleven he was driving me back to the children's school.

'Do you know the one about the two Anglican ministers?'

'No,' I said.

'There were these two Anglican ministers,' Mendel said. 'One had seven children. The other had none. The one with the seven children asked the other. ''How do you do it?''

' "I use the safe period," the other minister said.

' "What is that?"

' "When *you* go out of the house — *I* come in. It's safe then." ' And Mendel laughed.

'Here's another one. There was this Jewish tailor. He had an audience with the Pope. When he got back to Montreal they asked him — How was the Pope? A nice looking man, the Jewish tailor said. 36 chest, 32 waist, 28 inside leg . . .'

'Are you taking out Constance tomorrow night?'

'Yes,' I said.

I took her to a movie. We got on fine. On Sunday we went out in the country to ski. We skied for miles. We both seemed to have so much energy. We came to a hill. I went down first. She followed and fell at the bottom. I picked her up and we kissed.

'My father is worried that I'll be an old maid,' she said laughing.

I didn't think he needed to have any worries about that.

'He only lets me go out with Jewish boys.'

We kissed again.

'Am I going to have a baby?'

'You don't have babies that way,' I said.

'I know. But I have a girlfriend in Montreal. She told me that if you let a boy kiss you like that you can become pregnant.'

Although I was being thrown together with Constance (we went out often for meals, saw movies, had romantic night-rides in a sleigh, wrapped in fur skins, behind the swaying rump of a horse) and Mendel took me to several hockey games, it was Frieda who interested me. But so far I didn't have a chance to be alone with her. If Mendel was there, he didn't let anyone else talk. If Constance was there, I was expected to be with her.

I managed to get away from the children's school early one Wednesday and drove up to the house to find that Mendel and Constance had driven to his branch store in Three Rivers.

'I was just reading,' Frieda said when I came into the living-room.

She got me a drink. We stood by the glass wall looking out. It's a nice time, in winter, just before it gets dark. When the snow on the ground has some blue in it, so has the sky. She told me she came from Saint John, New Brunswick. Her father was a doctor. At seventeen her parents sent her to Montreal. 'Just the way we worry about Constance.' She met Mendel. He was working for his father who founded Rubins Department Store in Quebec. She was eighteen when they married and Constance came along when she was nineteen.

'After she grew up I found I had nothing to do with my time. And when I tried things — I found that I can't do anything well. That's my trouble.'

'You had Constance,' I said.

'Anybody can do that,' she said contemptuously.

'I tried to paint — I have all these nice pictures in my head — but look how they come out. I tried writing — but it was the same. Sometimes when I'm walking through the streets or in a restaurant I see something. It excites me. But what can I do with it? There's no one I can even tell it to. I hardly go out of the house now. I feel trapped.'

'Can't you leave Quebec City,' I asked, 'for a short —'

'I don't mean by this place,' she interrupted. 'I mean by life.'

This conversation was out of my depth. I didn't know what she wanted. But her presence excited me far more than did Constance.

'I taught myself French,' she said, 'so I could read Colette in the original. And I have my flowers. Do you like flowers?'

'Yes,' I said. 'I like the colours.'

She led me to her conservatory. It was full of orchids: yellows, purples, oranges, pinks, browns. There were other exotic flowers. I didn't know their names. There were several creepers overhead. And a smell of jasmine from the one in a corner. But it was mostly orchids, and in different stages. Some were only beginning to grow. They seemed to be growing out of stuck-together clusters of grotesque gooseberries. While outside the glass of the conservatory the thick snow had a frozen crust. It glittered underneath the street light.

She showed me a striped orchid on the table in the hall. Yellow with delicate brown stripes. It was open and curved in such a way that you could see deep inside the flower.

'Do you know how Colette describes an orchid?'

'No,' I said.

'Like a female genital organ — I have shocked you,' she said with a smile. 'I would be promiscuous if I was a man. I know it. I wouldn't be like my husband. He's so old-fashioned — telling jokes. But I can't do anything like that here. If I step out of line —'

She broke off again. She would talk, follow a thought then, unable to see it through, break into something else.

'Poor Mendel. He desperately gets in touch with every Jewish officer who comes to Quebec. Throws them together with Constance as much as he can. Then they go overseas. They promise to write. But they never do.'

I heard a car drive up. Mendel and Constance came through the door.

'Hello Jimmy,' he said, 'boy, it's a cold night.'

The other officers complained about the deadness of the place. They thought I was lucky. Some met girls through a church dance or YMCA do. A few could speak French. Most tried to pick something up.

Tucker and Fleming got into trouble accused of raping a waitress. But nothing came of the charge, except they were confined for three days to a make-believe cell in the children's school.

I tried to get Frieda alone again. The only time I did she was upset. The boiler for the conservatory had broken down.

'You must get a plumber,' she appealed to me. 'If I can't get a plumber the orchids will die.'

I got a taxi into Lower Town. Half an hour later I came back with a French Canadian plumber.

Our time was up. To see how we finally passed, the Air Force organised a ball at the Château Frontenac and all the eligible debutantes from Quebec and district were invited to be escorted by the officers. I took Constance. She looked very nice in a long white gown. We danced, made small talk, ate, passed the carafe of wine around. The dance band played.

> *To you he might be just another guy*
> *To me he means a million other things.*
> *An ordinary fellow with his heart up in the sky,*
> *He wears a pair of silver wings.*

Air Marshals made speeches calling us 'Knights of the Air', 'Captains of the Clouds'.

At half past two we left the Château Frontenac. In the taxi, driving back, she pressed against my side.

'Don't you love me a bit, Jimmy?' she said softly.

'I'll be gone in a few days,' I said.

She took my hand.

'Would you like to come up to my room? You'll have to be very quiet up the stairs. I'll set the alarm for six. You'll have to be out by then.'

I wondered how many times this had happened before.

'Is this the first time?' I asked.

'No,' she said. 'There have been other officers passing through.' She squeezed my hand. 'I didn't like them as much as you.'

'How many others?'

'Four. This will be my fifth time.'

She spoke too soon. After we went up the stairs, closed the door of her room, undressed, got into bed, turned out the light. I found I couldn't do a thing. And she didn't know how to help things along.

'Let's have a cigarette,' I said, 'and relax for a while.'

I lit one for her and one for me. We lay on our backs, the cigarette ends glowing in the dark.

I was wondering what to do when I heard a door open. Then footsteps. Someone was walking in the corridor. The footsteps stopped by the door.

'*Con, are you awake?*'

It was Frieda on the other side.

We both stopped breathing. I was aware of Constance's body becoming tense with fear.

'*Con — you awake?*'

She was lying beside me, not moving, breathing deeply and rapidly.

I waited for the steps to go away, the sound of a far door closing. I put out our cigarettes. And took her easily.

'That was the best yet,' she said softly. 'Goodnight darling. Wake me before you go.'

She lay on her side, away from me, asleep. And I lay on my back, wide awake. I listened to the ticking clock, her regular breathing, and thought of Frieda.

Just after five I got out of bed, dressed, disconnected the alarm, straightened the covers on Constance. And went out of the room, down the stairs, and out.

It was snowing. Everything was white and quiet. It felt marvellous walking, flakes slant, very fine. I didn't feel at all tired. I heard a church bell strike and somewhere further the sound of a train whistle, the two notes like the bass part of a mouth organ. The light changed to the dull grey of early morning and the darker shapes of a church, a convent, came in and out of the falling snow.

Next day we were confined to barracks and told to pack. That afternoon we boarded a train onto the waiting troop ship. Two weeks later we docked at Liverpool.

Those first few months in England were exciting. I moved around a lot. A week in Bournemouth in the Majestic Hotel. Ten days leave in London. Then a small station, in Scotland, for advanced flying on Ansons. Then operational training near Leamington on Wellingtons. Before I was posted to a Lancaster Squadron in Yorkshire.

Perhaps it was this moving around? Perhaps it was being twenty, away from Canada for the first time, spring, meeting new people, new situations? The uniform was open sesame to all sorts of places. And there were plenty of girls around. I had forgotten about the Rubins except to send them a postcard from London.

In the middle of May I had an air-letter, re-directed twice, from Constance.

Dear Jimmy,
    I hope this will reach you soon. Probably you are having all kinds of exciting things happen to you . . . meeting new people . . . doing things . . . and you have long forgotten me and the time we had together. I hope not.
    Now my news. We're just getting over winter. It's been a long one, cold and lots of snow. The next lot of officers after you was a complete washout. But the one now has three Jewish officers. Shatsky and Dworkin from Montreal. And Lubell from Winnipeg. None of them are as nice as you . . . but I like Shatsky best . . . he's fun.
    Don't forget to write when you can and take care. Mummy and Daddy send their regards. We all miss you.
                                              Love,
                                              Constance.
Two months later I received a carton of Macdonald cigarettes from Mendel. I bet he sent them to all the boys he had up at the house.

When the war was over I went back to Ottawa and to the job I had in the Government with the construction department. In my absence I was promoted. Now I'm assistant to the Head.
    I have not married. Nor have I been to Quebec City, until this winter when I had to go to New Brunswick to see about a proposed dam that the Federal Government was thinking of putting some money in. The plane stopped at Quebec longer than the usual stop to let off and pick up passengers. A blizzard was blowing. Flying was off. A limousine brought us from the snow fields of the airport to the Château Frontenac. We were told the next weather inspection would take place at three.
    I took a taxi to Lower Town. Down St Jean. Down the slope. Passed the cheap stores, the narrow pokey side streets, horses pulled milk sleighs, the bargain clothes hung out, the drab restaurants. An alligator of schoolgirls went by along the sidewalk with two nuns behind. Even with the snow falling, men

doffed their hats to priests.

I found Mendel standing in the furniture department. He looked much older and fatter in the face, the skin under the jaw sagged, and the small neat waves of hair were thin and grey.

'Hullo Mendel,' I said.

He didn't recognize me.

'I'm Jimmy Ross,' I said. 'Remember during the war?'

'Of course,' he said becoming animated. 'When did you get in?'

'Just now. The plane couldn't go on to Fredericton because of the snowstorm.'

'Let's go and have some coffee next door,' he said. 'It's been snowing like this all morning.'

We went to the Honey Dew and had coffee. The piped-in music played old tunes. And bundled-up people with faces down went by the plate glass window.

'I wish Constance were here,' he said. 'I know she would be glad to see you.'

'How is Constance?'

'She's living in Detroit. Married. He came over from Germany after the war. His name is Freddie. He's an accountant. They're doing well. They have four kids. And she's expecting another. How about you?'

I told him briefly what I had done.

'There were some good times during the war —' he said.

'How is Frieda?'

'She died a year and a half ago. I married again. Why don't you come up to the house and meet Dorothy.'

'I'd like to,' I said. 'But I don't want to miss the plane.'

'They won't take off in this weather,' he said. 'But here I am telling *you* about airplanes.'

'That was twenty-two years ago,' I said. 'I couldn't fly the airplanes today.'

We got into his black Cadillac with black leather seats. He drove through all white streets, the windshield wipers going steadily, to the house.

Dorothy was the same size as Mendel, plump, a widow, very cheerful.

'This is Jimmy Ross,' Mendel said. 'He was a young Air Force officer here during the war. He used to be much handsomer.' He went to the far cupboard to get some drinks.

The oil paintings, the creepers, the flowers, were gone. A rubber plant stood by the plate glass wall. Its bottom leaves shrivelled and brown.

'Would you like some sponge cake?' Dorothy asked.

'She makes an excellent sponge,' Mendel assured me.

'I had lunch on the plane,' I said. 'I can't stay very long.'

It had almost stopped snowing. Only the wind, in gusts, blew the loose snow up from the ground and down from the roofs.

'Where are you from Mr Ross?' Dorothy asked.

'Ottawa,' I said.

I felt awkward. It was a mistake to have come.

Mendel drove me to the Château Frontenac.

'Don't forget,' he said. 'Next time you're here let me know in advance. We'll have you up for dinner.'

'You used to tell me jokes, Mendel,' I said. 'Where did they come from?'

'From the commercial travellers. They come to see me all the time. All of them have jokes. I had one in this morning. What is at the bottom of the sea and shakes?'

'I don't know,' I said.

'A nervous wreck,' he said and smiled. 'Here is another. Why do cows wear bells around their necks?'

I said nothing.

'Because their horns don't work.'

He stopped the car outside the entrance of the Château Frontenac.

'When I write to Constance I'll tell her I saw you —'

An hour later I was back in the Viscount taking off from a windswept runway.

# South of Montreal

I see her now. In some kind of outer garment. Tugging at her lapels, as if it was falling off her shoulders. Her hair, a thin yellow-blonde, piled on her head. She was short. A pale white skin. A largish nose. Talking elaborately, closing her eyes, exaggerating her gestures. She could have been an actress in some melodrama. Her name was Madame de Wyssmann. She was French Canadian, a widow, a Huguenot. She wanted her nephew Paul to be taught English so he could go to Loyola in the autumn. That's how I came to Ile Aux Noix. I was to tutor Paul and two of his school friends — Jose and Mario — Guatemalans.

I am writing about the summer of 1947. I had just finished third year at McGill when I went down to the Placement Bureau to get fixed up with a job for the summer months. Madame de Wyssmann's letter giving me detailed instructions on how to get to Ile Aux Noix was written in the largest copperplate I had seen.

On Saturday I left Montreal, by bus, over the light green bridge. And soon we were on a straight highway that led to the United States border. The countryside was uninteresting. Flat

fields to the river that went parallel to the highway with a few
stilt-cottages along the bank. The river had overflowed, in the
spring, and the receding water left reeds wrapped around the
fence posts and around the trunks of the few trees.

I got off the bus by a telegraph pole that had a sign *Riverside
Hotel* pointing down a dirt track to the river. Further along the
highway was the white church steeple where the village began.
Across the road, this fine row of poplars, a nice lawn, and a
large stone house with white trimming.

'You had no trouble getting here?'

'No Madame. Your instructions were exact.'

'Would you like some coffee? This is *Madame*.'

She introduced me to a gentle old woman in a brown print
dress. She had bow legs and a small moustache. She spoke a
few sharp words of French to her.

'*Oui Madame*,' the old woman said and went to the kitchen. It
could have been the voice of a young child.

My room was the small room on the first floor. The staircase
was wide and wooden and it went up to a large tapestry on the
wall showing a battlefield. There were shelves of books, mostly
Balzac. And old *Geographical Magazines*. It was a fine house, cool
in the middle of the summer, high ceilings, with highly polished wooden floors. Downstairs, the dining-room was filled
with Japanese screens and other stage props.

'They were given to me by Tyrone Power, Senior,' Madame
de Wyssmann said at lunch. 'He and his wife had a cottage
next to us by the river. I taught young Tyrone Power how to
drive a car. We had fine times — but the interesting people
who were here are gone.'

Her nephew Paul wore glasses and had straight blond hair
that he combed back. He was tall but flabby. The two
Guatemalans were quite different. Jose had brownish skin,
curly dark hair. Until he met me he thought everyone in the
world was a Catholic. Mario was smaller, white skin, sharp
features. He mispronounced ham and jam at the breakfast
table. They both laughed and smiled a lot.

On the second day, after breakfast, when they had gone to
the village to collect the mail, Madame de Wyssmann came up

to me.

'Sir,' she said. 'Look what I have found in his bed.'

She gave me a rubber doll. It was a miniature nude woman about seven inches long.

'What am I to do?'

'Boys are boys,' I said.

'It's all he thinks about. He's got this little DP in St Johns. A little prostitute.' She closed her eyes and spat out the word. 'He thinks of nothing else.' Then she said something in French that I didn't understand. 'I was married. But we slept in different rooms. He had to knock if he wanted to come in.'

'Were you married long?'

'Six months,' she said. 'He was a lawyer. Much older. I came straight from the convent.'

At the end of the first week I realized why I was here. It wasn't only to get her nephew into Loyola. Madame de Wyssmann believed that English meant refinement. And French Canadian was coarse and provincial. I was expected to help her nephew make the change.

Lessons meant reading from *Vanity Fair* (it was the only English book she had on her shelves) and giving them words from my *Pocket Oxford Dictionary*. We had spelling classes. We had reading classes. We talked in English. Sometimes it was on the grass around the stone house with the poplars overhead. And I would hear Madame de Wyssmann playing Chopin on the piano. More often I would go with the boys down the dirt path to the river. And there, from a garage, take out one of the three boats: the sailboat, the canoe, the dinghy. And we'd go up and down and across the Richelieu River while they read or spoke English.

I liked the river. There were red and black buoys in the middle to mark the channel. But weeds had claimed most of it. And sometimes the boat got so tangled in them that it came to a stop. Towards dusk swallows would come over the water. And the beeches, the mountain ash, looked very pretty along the shore.

One Saturday afternoon, when there were no lessons, Paul and Jose and Mario came back to the stone house with a large white bird. They said they found it in a field by the river. It couldn't fly. Paul carried it very gently in his arms. Outside the kitchen door he tied its long thin legs to a fence post with a leather strap. Then pulled it by the neck until it stretched fully out, its whole length parallel to the ground, the wings hanging lifelessly by its sides. Jose came out of the kitchen with a knife and gave it to Paul. And Paul began to saw away at the neck. The wings began to beat the air. They were large wings. They made a swooshing sound and sent the dust on the ground moving. All the time he was fiddling away at the neck, the bird was stretched out as in flight, the wings beating powerfully, until he cut through.

At next day's lesson, in the sailboat, I had Paul alone. In the middle of reading Thackeray he said. 'I am French. Why should I try to be like the English.'

'It doesn't hurt to know another language,' I said not very convincingly.

But it was the end of that lesson. After that, Paul went through the motions. He was too polite for any more outbursts. But with his aunt, even when I was there, he spoke French. When she said.

'Paul. *Speak English.*'

He just smiled.

It had been the nicest summer I ever had in Canada. I had gone out fishing by myself, trolling for pike. I had gone out with old Lacosse (he did errands for Madame de Wyssmann). He taught me how to spear carp at night using a light. And I had gone with him in his old Ford when he collected the mail from the tin letter-boxes stuck crookedly to the wooden posts of the farms. And also on Saturday afternoons when he went for frogs. He had a sack and a stick. And he would knock the frogs and put them into the sack then sell them to a Montreal restaurant. One afternoon, late in August, the frogs began to leave the fields by the river and move to the higher ground. But they had to get across the highway. The cars killed most of them. There were thousands of dead frogs lying on the highway for the next few days.

In the first week in September the trees had started to change colours. The swallows flew lower over the river. And splashes of red settled slowly on the reeds by the shore. The nights were cold. One day the radio said snow was expected. Jose and Mario were excited. They had never seen snow. They wanted to stay up all night. So we all did. The moon was large and orange. It was cold. But no snow fell.

Next day it was time to go away. I thanked Madame de Wyssmann. I said I enjoyed the summer. Old Madame brought me some coffee. Paul and Mario and Jose shook my hand. Then we went outside and stood by the spot where Paul had killed the bird waiting for the bus to come.

'What are you going to do?' Madame de Wyssmann asked.

I said I would finish university. Then go somewhere. Where I didn't know.

'You are young,' she said. 'You still have your ambitions.'

# The English Girl

There was that first shy meeting on the Arts Building steps with
her folder of drawings and then going for a meal at the wind-
mill where it was dark and the woman played Strauss waltzes
on the cello and we had frankfurters and sauerkraut under a
bust of Bach. Then a film, and on the ride back from Notre
Dame de Grace in a taxi I leaned over and kissed her neck.

Later she said. 'I could tell it was going to be different. No
one ever kissed my neck, first.'

The taxi stopped outside Royal Victoria College. I walked
with her up the wooden steps. 'Let's meet tomorrow,' I said.

'All right.'

'— for breakfast.'

Before eight next morning we had breakfast together in the
Honey Dew on St Catherine. She was dressed in a skirt and a
leather windbreaker. She had her small hammer with her and
was going out on to the mountain for her geology period.

Afterwards, we met every day.

She would wait for me underneath the clock in the Arts
Buildings, or by the Roddick Gates. And I waited for her in the
Union, or in the sitting-room of Royal Victoria College, with

the silkscreen reproductions of Canadian landscapes, the maroon leather chairs, and others like myself waiting for their girls.

Then we would go for lunch.

To Ben's for smoked-meat sandwiches; to Fern's for spaghetti and meat-balls; to Chicken Charlie's; to Pauzes for oysters; to Slitkin and Slotkin for a steak. And in the evening to Aux Delices, the LaSalle Hotel, Mother Martin's, Brother Andre, The Bucharest, or to a restaurant in Chinatown . . .

We were both living away from home.

We met because I was editing the university's literary magazine and she wanted to do the illustrations. Later, when she darned my socks, she would return them neatly done up in a parcel with a small cartoon showing her darning socks and the balloon above her head said:

'Look you, I'm expensive.'

But she wasn't. Apart from the first month of meals out and drinks in hotel cocktail bars, we settled down to the Saturday night film, the late night meal. But we still spent most of our free time together. During the day, when we didn't have lectures, we went for walks or to various Honey Dews; or to some of the greasy spoon restaurants near the university for coffee.

She had come over to Montreal because her mother, a widow, didn't like what England was like after the war. And, I suspect, because it was easier to get into a Canadian university than into a good English one. She was tall, a longish face, dark eyes, a nice smile, black unruly hair. She hadn't made many friends at university. Others thought her quiet, reserved. They put it down to her being English. I found all this very attractive.

I had not long come back from wartime flying in Britain, a confirmed pro-Britisher — probably because I had such a good time there.

Wartime England meant, for me, a life of abundance, carefree good times, new experiences. I was attended by a series of batmen, all old enough to be my father. We ate in a fine mess. A string quartet played for us while we had our Sunday dinner. We lived well. We had lots of money to spend. The uniform gave us admission to all sorts of places. The English assumed that anyone who was an officer came, like their own, from the same kind of background. They didn't know our lot had spent a couple of months, before coming over, at a finishing school in Quebec City where we were taught how to eat with a knife and fork.

And when I came back to provincial life I didn't want the other kind of life to end. Going to university was just a means of filling in a few years until one could, somehow, return to England. So it was no accident that I was attracted to the English girl. I don't mean it quite like that. She was a person very much in her own right. But here was I, in Montreal, wearing Harris Tweed jackets, grey flannels, English shoes, reading English weeklies — marking time. And here she was, an English expatriate holding on to the things that reminded her of home. *The Times* calendar on the wall; the crumpled copies of *Punch*; the mementos on her clothes; Alexander, the frog, on the lapel of her tweed suit. Jeremy, the ladybird, on her green corduroy. We used to go through Montreal at night singing 'We'll Gather Lilacs in the Spring Again'. And I remember in a snowstorm going by the Ritz, arm in arm, doing a sort of Palais Glide and singing ' The Teddy-Bears' Picnic'. It was the thin book she gave me with her name inside, in a child's writing, that introduced me to *Winnie the Pooh*. And when Princess Elizabeth was to get married, she got up in the night to hear the wedding over the short-wave radio.

To be closer to her, and to be even more in an English atmosphere (though of another kind), I moved to the corner of Guy and Sherbrooke, to the large basement room of the Dean of Christ Church Cathedral (and you couldn't get more C. of E. in Montreal than that). She filled the walls of that basement room with watercolours. They had scissors stuck upright in the sand with eyes where the handles were. And others had large fish with fat human lips.

At Christmas we went to Mont Tremblant to ski. (We had to take another girl for a chaperon — but on the second day she fell for an American clothing manufacturer.) I had assumed she had been on skis before — why else go to Tremblant? We

went up on the chair-lift to the top of the steepest run. When
we got off, she could hardly stand up on the skis. She just stood
there, looking down the sheer slope, unable to move. I thought
the only way to get her down was to go with her across the
slope, have her stop by falling into the snow, turn around and
go across again, this time a few inches lower down. It took us
over two hours before we got down to the bottom. Also staying
at the ski lodge were two English army officers, on leave. We
sympathised with them at breakfast as they tried to hide behind
their papers, their tea, their toast and marmalade — while the
Americans, at the other tables, made breakfast sound like a
carnival. On New Year's Eve there was a series of dances at
different ski lodges. And going out in the hall around midnight
I saw her being kissed by an American. We had our first quarrel that night.

In spring we went to Ile Aux Noix — a French Canadian
village south of Montreal near the U.S. border and by the
Richelieu River. I had, the previous summer, tutored three
French Canadian boys in English at a large house and in the
summer cottage. The woman, who owned the house and the
dark-green cottage by the river, looked like those late
photographs of Colette. She said I could come down with 'my
English girl.' We spent the week-end there. I took out the
sailboat, but a storm came up and in trying to dismantle the
mast we nearly capsized. When we got back to the shore the
wind lessened and it began to rain, and there was the familiar
dark-green wooden cottage, with the piles of old *Geographical
Magazines*, the spinning wheel in the corner, the old piano. I
decided to break in. One wanted to do something reckless, to
show off. And along with that there was much that was tender
and full of hope . . .

She was a year behind me at university. And we took it for
granted that our lives would go on together, not in Canada but
in England — the England that we tried to keep alive in
Montreal. To make that possible I went in for a fellowship. I
had to go to Toronto for the interview. When I got back, Saturday morning, there was the telegram saying I had got it. We
knew somehow it would. One had a great deal of confidence in

the future. As far as one's past — she said once she wanted to meet my parents. But after telling me of things like going to Hunt Balls, of her nanny, of the country house in Suffolk — I thought it best if they didn't meet. So I killed them off. Along with the street of the peddlers' horses and wagons parked on both sides, the eyes of middle-aged women staring from behind lace curtains . . .

I think she changed me as much as anyone is changed by another person. And in turn she began to tell me things that she had kept bottled up inside. We were walking in winter by Westmount Park, our breath smoking in the crisp air, tears in her eyes as she told me how she heard her father was dead. She was taken away from school one afternoon, brought back to her house, and there was the urn of ashes.

For my graduation she bought herself a new dress, shoes, and a hat like a boater with daisies around it. We went to the Ball that night and she stuffed her bed with clothes and got another girl to sign in for her. We danced until three then went to the hotel on Dorchester. We had taken separate rooms. I knocked, she let me in. Not long after we heard a man opening a door, next to us, and walking down the corridor and returning and shutting the door. Then about five minutes later repeating the same. And it went on. We named him the hotel detective. Then she said, 'Listen.' But there was no sound from the corridor. It was the singing of birds. It came from the window. And then the window went blue. And the birds were singing as I suppose they do every morning, but never have I heard them as clear. And the blue became lighter, and you could see it growing. And we stood there watching, touched by some understanding that this was the end of something . . .

I saw her off next day. She was going for the summer with her mother on a car tour of the States. She wept and we kissed goodbye. Two days later I went down to the docks to catch the freighter for Newcastle.

Her letters came often. They came from down the Atlantic seaboard, to the south, then across to California — blue air-letters with cartoons at the end. I looked forward to the year passing quickly. For the England I had kept alive, with her,

had gone. Now it meant sharing with another Canadian a peeling flat that was falling to bits, queueing up once a week for the
cube of butter, the small Polish egg, the bits of cheese, the ten
cigarettes under the counter. Still, I thought this would change
when she came over.

That autumn she was back at university. The letters became
less frequent. She wrote that she was going out often, that she
was discovering North America and having a marvellous time.
And after the first formal dance she wrote that she had met
someone from Princeton and that she was going to the States
for the week-end to meet his parents.

I sat by the pub opposite Kensington Gardens drinking a
light ale by a rough wooden table, watched how the Japanese
cherry flowered pink, the cars and buses moving along
Bayswater. And felt my world had been shattered.

That happened fifteen years ago.

I heard she got back to England, married an Englishman.
That they have a house in town and another in the country. I
keep a letter in my drawer. It came quite out of the blue, about
a year ago, when she heard something of mine broadcast; it
was forwarded on. She wanted to know what I was doing after
all these years. And told me that they were just off for a winter
cruise to see the temples at Abu Simbel before they are flooded.

# A Canadian Upbringing

When people ask me why did I leave Canada and go over to England, the answer I give depends on the kind of person who is doing the asking.

If it is someone of my own generation, at some party, I tell them it was because of the attractive English girl who sat beside me at college and took the same courses as I did, and who was going back when she graduated. If it is someone like my bank manager, I say it was because of the five-thousand-dollar fellowship I got for postgraduate study. The only condition being that I had to do it at some British university. And if the question comes from an editor, I tell him that at that time I had just written a first novel and my Canadian publisher (to be) having read the manuscript said that I would have to go to New York or London to get it published, then he would look after the Canadian market.

All of these have something of the truth about them. But what was behind them, and which I could not admit at the time, was the work of Alexander Marsden.

I had never heard of Marsden until I went to McGill. In my second year, Graham Pollack, one of the English professors —

poor Graham, he's dead now. No one, apart from the handful of students who took his courses, gave him much credit for the range of his reading, nor understood the kind of humility he brought into the classroom. He lectured, in a weak voice, on Utopias throughout the ages; on science fiction; and on Comparative Literature. Wiping away with a large white handkerchief the sweat that broke out on his forehead.

His office, which he shared with an assistant professor, was swamped with his books. Not only were they around the walls, but in piles on the floor. And it was from one of these piles that he pulled out *A Canadian Upbringing* by Alexander Marsden.

'I think you might enjoy this,' he said, blowing off the dust.

I began to read it late that night — in that large basement room on the corner of Guy and Sherbrooke that I rented from the Dean of Christ Church Cathedral. And when I finished the last page I was far too excited and disturbed to go to sleep.

It's a small book, 112 pages. It was published in England in 1939. The first half deals with Marsden's growing up in Montreal. The rest with a trip he made across the country in the early thirties: by riding freight cars, by bus, hitch-hiking, and walking.

What first disturbed me was the shock that one gets when, without warning, you come across a new talent. But I was also disturbed by something else.

Although I was brought up in Ottawa — and Ottawa has, compared to Montreal, a small Jewish community — the kind of upbringing I had wasn't much different from the one Marsden describes in Montreal. He pinned down that warm, lively, ghetto atmosphere; the strong family and religious ties — as well as its prejudices and limitations. And when, at the end of the book, Marsden decides to leave Canada for England, not because he wants to deny his background but because he feels the need to accept a wider view of life, I knew that was the way I would go as well.

From Professor Pollack I found out what I could about Marsden, which was very little. Marsden had gone over to England in the late thirties, and as far as Pollack knew he had never come back.

I graduated that summer and set out for London. With my five-thousand-dollar fellowship; the English girl; the manuscript of my novel; and the well-marked copy of *A Canadian Upbringing*.

In London I soon discovered that I didn't care for the academic. And I dropped it. The attractive English girl went over to Paris and on the cross-Channel boat met an Englishman. And they married.

But I did get my novel accepted by an English publisher. And with this I decided to try and make, like Marsden, some kind of literary career over here.

I also tried to track down Marsden's whereabouts. But the publisher of *A Canadian Upbringing* was out of business. And it was only a chance remark by the librarian at Canada House that put me on his trail. She didn't know who he was, and had never heard of the book. But she remembered his name.

'I send him batches of Canadian papers,' she said. And pulled out a card from a file that had Alexander Marsden on top. And below, a series of crossed-out addresses. The last one she had was: The Little Owls, Mousehole, near Penzance, Cornwall.

I copied it into my address book and there the matter rested.

Until this summer. One of my short stories was bought up for a film. And with the money from that I bought myself a small English car, rented a cottage in Mousehole, and took my wife and kids for our first holiday in Cornwall.

It was very pleasant. The weather was marvellous. The kids played along the rocks at low tide. And found rockpools with sea anemones in them. Towards evening we drove down to Land's End, stopping off at the coves, the small coastal villages, on the way. Or over to Penzance where my wife did some shopping and the kids played on the lawns of the Morrab Gardens.

On the sixth day I couldn't put it off any longer. I asked the postman where Marsden lived.

The small greystone cottage, without a front garden, was easy to find. Across the unpaved road water flowed in the ditch. A few chickens were wandering about further up the road, from a field. And a black dog was stretched out in the sun.

I knocked.

The man who opened the door was about five foot ten, a little on the plump side. He had a sardonic, very pale, face. And a short pointed blond beard. He reminded me of one of those engravings of Shakespeare.

'Mr Marsden?'

'Yes,' he said gently.

'I'm a Canadian, and since I was in Mousehole I thought I'd come over and tell you how much I've enjoyed *A Canadian Upbringing*.'

The pale face looked very vulnerable.

'Come in,' he said quietly. 'How is Canada?'

'Fine,' I said.

'When were you last there?'

'Eight years ago.'

'What part?'

'Ottawa.'

I then told him my name, that I left for much the same reason as he did. And that since my college days I had carried around his book, like a Bible.

'Would you like some tea?' he said in that gentle detached manner.

'Yes,' I said. 'Thank you.'

'I'm sorry I haven't any spirits,' he said, as he disappeared into the back.

It was a small tidy cottage, very simply furnished. An unvarnished wooden table in the middle. A couple of well-made wooden chairs. A fireplace with some coloured post-cards on top.

Marsden returned with a tray that had a small teapot, two earthenware mugs, a loaf of bread, and a sliced lemon. Then he went back again.

'I've got a surprise,' he said.

He came back with a large salami that had 'Blooms' written across it, in white, several times.

'I get this sent to me once a month from a delicatessen in

London. I tried to get some rye bread, but they won't send it.'

He cut a thin slice of the salami and, spearing it with the knife, gave it to me.

'Delicious,' I said.

He made me a salami sandwich and one for himself and we had tea and sandwiches sitting by the bare wooden table.

'That's what I miss most, the food,' he said, and for the first time he sounded enthusiastic. 'I tried to make gefilte fish. It turned out uneatable. I tried to make putcha and finally persuaded the local butcher to get me some calf's legs. But the thing looked like jellied dishwater, and I threw it away. Where are you staying?'

'In a cottage across from The Coastguards. We rented it for two weeks.'

'Married?'

'Yes,' I said. 'I've got two kids.'

'I never did,' he said, and seemed to go off again on some private thought. But I wasn't going to let this meeting play itself out in small talk about food. I had rehearsed this occasion during too many sleepless nights. I wanted to talk about *A Canadian Upbringing*. And how he had made me aware of my background and why it was necessary to leave it.

'Go home,' he said suddenly. 'Go home while you are still young.'

'But I thought you were critical of Canada?'

'Maybe. But I care less about England.'

He cut some more salami, very carefully, and made another two neat sandwiches.

I decided to change the subject. 'How is your work going?'

'Fine. I do that upstairs. Would you like to see my workroom?'

I said I would and felt somewhat flattered. Writers' workrooms are usually private things.

I followed him up the stairs — I noticed he wore brown leather slippers — to a largish airy room that had planks of wood on the floor, some packing cases, an electric saw, several planes, several chisels, tins of glue and paint.

He led me to the far side where, in what looked like former

bookcases, were standing brightly painted toys.

'I make roundabouts,' he said, picking one up for me.

They were the gayest roundabouts I have seen. Bright blues, crimsons, oranges, yellows, greens — with a barber-shop pole in the middle around which farm-yard animals went to the tinkle of a small silver bell.

'I make these for various toy shops in London, and they go all over —' Marsden said.

He saw me look at the Canadian newspapers on the floor.

'I get those sent from Canada House. They're handy for packing.'

He had a large mirror on one wall with various post-cards stuck along the inside of the frame. They showed Piccadilly with the Guinness clock and several red buses; the midnight sun over a lake of Landego, Norway; a snow scene in Obergurl, Austria; a bull elephant from Kenya; and the Peace Tower and the lawns in Ottawa. On the backs of the cards was written much the same sort of message.

> I think your roundabouts are
> wonderful. They have given my
> children much pleasure. Thank you.

I told Marsden that I thought the roundabouts were splendid.

'Do you make any other kind of toy?'

'No,' he said, 'just this one model.'

Downstairs. The tea was cold. He had put away the salami and we had smoked all my cigarettes. I stood up and shook hands and said I would see him again before we left. He opened the door for me.

'I'm very glad you called,' he said, in that gentle, unemotional way of his.

For the next few days I didn't go and see Marsden but thought of little else. I have not had many heroes lately and as I grow older they get less. But Marsden had meant something personal to me. And I felt I had been cheated. Of what exactly I didn't know. But the man who wrote *A Canadian Upbringing* no longer existed as far as I was concerned. And I was quite prepared to leave Cornwall without seeing him again.

But on the morning we were to leave, and as we were packing things to take back in the car, he turned up, looking very elegant in light cream trousers, brown sandals, yellow socks, and a maroon shirt.

'I hope you don't mind,' he said. 'I thought your children might like these.' And he gave each of the kids a roundabout.

Their reaction was immediate. They kissed him. They jumped around him. They gave little squeals of delight. And Marsden was enjoying it as well.

For my wife he had an enormous bunch of anemones — and my wife is a sitting duck when it comes to flowers.

He played with the children while I and my wife finished bringing the packed things from the cottage into the car. I was trying to close the back when Marsden came up.

'Can I help?'

'Thanks,' I said, shutting it. 'It's all finished.'

'It was good of you to come and see me,' he said. 'You're the first author who has.' He was, I think, going to say something else, but the kids came running around. So we shook hands, and we all got into the car.

'I'll send you some rye bread,' I said starting the engine.

'I don't want to put you to all that trouble, but if you could send me a couple of loaves, just once —.'

And he waved.

And we were waving as I drove away. Around the first bend he disappeared from sight. The road went by some large blue rocks and by the briny sea that lay flat to the horizon. It made everything, suddenly, seem awfully silent.

# Part Three

# English for Foreigners

The classrooms were above an optician, by a seedy restaurant, overlooking a large bare cathedral. When I started, at the beginning of May, the season had not begun. I had eight pupils, the intermediates. If anyone could carry on a few sentences in broken English he left the beginners — which was crowded — and stayed in the intermediates until there was room for him in the senior class. Each class consisted of a small room with tables pushed together in the shape of a horseshoe. I sat behind a desk, at the open end of the horseshoe, by a portable blackboard. The windows had to be closed because of the traffic noise. On a warm or a rainy day, the room was stifling.

On the first day I wondered whether my Canadian accent would matter. 'Ladies and gentlemen. I'm your new teacher. I'm a Canadian. And the kind of English I speak is not the kind that Englishmen speak. So if you have any trouble understanding what I say —.' But I was interrupted by an Italian girl who beamed and said how clear my diction was. And they all said they understood me and complimented me on how clear I spoke. I was getting to feel quite good. But I found out, on the second day, that the Englishman I replaced had a speech impediment. He left without saying goodbye. That was one of the occupational hazards. One was hired without references and left the same way.

Teaching consisted mainly in giving them new words, correcting their pronunciation, dictating to them small pieces of anything I happened to see while looking out of the window. And reading excerpts from Conrad. Or else we played games. I would borrow one of their watches with a sweep second-hand and say:

'Miss Laroque. You are walking in Brighton from the Steyne to the West Pier. Tell me, in one minute, all the words beginning with the letter 'M' that you would see. *Now.*'

'Mouse . . . Mutton . . . Murder . . . Mister . . . Missus . . . Miss . . .'

'Sir. That's not fair.'

'Six, Miss Laroque,' I said, 'twenty-five seconds to go.'

'Mimosa . . . Macaroni . . . Man . . .'

They were mainly young girls. Some were there for business reasons: to be a receptionist in their father's hotel; another was going to be an air-hostess; another to work in an export office. But the majority were there for a holiday.

I had been there three weeks when Mrs S—— came in. The age of the students didn't vary a great deal; they were in their teens or early twenties. But Mrs S——, a handsome-looking woman, with grey hair combed neatly back in a bun, and very light-blue eyes, was in her seventies. The immediate reaction to her presence was to subdue everyone. And we got a lot more done. She sat half-way up the left of the horseshoe listening to what I was saying. Sometimes she took out a handkerchief and wiped her eyes. I took it that she had some allergy. When it was her turn to read she read softly and very slow, and apologised at the end for not doing better.

At eleven we had a ten-minute break. The teachers would go into the office and have coffee. The students would either go to a small café nearby or stay in the room, open the windows, lean out and smoke. One morning I came back early and a new student, a Mexican, offered me a cigarette.

'Sir. You like Turkish?'

I said I did.

Two weeks later, on a Friday, Mrs S—— came up to me. 'Thank you very much,' she said graciously. 'This morning was my last lesson. I enjoyed myself very much. I have a small present for you.'

We shook hands. And I went down the stairs holding my books and this package carefully wrapped in white paper with a neat red ribbon.

In the office I unwrapped it. It was a large package of Turkish cigarettes. I was deeply touched. None of the others had bothered to say more than 'goodbye'. Perhaps, I thought, it's just old age that feels it has to pay for even the briefest encounter.

I asked the secretary in the office about Mrs S——. She said that Mrs S—— was a widow. That she was part of *the* S——'s, in Germany. They were extremely wealthy. Her son had died and the doctors advised her to get away and do something to take her mind off things.

And as the secretary was talking I remembered that the words I introduced to the class during her stay — the passages I chose to read or dictate — for some reason kept harping on some aspect of death: on cemeteries, gravestones, funerals, coffins.

But this was Friday and there was little food in the house and I knew that I would have to walk back the three miles. If I had breakfast that morning, I didn't mind the walk. After Preston Circus it was very pleasant. There were the small gardens, each one with the name of an English city and with a single stalk of corn growing incongruously in their middles.

I went into a large tobacconist and told the girl behind the counter that I had bought this package of Turkish cigarettes for a friend as a gift, and I found out that he doesn't smoke. The girl examined the box closely. Finally gave me fourteen shillings.

I went out and bought half a dozen eggs, a tin of luncheon meat, a loaf of bread, some sugar, tea, cheese, a newspaper, and took the bus back.

But that afternoon — though I watched my wife and children eat — I felt I had betrayed something.

# I Like Chekhov

It was a warm afternoon in July. And in the Yorkshire town the sheep were grazing on the grass of the school lawns that sloped to the river. Chester Conn Bell walked along the footpath under the avenue of heavy trees. He was twenty-nine, blond and with a fine profile, he looked more like an actor than a schoolmaster. Beside him the river had little water in it. It was mainly mudbanks with beached rowboats and old bits of wood.

He turned off the footpath, as he had done five days of the week for the past nine months, and went through the small park with its scented gardens of lemon thyme for the blind.

It's over, thought Chester. And then a sudden light feeling of release. How marvellous to be free again.

Tomorrow he would leave this provincial backwater with its bad library and deadness at night. He didn't mind the teaching as much as he disliked being reminded that he was a teacher. When he walked through the streets the schoolboys were always there touching their caps with their hand.

'Good morning, sir.'

'Afternoon, sir.'

'Good evening, sir.'

By the church with the slate spire he left the park and walked along the side street that brought him into a residential area. On both sides were pale yellow brick houses. Halfway down, on the left, lived Miss Fort who was in her sixties. She taught music. And Chester rented her front room. As he opened the front door he heard the piano and a girl's thin voice singing 'A lover and his lass'.

He took off his navy blue blazer, loosened his dark blue tie, undid his collar button, sat down in the comfortable chair, lit a cigarette. And listened to the singing and the piano. And he began to think that no more would he be coming back to this room. Nor early mornings going out for coffee and toast. Then through the park, by the cemetery, the mist hanging over the river in the winter. Nor going on the stage and singing solemnly the morning hymns. Then the roll calls, detentions, telling them to stop talking. He had hated it all the time he was doing it. But now that it was over.

The singing and the piano stopped. It was five-thirty. He knew he would like to round off his teaching days and his stay in this town with some kind of gesture. And he was looking forward to seeing the Latin Master and the Geography Master later that evening in the Antelope.

It was the Latin Master's idea to go to the Antelope. He had told Chester about Sophie Jewtree, the proprietress, who served behind the bar. And Chester had also heard from the others in the staff room about Sophie and the Latin Master.

Sophie Jewtree was one of the attractive women in the town. When she was behind the bar there were, at various times in the evening, five or six married men who left their wives to be with Sophie. Her husband, a stocky retired RAF officer, did not mind. (The men came regularly, talked quietly, stood together in a small group, like overgrown schoolboys.) He called them Sophie's admirers. And the most consistent of all the admirers was the Latin Master.

He was a lean, taut, man with rimless glasses, small neat moustache and thin lips. He spoke quietly and precisely. But when he became angry with a pupil, his face would flush and leave him speechless.

Every Monday to Friday the Latin Master went to the Antelope to have a few drinks and to see Sophie. They talked quietly, and kept looking at each other. Then the Latin Master went back to his wife. It had gone on like this for three years.

The Geography Master was different. He looked like a corpulent schoolboy whose suits were always in need of a press. And he couldn't shake off the classroom. Away from it he continued, in his conversation, to explain the obvious. He was married with five small children. And while the Latin Master lived with his wife in a neat rented flat, the Geography Master inherited money and owned one of the finest houses in the town.

What held these two together was that they both went to Cambridge. While the rest were graduates of provincial universities. And Chester, being Canadian and socially unclassifiable, was accepted by both sides. He was invited to the Latin and Geography Masters' homes for dinner — a thing they had never done with the other masters. And when Chester went out to a pub with some of the masters from the provincial universities they told him how stuck-up the two Cambridge men were.

The Antelope was a combination pub and hotel. It had one long copper bar that stretched most of the width of the room and some wooden cubicles against the wall opposite the bay windows.

When Chester came in the two were already there.

'What are you having?' the Geography Master asked.

'Whisky,' Chester said, '*Teachers*.'

They laughed.

'This is Chester,' the Latin Master said to the woman behind the bar.

'I heard a lot about you,' she said.

She looked handsome but vulnerable. A tallish woman with brown loose hair that she kept pushing back from her eyes. There was something about attractive women that drew Chester to them. Unlike the other masters, Chester felt more comfortable in the presence of women than of men. And women soon realized this.

'You look different,' the Geography Master said to Chester.

'All people look different when they are going away,' Sophie said.

While she was serving at the other end of the bar the Latin Master asked, somewhat proudly. 'What do you think of Sophie?'

'Wish I'd come here before,' Chester said, noticing how her belly pushed out against the tight stone-tweed skirt.

'— years from now we'll be saying,' the Geography Master said, '*remember the time Chester Conn Bell . . .*'

'Couldn't you teach, and write in your spare time?' Sophie said.

'I tried,' Chester said, 'but I didn't do any writing all the time I was here.'

'Have you had things published?' she asked.

This was a sore point with Chester.

'I've had some stories, in a magazine, in Canada.'

Sophie said her husband was born in New Zealand (he was away in London) and told them how they met in London in 1944 when she was a WAAF. And what a gay exciting time she had when she ran her own MG and met new people nearly every day.

'You must miss that — living here,' Chester said.

'When I do I go to see my doctor,' she said. 'He tells me I have good legs.'

'The thing I missed most in this town,' Chester said, 'was not being able to get a decent book. The library here is terrible.'

'I've got books,' said Sophie.

'What kind of books?'

'Chekhov — Tolstoy —'

'You have books like that?'

'Yes,' she said. 'I like the Russians. They're in the back. Would you like to see them?'

The Latin Master didn't like the way the conversation was going.

'You can see them tomorrow.'

But there was no confidence in his voice.

'I'll be gone tomorrow,' Chester said.

'We'll only be a minute,' Sophie said to the Latin Master, and touched his hand as she went by.

She led Chester into an adjoining room. She put on a wall-light that kept most of the room in shadows. Then walked over to the bookcase. There weren't as many books there as Chester expected. He bent over to read the titles. There was a thin olive-green volume of Chekhov's short stories — books of poetry — Browning — some wartime anthologies — Penguin *New Writing*. She was bending over beside him, he could smell her scent. Their hips touched. He turned and they kissed gently on the mouth. Then they straightened out. And they kissed several times, not gently.

'I think we'd better go back,' she said, after a while.

The light in the bar was hard on their eyes as they came in. The Latin Master looked annoyed and puzzled. The Geography Master: as if he had been told a dirty joke and had just got the point.

'She's got some good books,' Chester said to them. Then to Sophie, who was now behind the bar, 'I like Chekhov. He understands people.'

But the atmosphere had changed. And there was something noticeably uneasy among them now. They finished their last drinks in a series of silences and said goodbye to Sophie.

As soon as they were out on the gravel drive the Latin Master came up to Chester.

'What did you do in there?'

'We kissed,' Chester said.

A flush appeared on the Latin Master's face. He looked at Chester but said nothing. Then turned, walked over the gravel to his bicycle, and rode away.

'I'll drive you home,' the Geography Master said quietly.

'Thanks,' Chester said. 'It's my last night. I think I'll walk.'

'Don't forget us,' the Geography Master suddenly called out from the car, as he drove away.

Chester began to walk down the slope. The moon was out and it shone on the water, on the stone bridge, on the small park and the town behind it. A breeze from the river. He turned the collar of his jacket up and put his hands in his trouser pockets and began to whistle. He felt very happy as he walked through the empty provincial streets and heard the echoing sound of his own footsteps. 'It's nice to be on the move,' he said to himself.

# Ringa Ringa Rosie

The Buchanans' fourteenth move in five years was to a semi-detached brick cottage in Bogtown. The front faced the main road. The back had long gardens, then a cricket field which sloped down to brush and a river.

Moving had, by now, become an accepted but reluctant part of their lives. Whenever they moved into a new address no serious attempt was made to change the place or impose on it any sense of possession. All Sheila did was to take down a few of the pictures from the walls and cover with cloths the tin trunks and tea chests until they became part of the set furniture.

Bogtown was a row of labourers' cottages on one side of the main Guildford-Horsham highway. At both ends were filling stations and two pubs. One would have long gone out of business had it not also been a rest point for the coaches plying between London and the south coast. On Sundays the village boys sat on their motorbikes in front of the filling stations and watched the cars go by. At night the place was lit up by a yellow-glass *Shell* sign, above a garage. When the garage closed the village was in darkness except for the sweeps made by passing headlights and the glow from thrown-out cigarettes on the road.

The Buchanans came here, as they did in their previous moves, out of necessity. They were unsatisfactory tenants. They were always behind with the rent. The electricity never received payment until they were threatened with disconnection. And since most of the time they were just trying to make sure that there was enough for the day's food — there was little inclination or time left in seeing that the garden was looked after, or the place kept tidy. In any case the furnished accommodation which they could afford, by the time they had moved into it, had already become run down and seedy.

This time they had moved from a partly furnished semi-detached suburban house in East Finchley. At two pounds ten a week the cottage was exactly half of the rent of the house. But even at that price they were being taken.

The rooms were damp. Patches of grey clotted the ceilings and the walls. The furniture was uncomfortable — a collection of junk that was picked up at various auction sales. And until the cold weather came the place had fleas.

On their second day the Buchanans went on a tour of inspection. In the long back garden dead stalks mixed with new shoots. The grass was overgrown. The rhubarb was wild. There were weeds and two dead apple trees. The middle of the garden was a rubbish dump. And from the rubbish and from every other mound where previous tenants had emptied the lavatory bucket, giant nasturtiums with thick fleshy-white tubular stalks twisted magnificently up. The nasturtiums were enormous. The white of the stalks swamped the yellow orange brown of the petals. They crawled and twisted over the ground like a series of swollen blood vessels.

In the neighbouring gardens the grass was cut, the dividing hedges trimmed. There were small greenhouses and rose-bushes and apple, plum, and pear trees. There were cultivated blackberries, strawberries, and straight rows of vegetables.

'We always seem to move —'

Sheila said, watching three blue tits on the other side of the hedge — faces like Indians with war paint — picking at a piece of fat dangling from a wooden post.

'— into places where the gardens on either side are always neat and well looked after.'

When the wind dropped there was a smell of decomposition.

He was writing a new book. And she, besides housework and trying to make ends meet, also kept the children out of the cottage by taking them for long walks so he could work in quiet; and on the way filled the second-hand pram with bits of wood which she would hide with the raincover so that the neighbours wouldn't see. And wrote a weekly air-letter to her parents in Ottawa, which was a form of blackmail, for only on that basis did they send her ten dollars every week. Besides this their only other income was the eighteen shillings family allowance.

George and Sheila had never lived in the country before. They had grown up in Kingston and had come over after graduating from Queens for their one trip abroad. But this was extended when Sheila became pregnant. They married. And George refused to return until he had a book published. So far their lives consisted of changing addresses, from one of the outskirts of London to the other, leaving small debts behind. But never had they allowed themselves to be cut off in the way they were now.

In the country when they couldn't pay the monthly newspaper bill — they had to go without newspapers. And likewise when the coal ran out. There was no alternate choice. The coal-man lived five cottages away and when George promised that he would pay at the end of the week, and then couldn't, the coalman said, 'I'm a man of principle.' And refused to deliver any. George then took an old sack, went across the snow-covered cricket field, and into the drifts of the brush.

The wind blew the loose snow on to his face and against his eyes. In the fields across the river he could see horses. They swirled in and out of focus, manes blowing. It was, he thought, like a scene in a Russian film. He went to the river, which was frozen, and began to pull the dead branches from the trees, breaking easily the very green, strong smelling light wood with his foot and then throwing the pieces into the sack. And carrying the sack on his back, like the coalman, he went back through the gusts. He thought that this should make him hate this kind of life. That it ought to give him some incentive, to do something else. Instead, he looked at the drifting snow, the staring horses, the backs of the cottages, the blurring gardens, and thought it was fine. Someday he would write about it.

It was fine until he brought the sack inside the cottage. The two small children were there with running noses, and they had brought the cot down for the baby as this was the only room they could keep warm in winter. Nappies were around the fireplace, and drying clothes hung on a line from the ceiling across the room. But the wet wood only filled the room with smoke.

They had been living in Bogtown five months. It was a Saturday morning, the middle of February, when she came upstairs and said, 'There's no food for the week-end. You'll have to do something.' He hitch-hiked into Horsham and pawned his typewriter. That lasted them a week.

The following Saturday it was raining when she walked, without her usual knock, into his room. 'The baker is outside. I'm not answering the door. We've no food for the week-end. And the milklady isn't going to deliver anymore unless we pay a pound tomorrow. You'll have to do something.'

So he came down and fumbled with the broken kitchen-door handle. When he finally opened the door he made a joke about the broken handle. But the thin, dark man in white uniform, did not find it amusing. He stood there, one hand held the wicker basket, the other his book. George took a plain white loaf. 'We'll pay next week.' The man didn't say anything. He closed his book. But when George put his hand out again to get another loaf, the man said, 'I was told that all you could have was one bread.'

George went back upstairs to his room, sat down in the chair, and looked out of the window. The garden was muddy and drab. The cricket field very green. He saw a large bird at the end of the field, by the river, gently flapping enormous wings. It had a small black body. Then he realized it was a man carrying a long plank of wood on his shoulders. And made a note of this in his notebook.

Downstairs he could hear Sheila becoming irritable with the children. And for his benefit she kept saying out loud, 'It's all right. Daddy will do something.'

He came down again.

'There's nothing I can do,' he said quietly. 'It's raining too hard. I've got nothing to sell.'

'How about the printer?'

'He's away for the weekend. Gone to see his sister at Bognor.'

He went over his list of what he could do. When there was nothing, he could usually borrow ten shillings from the printer down the road. Once, when they were hungry and living in Clapham he did a song and dance for them, crossing his hands while he moved his knees together and apart. It made them laugh. And laughing they went to bed. But this time she was becoming hysterical.

'You gotta do something.'

'But what can I do.'

The baby fell over a broken plastic flute and began to cry then ran up to him and buried her head between his legs. The rain came down from the roof, and down the windows, and into the barrel by the drain. It overflowed on to the sogged earth forming pools in the depressions.

'I don't care what. Long as you do something.'

He went upstairs and looked through his room. Only a few used paperbacks were left on the bookshelves and an old copy of Gulliver's Travels that the secondhand bookseller in Horsham had refused to buy. He came down carrying a small green address book and began to telephone. Sheila and the children just stood and watched.

'Hello Bill. This is George Buchanan. How are you? I bet you are. We're fine. Sheila and the kids. Look Bill, the reason I rang. I'm hard pressed at the moment. Could you send me ten pounds. You'll have it back by the end of the month . . . I see. Sure, I understand. How's Tangier? No, just raining. I'll tell Sheila. Any time you come to England, drop in. I don't know. Maybe I'll go back home next year. Sure. Bye.'

He hung up. Looked through his address book. Then he was

talking again.

'May I speak to Paul de Secker-Remy? Hello Duke. Guess who this is? No. George Buchanan. Bucky, the genius. Long time no see. I bet you are. Me too. Three, girls. We're living in England. I hear you've got yourself some hotel in the Laurentians. Paul, the reason I called. I'm in a spot at the moment. Could you telegraph a money order for fifty dollars. You'll have it back by the end of the month. Rose Cottage, Bogtown, near — Twenty-five will do. No. . . . I didn't. I don't worry too much about income tax. Yeh, sure. Sounds like a nice car. I understand. Bye.'

He continued to go through the pages of his address book, calling up people, and he was getting near the end when Kate, the three-year old, said:

'What Daddie doin'?'

'I'm doing something.'

'What Daddie doin'?'

'Talking on the telephone.'

'Don't be silly Daddie that's only the top-end of my toy-iron,' Cassie, the eldest, said — a blue-eyed girl of five with blonde, curly hair.

'Daddie funny,' Kate said. 'Daddie pretendin'.'

He had gone through to his last address when Kate ran to him and took his hand. For her that game was over. She began to pull him. 'C'mon, Daddie, play inga-inga-osie.'

Now Cassie took his other hand. And Sheila, standing by the stairs, began to weep. For a short while Cassie didn't know whether she should join her mother and cry as well. But Kate pulled him, then her, and then went over and held out her hand for Sheila. She took hold. And the four of them went around the room in a circle singing loudly.

> *Ringa — ringa — rosie.*
> *A pocketful of posie.*
> *A tishoo. A tishoo.*
> *We all fall down.*

And they all did, laughing.

# I'll Bring You Back
# Something Nice

Gordon Rideau's eyes were closed and he could hear the trucks going by outside the window on the main London to Guildford road. And in between the trucks the alarm clock on the floor. At his feet the hot-water bottle was cold. He shoved it to the edge of the bed. Then he opened his eyes and saw the wallpaper: wide yellow bars separated by thin black lines.

His wife, Coral, lay with several blankets over her so that just her dark hair was sticking out. Between them a National Health orange bottle was wrapped in a nappy to keep the milk inside it warm in case the baby woke during the night.

He could hear Kate walking down the stairs. The hall light was on. The brown curtains across the bedroom were drawn. The room was cold. There was a pitcher standing in a large basin, both had a red rose painted on the enamel. And a large bedpan with an old copy of *Vogue* on top. A small triptych of three angels stood on the mantel above the small fireplace which was stuffed with newspapers, cardboard, and bits of coloured crepe paper. All this they had inherited from the owner of the cottage. Their belongings: a steel trunk was open in a corner, in another corner two smaller trunks. Inside were clothes jumbled and spilling out.

Coral sat up quickly, turned back the cover, and looked closely down one leg. Near the ankle she picked off a flea and, carefully, crushed it between her fingers. Then she left the bed.

Gordon watched her. There is nothing graceful about her movements he thought. She was wearing a grey sweater and put on a blue skirt. She took the nappy with the makeshift milk-bottle, the alarm clock, and went downstairs.

Now he lay in bed in a sense of luxury. He was alone, staying in. He drew his knees up to keep warm. He heard the radio downstairs playing dance music. And lay there wondering whether she would bring him a cup of tea.

A door opened below and Kate called out,

'Breakfast is ready Daddy.'

'Coming,' he said.

And remained in bed knowing that in a few minutes she would open the door again and say,

'Breakfast is ready Daddy.'

And he would say,

'I'm just getting my socks on.'

But he had them on all night, and his shirt, and a heavy black sweater.

The child came lightly up the stairs. She had just turned four. A shy attractive child with blonde straight hair and fine small features.

'OK,' Gordon said as she came into the bedroom. 'I'm coming.'

'Post, Daddy.'

She gave him a brown envelope.

He opened it. It was a letter from the electricity company saying that a man had come yesterday to disconnect the electricity but no one was in. He was going to come on Friday at eleven unless they could pay £12. 5s. 2d.

It means a trip to London, Gordon thought. And that was enough to make him get up.

He dressed and went to the window and pulled back the brown curtain. The diagonal crack in the glass was like a scar. The fields, across the road, muddy and drab. The trees on the

border of the field — misshapen by the ivy that was slowly killing them — looked very pretty. He watched a motorcycle
accelerate as it went by splashing mud on either side and with a
muddy wake. Then he closed the light in their bedroom and
went down a narrow passage. By the children's open door: the
smell of urine, the camp bed, the mug of water, the comics and
books on top of an overturned orange case. He turned sharply.
Down the narrow stairs. At the bottom he opened a door and
immediately felt the warm air. It was the one room that was
warm. A coal-fire was going in the fireplace. Beside it, in a corner, was a baby's cot.

Kate stood by the cot dressed in a jumper, a red sweater,
which someone had given them when their own children had
grown out of the clothes. She was talking to the baby. 'Ah
goolie goo Rachel. Ah goolie goo.' The baby stood up in the cot
grasping the wooden struts and gurgled back a couple of
vowels. She looked like something caught in a cage.

'Good morning,' Gordon said cheerfully to the children and
went into the kitchen.

Coral was at the stove. 'High keeps changing,' she said. 'I
don't know if the hot plate is off or on.'

'Use the Master Switch.'

Then he decided it would be better to show her. 'Off' he
said and put the switch up. 'On' he pulled it down.

'What do you want,' she said. 'There's a bit of cheese — I
could make toast.'

'Fine,' he said and went into the other room. Kate was playing with some pieces of paper and a pencil. The baby was
crawling on the floor to the coal bucket. She took pieces of coal
and tried to put them in her mouth. Her lips were black. Gordon took the bucket away and put it by the side of the fireplace,
behind a chair. The child crawled after it.

'What post did you have?' she said bringing in the toast and
cheese.

'A reminder from the electricity.'

'When are they coming?'

'Tomorrow.' He tried to appear casual. 'I guess I'll have to
go to London.'

'Where Daddy going?' Kate said quickly.

'To London — I'll bring you back something.'

'A dolly,' the child said excitedly.

'What will you do?' Coral said.

'I'll try the bank first — I'll find a way.'

'You know how I hate this place.'

'I know.'

And he prepared himself for her to follow with: you can always get away but I'm stuck here . . . my hands are tied . . . I'm the one that's always left behind. Instead she said, 'When you're up could you look around.'

'I'll go and see some real estate people.'

'Try somewhere near a park.'

'I'll try darling.'

'This isn't just you saying things to keep me happy? You will do something.'

'Yes,' he said quietly.

'We've got less than two months.'

'You know how I work,' he tried to sound convincing. 'Leave things until the last week. Then I get something.'

She didn't reply. He was nearly there, he thought.

'You won't forget.'

And he was safe now.

'I'll do my best darling,' he said and got up. 'I'd better shave.'

There was some hot water left in the kettle. He emptied it into a tin mould that she used to make cakes in, mixed a bit of cold water from the tap, and shaved in front of the mirror, above the dishes.

He tried to tidy his sideburns and realized that his face looked odd. It was the eyes. The left one set at an angle. He saw it as well in the baby. Around the small mirror was the kitchen window with old spider webs. Cuts in the snow skiers made climbing a hill sideways. And for a moment he was back to the pressure the cold made on his forehead. He was in a sleigh sitting behind the swaying rump of a horse held in its tight harness, with Holly. Past white fields with the telegraph poles just protruding. I could tell, she said, when you held my hand to take my coat off. And Jasmine. It snowed all that day in Montreal. After the lecture we went to the Berkeley and drank Brandy Alexanders until it was time to go. The expensive gloom of her parents' apartment. The thing like a curled bulrush that she took from out her hair. And Lily. How quick it was with her . . . she had her own car. Her father owned an entire small town in Northern Ontario. He wondered what would have happened to his life had he made one of them pregnant.

'Don't forget to empty the bucket,' Coral called from the other room.

He took a spade from the shed, walked along the path to the back garden. Halfway down he selected a part of bare earth and began to dig. He emptied the almost full black bucket into the hole he made. Then shovelled the earth back into the hole. It splashed gently. Then the liquid overflowed and stained the earth. He came back into the kitchen. 'I've emptied the bucket,' he said to Coral. He washed his hands. 'Is there anything left?'

She went to the dresser with the few dishes and from a Peter Rabbit saucer took out a halfpenny and a 3d. stamp. He put the halfpenny in his pocket. Then went upstairs, into his room, and put on his one clean white shirt. He took down his trousers hanging from a hook on a hanger in the corner. They were the trousers of his one remaining suit. He saw how frayed the bottoms were. He took the small scissors from his desk and cut some of the hanging threads. He put on the trousers, his tie and jacket. And came down carrying the black winter overcoat that he bought twelve years ago when he was at university. He put it on. Coral brushed him down. The children were crowding around him.

'You look nice Daddy,' Kate said.

'You will look around,' Coral said.

'Yes,' he said, then smiled to the children.

'I'll bring you back something nice.'

'A dolly?' Kate said.

'Something to eat.'

Coral picked up the baby.

He kissed them all goodbye.

They went with him to the front gate. And watched him walk along the road away from them. Kate climbed up the wooden gate and said goodbye several times. And they waved to each other.

From a distance of ten yards, Coral thought, he was still handsome and looked neat and successful. There was the confident manner, the upright walk. He turned and waved back to them. From some thirty yards, she thought, he looked even better. He might have been an executive going off to the office, to work.

He looked for darkness in the windshield. He could tell quickly by the amount of darkness, the outline (like those outlines they had trained him to look at in a tenth, a twentieth, a fiftieth of a second), whether the driver of the coming car was alone or not. He didn't bother to put up his hand if there were two.

From Piccadilly Gordon walked down Lower Regent Street and into the bank, across the light marble floor, to the short teller with the Italian-sounding name. They shook hands and asked each other questions as if they knew one another well.

'I've just come up for the day,' Gordon said.

'How is the family?'

'Fine. And yours?'

'They're fine. We went to Connemara for a holiday.' He smiled and took out some photographs. 'It was wonderful — the best holiday we had.'

There were photographs of some children by a pony, by a cottage. And the bank teller in a pair of shorts.

'May I see the manager?'

'I'll see if he is free.'

He left his cage and out of it looked even smaller but long in the arms.

He came back smiling. 'The manager is busy. But our assistant manager Mister Henderson will see you.'

'Come in Mister Rideau.'

The assistant manager, unlike most North Americans, looked much older than his forty-two years. But his: 'Sit down

Mister Rideau. Cigarette?' had a professional warmth. 'Now, what's the trouble?'

'I have an electricity bill just over twelve pounds that I must meet tomorrow or else they'll cut us off. Could the bank let me overdraw fifteen pounds? It will only be for a short time. I've got money coming in.'

'I'm sorry. It's impossible,' the assistant manager said. 'I can't let you have a pound.' He lowered his voice. '*He* gave me strict instructions.' And his eyes indicated the frosted glass partition of the other room.

'But I've been with the bank for seven years.'

'*He* doesn't consider you a banking proposition.'

They were both silent. The assistant manager looked uncomfortable. 'Are you a veteran?'

'Yes,' Gordon said, 'I was in the army.' And remembered a time in Montreal, after taking a girl home to the Town of Mount Royal he flagged a cab and found he didn't have enough money to get back. He told this to the driver. 'Are you a veteran?' the driver asked.

'I was in the air force,' the assistant manager said. He crushed his cigarette in the green-glass ashtray. Then stood up and walked away from his desk. Gordon also got up. The assistant manager put his hands in his trouser pockets.

'I'm sorry I can't let you have the money. Take this. Pay it back when you can. *Please.*'

'Thanks. I'll pay it back soon as I can.'

'There's no rush.'

He wondered if the assistant manager was now going to give him a lecture. But they shook hands and said goodbye.

Outside, walking up the Haymarket, Gordon took the bill out and saw it was a five-pound note. He was delighted. Imagine getting money from an assistant bank manager I had never met. But a moment later it also registered on him that the probable reason he got the money was because the assistant manager had never laid eyes on him before.

At a small kiosk he bought a pack of tipped Gauloises, a box of matches, an *Evening Standard*. Then walked along Piccadilly to Lyons Corner House. He went into the Wimpy side, found

an empty table by the wall, ordered two hamburgers and a
black coffee. Around the centre counter North Americans were
staring at other North Americans. It might have been the
drugstore back home, except they were on good behaviour.

The alarm clock woke Mr and Mrs Black at seven even though
Mr Black wasn't going to work. He went to shave. And used
the foam lather of the company whose assistant accountant he
was. Then he sat down in the room with the Van Gogh print on
the wall, the souvenir ash-tray from Clovelly, the silver napkin
rings, the photograph of himself in the Home Guard, while
Mrs Black did his porridge and the two pieces of toast in the
kitchen.

'You won't get excited,' Mrs Black said as they were having
their second cup of tea.

'No dear.'

'She could have her old room. The children could sleep in
the spare room. And there's the camp bed.'

Mr Black put on the jacket of his dark suit, the Homburg
hat, the black coat. He was a handsome if stern-looking man
with dark straight hair, a lean face, but there was a strain about
it, the result of a lifetime of bronchial trouble.

'Do you want to take anything for the train?' Mrs Black
said, standing by the glass-enclosed cabinet with her Mary
Webb novels and his Lord Jim, James Agate, Quest for Corvo,
the books on accountancy.

'I have the paper.'

'I hope it goes all right,' Mrs Black said at the door.

'I'll be back for tea. Goodbye dear.'

The train went by Eltham, Kidbrooke, Lewisham. Mr Black
turned to the Telegraph's crossword. '— — — — — — —
is mortal's chieftest enemy' *(Shakespeare)*. He tried 'dying'. But
that wasn't long enough. Neither was 'boredom'. 'Tempta-
tion' was too long. . .

At Charing Cross he changed to a tube that took him to Victoria and here he had to wait another ten minutes for a train to
Horsham. At Horsham he took a taxi to the cottage. It was
10:20 when he opened the front gate, but he didn't go to the

front door. He went around the side of the cottage where he surprised Coral hanging up the children's washing.

'Hullo,' he said quietly.

They smiled, then they kissed. And one could see a family resemblance.

She opened the kitchen door and led him into the warm room where he took off his coat.

'How is Mummy?'

'She sends her love.'

He gave the children some toffee candy.

'Gordon is in London,' she said. 'He had to go up on business.'

'Daddy is going to bring me a dolly,' Kate said.

'We haven't had our milk,' Coral said. 'I could make tea without it.'

Mr Black sat in the worn red chair. His breathing was audible. 'You can't go on like this,' he said quietly.

Coral quickly took the children into the next room and closed the door behind them.

'Why don't you leave him,' Mr Black said. 'I'll see that you and the children are looked after. I'll get you a house —'

She didn't reply.

'He's no good,' he said. 'He'll only drag you down.'

'I can't leave him,' she said.

'If he wants to go on like this there's no reason why you and the children —'

'He's got no one except me and the children.'

'I'll get you a house—' he began, but he knew it had not gone right. This wasn't the way he had rehearsed it.

'I think you must hate me,' Coral said.

'I don't hate you,' Mr Black said. But he was at a loss as to what to say next.

Kate came into the room followed by the crawling baby. Kate had a drawing. 'This is for you Grandpa.' He took the drawing and gave the child a half-crown. He also gave Coral three one-pound notes. She immediately went next door to the grocery and came back with milk, sugar, and some biscuits. They sat in the warm room and had tea while Mr Black told

her about a cousin who had gone to Rhodesia to run an Outward Bound School. That an uncle had become manager of a
bank in Plymouth. And another cousin had gone to Canada as
a physical training instructor. It was time, he said, he was leaving. They walked slowly up the road to the Shell garage where
Mr Black took a taxi. Kate kissed him. So did Coral. 'Goodbye Daddy,' she said.

For half an hour Gordon sat in the cubicle by the wall of the
Wimpy watching other people. Then he went downstairs to the
washroom. He turned the hot tap of the sink and began to wash
his hands.

'You can always tell a McGill man. He washes his hands
*before* —'

Gordon turned to see a grinning boyish face. I don't know
him, he thought. Aloud he said, 'Of course. It's —'

'Not fair surprising you like this. I'm Hugh Finlay,' the man
said still grinning.

'Hugh Finlay,' Gordon said. They shook hands. 'What are
you doing over here?'

'Passing through. I'm on the way south, to France.'

They were both in their middle thirties, McGill graduates, in
London, but there the resemblance stopped abruptly. Hugh
Finlay was blond, ruddy, and radiated bodily comfort.

'I heard you were over here,' Finlay said. 'I was going to go
to the bank to get your address. You know we're having a
reunion?'

'No,' Gordon said. 'No, I didn't.'

'It's our tenth anniversary.'

They returned to the cubicle and ordered two coffees.

'You've worn well, Hugh,' Gordon said.

'The reward for leading a healthy life,' Finlay said. 'You
married?'

'Yes. We've got two kids.'

'Do I know her?'

'No. She's an English girl. We live in the country. How
about you?'

'I was engaged to Sally Boston. The Boston Biscuits. They

give a quarter of a million each year *anonymously*. But she was too good. She's like an angel. If she saw somebody poor, she'd cry.' He took out some coloured snapshots from his jacket pocket. 'This is my yacht at Cannes. Here's a picture of Garbo on it. Here's some of the girls I had on board last summer. She's only sixteen. Hard to believe. Do you know any addresses of girls?'

The pretty West Indian waitress came with the two cups of coffee. Gordon insisted on paying.

'How about coming to the reunion?' Hugh said suddenly. 'Lot of the gang you know will be there.'

'Do you think it will be all right?'

'I know it will. I'll phone Charlie Bishop.'

While he was gone Gordon tried to remember Hugh Finlay at McGill . . . but he couldn't.

'I talked to Charlie. He said sure, swell. We've a couple of hours. How about if we got some fresh air. I've a rented car outside.'

They were driving through Hyde Park when Hugh Finlay said, 'I saw a friend of yours last week. Mary Savage. Except she's not Mary Savage any more she's Mary Troy. Remember Jack? You'll see him at the reunion.'

'How is Mary?'

'Exactly the same. She does some kind of social work.'

'What's Jack doing?'

'Selling beans . . . millions of them. They've got a place by the river. Fifteen rooms but no kids. I think they're planning to adopt one.'

Because her father left her the money Coral decided to go into London with the children. She washed them and herself, got them dressed, caught a green bus to the station then a train to Victoria.

From Victoria she took a bus to Kensington Gardens. And walked through the Gardens. A man was flying a kite, ducks flew over. The children chased the wood pigeons. She liked London. It was the only place she wanted to live. But what chance had they? She decided to try the Town Hall. The recep-

tionist led her into a separate office where a single yellow rose
in a thin glass vase stood on the wooden desk. 'Mrs Troy will
be here in a minute.'

A tall angular woman with dark hair and glasses came in.
The woman was about the same age as Coral, perhaps a year
or two older. 'What's the problem,' she said.

'We have to get out of the place we're living in . . . in Sussex
. . . and I wonder if you can help us find somewhere in
London?'

'You have no alternative accommodation?'

'No.'

'Have you funds?'

'No. We haven't.'

'Does your husband live with you?'

'Yes.'

'I'm sorry. I'm afraid I can't help you. We can only help if
your husband leaves you.'

Coral came out with the children and walked along Kensington High Street. Everyone it seemed would help her if he left
her, or if she left him. Otherwise, what was the future? Moving
from one rented place to another, from country village to country village or, with luck, to a provincial town. And she hated
living in other people's houses.

She caught a bus to Trafalgar Square and walked among the
pigeons. The children clung to her. Then along the Mall. She
bought some choc-ices and they had a little picnic of choc-ices
on a bench in St. James's Park. She wondered where Gordon
was, who he was seeing, what he was doing. He always came
back with money and food from these trips to London. But she
suspected that he never told her the whole truth as to how he
got it.

She was walking through the Park — the baby in the push-
chair, Kate holding her hand — when a truck, with a camera
on the roof, stopped. A man and woman were inside. The man
said, 'Do you mind being in a film? Just like you are . . . with
your children. Can you do that again? Thank you. Thank you
very much.' A few minutes later, further into the park, she sat
on the grass, underneath a beech, by the water. The sun was

out. Kate was feeding the ducks, the baby was on the grass watching. She suddenly felt extraordinarily happy. She hoped the truck would come back and take a picture of them now.

Well dressed men in their middle to late thirties were standing under the hanging flags or by the windows looking out to Trafalgar Square. They greeted one another enthusiastically. They came up to Gordon Rideau.

'Hi, Gordy old man.'

'Where have you been hiding?'

'Hello Gordon,' Charlie Bishop said and shook hands. 'Nice of you to come. It has been a long time.'

'Ten years.'

'You don't look any different Gordon.'

Mike Gagnon an energetic head of a publishing firm who was tipped while an undergraduate to be the next Prime Minister came up. 'Let us in on the secret Gordy. How do you keep so slim? You wearing a corset?' Mike's fine features were slowly being undermined by fat. 'I go to the Y three times a week but I've still got this rubber ring.' And he playfully slapped his middle.

Charlie Bishop hit his glass with a spoon and called Quiet. Quiet. A short stocky man with glasses, almost bald, but hardly a line in his face. He was a director in the London branch of his grandfather's tar company.

'As you know,' he said confidently, 'this is something of an occasion. Our tenth anniversary. And while the main one is being celebrated in Montreal it is fitting that we in London should get together and remember when we all were . . .'

'Single,' someone shouted.

'*And* broke,' another replied.

He waited. 'The bond we established at McGill was something special. It's a different kind of loyalty to anything else. It's different from the wife or the kids. And I know that every time we come and get together like this that bond is strengthened.'

'Hear, hear,' came from several tables.

'This year I have a surprise. And by now you all must know

who the surprise is. He's sitting here beside me. . . Somebody has pointed out that our year was a vintage year. And it's true. We've got more people in the Canadian edition of *Time* than any year since. But the only literary man we produced was Gordy. He has lived in England, in the country, since he left us. And he is difficult to get hold of. But when I heard he would be in London today I didn't have to do much persuading to get him to come to this reunion. Fellow classmates, I'm very proud to give you Gordon Rideau.'

There was generous applause. Gordon got up.

'I first would like to say how pleased I am to be back with you.'

'Hey, where did you pick up that Limey accent?' Jack Troy called out. Charlie Bishop detected something else in Gordon's voice and wondered why he was so nervous.

'Although this is the first reunion that I have attended, I've often thought of my college days,' he said hesitantly. 'I really had a good time. And I was just old enough to know it. . . I think what made us different from the other years was because we were all returning veterans. And it was difficult to pretend we were college kids straight from high school . . .'

He's not a good speaker, thought Charlie Bishop. His voice is too monotonous. But he seems to have the right idea. It looks like a short speech.

'. . . and that nice secure feeling of walking under the avenue of black trees in winter or in the fall sitting on the grass under the willow . . .'

Hugh Finlay seemed, at that moment, to be sitting on the grass under the willow tree watching the grey squirrels, the fallen leaves, on the lawns: and waiting for a two o'clock lecture.

'One is always disappointed by change,' Gordon said coming to the end. 'And these reunions remain a tribute. To one's youth. To gaiety. To optimism. When things seemed continually fresh. And life was a pleasure. And it was all so very easy.'

He sat down quickly to loud applause. Charlie Bishop leaned

over and shook Gordon's hand. So did Mike Gagnon from the
other side.

Then Charlie Bishop got up, thanked Gordon for his speech.
'Before we leave the formal side,' Charlie said, 'I'd like us all
to stand and remember those classmates who are not here with
us.'

They got up, some bowed their heads slightly. Charlie
waited then nodded to Jack Troy. And Jack began to sing.
Holding hands the rest joined in. There were tears in Hugh
Finlay's eyes as, with the others, he sang.

> *For auld lang syne, my dear.*
> *For auld lang syne.*
> *We'll drink a cup of kindness yet*
> *For the days of auld lang syne.*

They broke up into small groups around separate tables. And
as the afternoon went on, the food, the drink, being guest of
honour did something to Gordon Rideau. He went around
gaily from one group to another. And he found himself
boasting about things that hadn't happened.

'The Russians have brought out my last two novels,' he
said, cutting into one group's conversation. 'But I can't spend
those roubles unless I go there.'

To another. 'They're making a film in Ireland. It's called
*The Millionaire.* I did the script. It's an original.'

A few moments later he tried again. 'I won some prize in
Australia. But I don't believe it. How can you believe a
telegram that's signed Johnny Soprano?'

But after a while of this he felt their lack of interest. And that
he was being left out of their conversation. The others were
talking away and they wouldn't let him come in. He had the
feeling that he was no longer wanted. . .

If anyone was watching this convivial gathering he would
have seen, through the smoke of cigarettes and cigars, Mike
Gagnon get up from the table shortly after five and make his
way across the room to the toilet. Gordon Rideau got up and

followed him. They were in there for a few minutes. Then they came out together, not talking. Some ten minutes later, Charlie Bishop made his way to the toilet. And Gordon left his chair soon after Charlie disappeared. They came out together. Charlie somewhat red in the face.

In the next half-hour Gordon followed three more into the toilet, and reappeared with each one.

The talk around the table where Gordon Rideau sat was noticeably subdued. A short while later he got up and said he had to go. 'It's a great reunion,' he said to Charlie Bishop. He wanted to shake Charlie's hand, but Charlie withdrew his. 'See you . . .'

After he had gone, Charlie Bishop, Mike Gagnon, Jack Troy, Hugh Finlay, sat around without saying anything. They looked tired.

'Our great author,' Mike Gagnon said finally.

'Maybe he's had a run of hard luck,' Jack Troy said.

'How much did he hit you?'

'Three pounds.'

'He got that from me.'

'That four-flusher —' Hugh said, his voice shaking.

'You guys got off easy,' Charlie Bishop said. 'He hit me for five.'

'*That little four-flusher.*' Suddenly Hugh lashed out at a glass on the table. Then he saw it was on the floor in pieces.

'Don't take it so hard,' Charlie Bishop said. 'There's another one next year. I won't make the same mistake.'

'But why . . .?' Hugh said. 'Why did he spoil everything?'

# We All Begin in a Little Magazine

We live in a small coastal town and in the summer, when the place is looking its best, it becomes overcrowded with people who have come away from the cities for their annual holiday by the sea. It is then that we leave and go up to London for our holiday.

My wife usually finds a house by looking through *The Times*. In this way we had the house of a man who built hotels in the poor parts of Africa so that wealthy American Negroes could go back to see where their grandparents came from. Another summer it was an architect's house where just about everything was done by push-button control. A third time, it was in a house whose owner was in the middle of getting a divorce — for non-consummation — and wanted to be out of the country.

This June she saw an ad saying: DOCTOR'S HOUSE AVAILABLE IN LONDON FOR THREE WEEKS. REASONABLE RENT. She phoned the number. And we agreed to take it.

The advertised house was central, near South Kensington tube station, not far from the Gardens. The taxi took us from Paddington — how pale people looked in London on a hot summer's day — and brought us to a wide street, stopping in front of a detached all-white house with acacia trees in the front garden. A bottle of warm milk was on the doorstep. I opened the door with the key and brought our cases inside.

The phone was ringing.

'Hello,' I said.

'Is this *ABC*?' a youthful voice asked.

'I'm sorry,' I said. 'You have the wrong number.'

'What is your number?'

'Knightsbridge 4231,' I said.

'That *is* the number,' the voice said.

'There must be some mistake,' I said. 'This is a doctor's house.'

'Is the doctor there?'

'No,' I said. 'He's on holiday.'

'Can I leave a message for him?'

'Are you ill?'

'No,' he said. 'Tell him that David White rang. David White of Somerset. He has had my manuscript for over six months now. He said he would let me know over a month ago. I have written him four times.'

'I'll tell him,' I said.

'If he needs more time,' the young man said hesitantly, 'I don't mind —'

'OK,' I said and hung up.

'I don't know what's going on here,' I said to my wife.

But she and the children were busy exploring the rest of the house.

It was a large house and it looked as if it had been lived in. The front room was a children's room with all sorts of games and blackboards and toys and children's books and posters on the walls. There was the sitting-room, the bottom half of the walls were filled with books in shelves. There were more books in the hallway, on the sides of the stairs, and in shelves on every landing. There were three separate baths. A breakfast room where a friendly black cat slept most of the time on top of the oil-fired furnace. And a back garden with a lawn, flowerbeds on the sides, a pond with goldfish, water-lilies, and a copper beech tree at the end.

The phone rang and a shaky voice said.

'May I speak to Doctor Jones?'

'I'm sorry, he's on holiday.'

'When will he come back?'

'In three weeks,' I said.

'I can't wait that long,' the voice said. 'I'm going to New York tomorrow.'

'Would you,' I said, 'like to leave a message?'

'I can't hear what you're saying,' the voice said. 'Can you speak up? I'm a bit deaf and have to wear a hearing aid. The doctors have a cure for this now. If I'd been born two years later I would have been all right.'

'I said would you like to leave the doctor a message?'

'I don't think that will do any good,' he said. 'Could you look in his office and see if he has a poem of mine? It's called "Goodbye". If it is in proof, don't bother. I'll wait. But just find out. I am going over to teach creative writing in night school so I can make some money to come back here. The poem will probably be on the floor.'

'Hold on,' I said.

I went into the office at the top of the house. The floor was cluttered with papers and magazines and manuscripts with letters and envelopes attached. On a wooden table, a large snap file had correspondence. A box had cheques for small amounts. There were also several pound notes, loose change, a sheet of stamps, and two packages of cigarettes. (How trusting, I thought. The doctor doesn't know us — supposing we were crooks?) There was typing paper, large envelopes, a typewriter, a phone, telephone directories, and some galleys hanging on a nail on a wall. A smaller table had an in-and-out tray to do with his medical work, more letters, and copies of the *Lancet*. The neatest part of the room was the area where stacks of unsold copies of *ABC* were on the floor against the far wall.

'I'm sorry,' I said on the phone. 'I can't see it.'

'Oh,' he said. He sounded disappointed.

'Well, tell him that Arnold Mest called. M-E-S-T.'

'I've got that,' I said.

'Goodbye,' he said.

'You won't guess,' I told my wife. 'The doctor edits a little magazine.'

'We can't get away from it,' she said.

Early next morning the doorbell woke us. It was the postman. He gave me several bundles. There were letters from different parts of England and Europe and air mail ones from Canada, the States, Australia, and South America. There were two review copies of books from publishers. There were other little magazines, and what looked like medical journals, and a few bills.

As I put the envelopes and parcels on the chair in the office and saw the copies of *Horizon* and *New Writing*, the runs of *Encounter, London Magazine*, and a fine collection of contemporary books on the shelves right around the room — it brought back a time twenty years ago when I first came over.

There was still the bomb-damage to be seen, the queues, the ration books, the cigarettes under the counter. And a general seediness in people's clothes. Yet I remember it as one of my happiest times. Perhaps because we were young and full of hope and because we were so innocent of what writing involved. A lot of boys and girls had come to London from different parts. And we would meet in certain pubs, in certain restaurants, Joe Lyons, the French pub, Caves de France, the Mandrake. Then go on somewhere else. I remember going over to see another Canadian, from Montreal, who was writing a novel. He had a studio, by the Chelsea football grounds (we could always tell when a goal was scored). I remember best the cold damp winter days with the fog thick — you could just see the traffic lights — and then going inside and having some hot wine by the open fire and talking about writing, what we were writing, and where we had things out. We used to send our stories, optimistically, to the *name* magazines. But that was like taking a ticket in a lottery. It was the little magazines who published us, who gave encouragement and kept us going.

I remember Miss Waters. She was in her late forties, a pale woman with thinning blonde hair and a docile tabby cat. She edited a little magazine founded by her great-grandfather. She had photographs of Tennyson on the wall, of Yeats and Dylan Thomas. And wooden pigeon-holes, like the sorting room at the post office, with some of the recent back issues. She didn't know when I was coming. But she always greeted me with:

'How nice to see you. Do come in.'

She walked ahead, into the dark living-room. Suggested that I take my winter coat off. Then she would bring out a decanter of sherry and fill a glass. Then take out a package of *Passing Clouds*, offer me a cigarette.

I was treated as a writer by this woman when I had very little published. And that did more than anything to keep up morale. And after another sherry, another *Passing Cloud*, and she had asked me what I was working on and seemed very interested in what I said, she told me that her great-grandfather paid Tennyson a thousand pounds for one of his short poems, and two thousand pounds to George Eliot for a short story. (Was she trying to tell me that there was money to be made out of writing?) Then she stood up. And we went into the other room. It was very neat and tidy. Magazines on a table laid out as at a news agent's, books as in a library.

'Is there anything you would like to review?' she asked.

I would pick a novel or two, or a book of short stories.

Then she would say. 'And help yourself to four books from that pile.'

That pile consisted of books that she didn't want reviewed. She had told me, the first time, to take these books to a book-seller in the Strand who would give me half-price for them, and later sell them to the public libraries. But before I could get the money from him I had to sign my name in what looked like a visiting book. And I saw there, above me, the signatures of the leading Sunday and weekly reviewers — they were also selling their review copies for half-price.

And I remember how I would come to her place — with the brown envelopes lying behind the door — broke and depressed. And when I left her, I left feeling buoyed up, cheerful. There would be the few pounds from the review copies. Money enough for a hamburger and a coffee and a small cigar. And there was something to do — the books to review. She always paid in advance.

And before Miss Waters there were others. The press officer at the Norwegian Embassy — he ran a Norwegian little magazine, in English, from London. And another one, from India, also in English. My early stories appeared in both. And when I got a copy of the Indian magazine I saw that my Canadian characters had been turned into Indians. And there was another editor who would ask to borrow your box of matches. Then when you got back to your flat you found he had stuffed a pound note inside the box.

They are all gone — like their magazines.

And something has gone with them.

Those carefree days when you wrote when you felt like it. And slept in when you wanted to. And would be sure of seeing others like yourself at noon in certain places.

Now in the morning, after breakfast, I wait for the mail to come. Then I go upstairs and close the door behind me. And I make myself get on with the novel, the new story, or the article which has been commissioned by a well-paying magazine. I take a break for lunch, then come back up here until four. Once in a while I might take a day off and go on a bus to see what the country is like. I forget that there is so much colour about. Or, for a change, take a train for the day to Plymouth. But otherwise, it is up the stairs to this room. All my energy now goes into work. I light up a small Dutch cigar, and sometimes I talk to myself. I feel reasonably certain now that what I have written will be published. Writing has become my living.

Of course there are still the occasional days when things are going right and the excitement comes back from the work. Not like in those early days when writing and the life we were leading seemed so much to belong together. I had complete faith then in those little magazines. What I didn't know was that what they bred was infectious. They infected a lot of young people with the notion that to be involved with literature was somehow to be involved with the good life. And by the time you learned differently, it was usually too late.

On Friday I had to be up early. In the morning I was to be interviewed, in a rowing-boat on the Serpentine, for a Canadian television programme on the "Brain-Drain". And later I was to meet my publisher for lunch.

It was very pleasant on the water early in the morning. The sun made patterns. People going to work stopped to watch. While I rowed the interviewer, the cameraman, the sound-recordist, and their equipment — and was asked why wasn't I living in Canada, and why did I write?

I met my publisher in his club. He is an American, from Boston, bald and short. We had a Martini. Then another. Then we went into the dining-room. Smoked salmon followed by duck with wine, then dessert. And ending with brandy and a large Havana cigar.

He asked me what type would I like for the book, could I send him the blurb for the dust-jacket? He told me the number of copies they would print, that one of the Sunday papers wanted to run a couple of extracts before publication. He told me some gossip about other writers, publishers, and agents. And what was I writing now? And which publishing season would he have it for?

I left him after four and caught a taxi back to the house.

'How did it go?' my wife asked.

'OK,' I said. 'How was the zoo?'

She began to tell me when we heard a noise. It sounded as if it was coming from the front door. We went to look and surprised a man with a key trying to open the door. He was in his late fifties, short and stocky and wearing a shabby raincoat.

'Is the doc in?' he said timidly.

'No,' I said. 'He's on holiday.'

'Oh,' he said. 'I've come up from Sussex. I always have a bed here when I come up.'

He spoke with an educated accent.

'I'm sorry,' I said. 'But we have the place for three weeks.'

'I always have a bed here when I come up.'

'There isn't room,' I said.

'My name is George Smith,' he said. '*ABC* publish me. I'm a poet.'

'How do you do,' I said. 'We'll be gone in ten days. Come in and have a drink.'

While I poured him a brandy, I asked what was the name of his last book.

He said he had enough work for a book and had sent the manuscript to — and here he named a well-known publisher.

'But I haven't heard,' he said.

'That's a good sign,' I said.

'Perhaps they have lost it,' he said. 'Or they are, like Doc, on holiday.'

He brought out a small tin and took some loose tobacco and began to roll his own cigarette and one for me.

'How long,' I asked, 'have they had it?'

'Nearly five months,' he said.

He finished his brandy. I poured him some more.

'I would ring them up and find out,' I said. 'Or drop them a line.'

'Do you think I should?'

'Yes,' I said.

I went to the door to see him out. And instead walked him to the bus stop.

The street was full of mountain ash and red berries were lying on the lawns, the sidewalk, and on the road.

'I had a letter from T.S. Eliot,' he said. 'I kept it all these years. But I sold it last month to Texas for fifty dollars,' he said proudly. 'My daughter was getting married. And I had to get her a present.'

I asked him where he would stay the night.

'I have one or two other places,' he said. 'I come up about once every six weeks. London is my commercial centre.'

I went and bought him a package of cigarettes.

'Thank you,' he said.

The red bus came and I watched him get on.

When I got back my wife said.

'Well, do you feel better?'

'No,' I said.

It went on like this — right through the time we were there. An assortment of people turned up at the door. There was a young blonde girl — she wanted to lick stamps for literature. There were visiting lecturers and professors from American and Canadian and English universities. There were house-wives; one said, over the phone, 'I'll do anything to get into print.' There were long-distance telephone calls. One rang after midnight and woke us up. 'Nothing important,' the voice said. 'I just wanted to have a talk. We usually do now and then. I've had stories in *ABC*.'

There was, it seemed, a whole world that depended on the little magazine.

I tried to be out of the house as much as possible. I went to see my agent. He had a cheque for four hundred dollars, less his commission, waiting for me, for the sale of a story. He took me out for a meal. And we talked about the size of advances, the sort of money paperback publishers were paying these days, the way non-fiction was selling better than fiction. I met other writers in expensive clubs and restaurants. We gossiped about what middle-aged writer was leaving his middle-aged wife to live with a young girl. And what publisher was leaving his firm to form his own house. I was told what magazines were starting — who paid the best.

Then I would come back to the phone ringing, the piles of mail, and people turning up at the door eager to talk about the aesthetics of writing. I didn't mind the young. But it was the men and women who were around my age or older who made me uncomfortable. I didn't like the feeling of superiority I had when I was with them. Or was it guilt? I didn't know.

Meanwhile my wife and kids enjoyed themselves. They went to the Victoria and Albert Museum, the National Gallery, the Tate. And came back with post-card reproductions that they sent to friends. They went to a couple of Proms, to a play, had a day in Richmond Park, Hampton Court, and a boat ride on the Thames.

When the time came to go back — they didn't want to.

But I did.

I had passed through my *ABC* days. And I wanted to get away. Was it because it was a reminder of one's youth? Or of a time which promised more than it turned out to be? I told myself that there was an unreality about it all — that our lives then had no economic base — that it was a time of limbo. But despite knowing these things, I carry it with me. It represents a sort of innocence that has gone.

On the Saturday morning waiting for the taxi to come to take us to Paddington Station, the phone rang. And a young girl's voice wanted to know about her short story.

I said the doctor was away. He would be back later. She ought to ring this evening.

'What time?'

'After nine,' I said.

'Have you read the story?' she asked. 'What do you think of it?'

'We just rented the house,' I said. 'We were here for a holiday.'

'Oh,' she said. 'You're not one of us?'

'No,' I said.

Then the taxi came. And the driver began to load the cases into the back of the car.

# Part Four

# I Don't Want to Know
# Anyone Too Well

I first heard of Al Grocer as a legible signature at the end of this typewritten letter.

Dear Mr. Bonnar,

I should like to ask you quite well in advance if you would be agreeable to act as my guide while I'm in Cornwall for a week at the beginning of September. I operate an original service for independent radio stations throughout Australia. We offer them tape-recordings of various aspects of European life. For the 1967 season our project is a series of journeys. And after reading your excellent article on Cornwall we have decided to include *A Journey into Cornwall* on our list.

I hope you can come with me, and together we can shape a thirty-minute travel-interpretation of this (your) region. I would be prepared to pay for your services. And I think it would be fun to do. And I hope you can find time to do it with me. By the way, to lug the equipment (and ourselves) around, I'll rent a car because I think of this in terms of my own pleasure and comfort, plus the great benefit of being mobile in our work. At any rate, may I have your initial reaction at this time.

Cordially,
Al Grocer.

I wrote back saying I'd be delighted. It seemed a fine way of seeing the country and having a holiday as well. For though I've lived in Cornwall for five years I haven't been around much. I don't drive.

On Friday I got Sam England to take his taxi and we drove over to St Erth to meet the train. It was a fine blustering kind of morning with white caps in the bay. And I could see the shadows of the low clouds moving over the far shore fields leaving patches of light green, dark green, and brown. Al Grocer had sent me a brochure of his company. It included a photograph. From the photograph he looked to be an undistinguished crew-cut, in his thirties. But the man I finally approached — the only one left standing on the platform — was clearly in his fifties. Medium height, stocky, bald. He was neatly dressed in a navy blue blazer, grey flannels, a white shirt open at the neck. And on a pale face he had very large black sunglasses.

'Mister Grocer?' I said. 'Good to see you.'

'Ditto,' he said, dragging the word out. And his accent had a trace of central Europe in it.

He smiled. And his mouth showed, contrary to what I expected, one of the finest sets of teeth I have ever seen. We shook hands firmly. Then he put his arm around my shoulder and left it there. Something I do not entirely take with strangers. It was, I discovered, one of his mannerisms. A few days later I introduced him to my bank manager to cash a personal cheque of his as he was running short. In less than five minutes after meeting the manager he was putting his arm around the bank manager's shoulder.

'Call me Al,' he said. And changed his glasses for another pair that he brought out of his blazer pocket. I caught a glimpse of bulging eyes. 'I better make sure the porters don't throw the equipment around, it's sensitive.'

There were no porters. The portable recording machinery was dumped on the platform, and the train moved off to Penzance. I helped him carry the equipment up the steps and across the covered, brown, wooden bridge above the tracks. He was breathing hard and I could smell scent, a kind of bay rum.

'How was the trip?'

'Not bad,' he puffed. 'I really go for these toy English trains.'

'Your first time in England?'

'No. Twenty-five or thirty years ago I lived in Southampton — for three months. Someone got a disease on the boat taking us to Australia. They took us all off the boat and put us in quarantine. Until we all got the disease. Guess who got it last . . .?'

On the way back we had to share the taxi with an elderly couple who were staying at the Tregenna Castle. We drove up the long drive of trees, to the plateau, and the taxi stopped. Mister Grocer opened the taxi door and got out, surveying the grounds, the country-house of a hotel, the fine view of St Ives with the harbour, bay, and the Atlantic below.

'I'm going to like this place,' he said, taking off his glasses and inhaling the air.

'This isn't where you're staying,' I said. 'This is the most expensive hotel here. You asked for bed and breakfast. I've got you a place for fifteen shillings a day — it's clean.'

He put his dark glasses back on and returned into the taxi visibly disappointed. I had a feeling this kind of thing had happened to him before. And for some inexplicable reason I wished there and then that Mister Grocer could have stayed at the Tregenna Castle.

My wife took an instant dislike to him. She had gone to some trouble and expense to get a duck and spent most of the day getting it ready.

'What's this?' he said, 'rabbit?'

'No,' my wife said, 'it's crow.'

He looked so startled that I found myself saying. 'It's duck. It's been done in wine.' And for my wife's benefit. 'It's delicious.' But the damage had been done.

Next morning he came around after breakfast. He had changed and was wearing a fawn gaberdine jacket over a dark blue sport shirt, light-blue sport trousers, and the black sunglasses. Apart from his bulging eyes his other features were fine, though age and fat had started to undermine them. 'How do you like the bed and breakfast place?'

'Just fine.'

I fixed him up with a place run by a couple of artists. They had a terraced house and took in people, since they couldn't make a living from painting. But I was a bit worried if Mister Grocer would take to their bohemian ways.

'Would you like a walk?' I said.

'You're now about to get one of Bonnar's Conducted Tours,' my wife said sarcastically from the kitchen. I had never known her to take such an instant dislike to anyone.

We were walking towards Carbis Bay — it's a pleasant walk: on the side of a slope, overlooking the bay, alongside flowering gorse, blackberry bushes, and wild garlic — when he said: 'William, you having trouble in your marriage?'

'No.'

'It's no good William, I can tell. I'm sensitive to people's voices. I can walk into a room and spot immediately by the way a person talks whether he likes me or not. And I could tell from the way your wife spoke that you've just had a row. . .'

'But we haven't.'

We walked on, through a stile, in silence.

'You married?'

He shook his head. 'I had a girl once, in Poland. When the war came an uncle in Adelaide said he would bring her out for me. I would come later. He did bring her over. Three years later he helped to bring me. When I came, I found my girl married to his son.' He stopped, plucked a wild garlic. 'I made films in Poland,' and put the green stem in his mouth, 'before the war, historical pictures — I used to be quite well known.'

After about a mile the path leads to the door of the Carbis Bay Hotel. It was a very hot day, the tennis courts were deserted, there wasn't anyone on the close-cropped lawns. We went inside the hotel. No one there either. I suggested that he wait while I try to find out if we could have some tea or coffee or a beer out on the lawn or the balcony. I finally found a student in the kitchen who said he was working here for the summer. He said they didn't provide refreshments for non-residents during the season. I told this to Mister Grocer. But it was obvious that he had his mind on something else.

'Is there anyone about?'

'No.'

He walked behind the reception-desk and calmly helped himself to a considerable number of hotel envelopes and hotel writing paper. Then he sat down by a table in the empty lounge, made himself comfortable, and began to write a letter.

'I like good hotel stationery,' he said.

When we returned to St Ives he fumbled in his fawn jacket pocket.

'I've lost my Biro.'

So I took him to Woolworth's. He tried out several plastic pens at a shilling each, but didn't like them. 'They are much too cheap.'

We came out and walked along the front.

'I think we can get a Biro,' I said, 'in Literature and Art.'

*'But I've got one.'* And he brought out from his fawn jacket pocket one of the plastic pens that were on sale in Woolworth's. 'What's the matter,' he said good-humouredly. 'Haven't you ever taken something with*out* paying for it?'

We rented a car from the North Star Garage. We planned to start next morning. For the first day we would go outward to Land's End along the North Coast, and come back by the South. We decided it would be best to start early and return to St Ives, from wherever we were, to sleep.

We met in the car park by the cemetery. He was there, looking closely through a copy of *The Times.* And he encircled with his pen possible stories that he might record. *The oldest water wheel in England was in the West Country* — that would make an item, he said. *The man who breeds worms for a living.* Then he transferred these into a notebook that was marked *Ideas.* On its front page in his large clear writing was

*What is precious is never to forget*
*The essential delight of the blood.*

'I've got the front of this book full of quotations and jokes,'
he said, turning the pages. 'Listen to this. What did the young
rabbi say to the old rabbi in the French pastry shop as he
passed the cakes: *Have another Ghetto.*' And he laughed infec-
tiously.

It was raining when he drove out of St Ives and in a matter of
minutes we were on the moors. The sea was beside us on the
right. The moor on the left. And the rain kept coming across
like folds of a pale white curtain.

'It's wet in England,' he said thoughtfully.

Our first stop was at a filling station. The man who ran it
was an oldtimer, one of the survivors of a mining disaster.
Mister Grocer came in carrying his portable tape-recorder in a
green sling over his shoulder. And he began to flatter the man.
But the oldtimer stopped him. 'I've been interviewed many
times on radio and television. You just tell me what you
want . . .'

Mister Grocer asked him questions. They rehearsed, twice.
Mister Grocer checked his equipment. He locked the door. He
stuffed paper into the door bell. He put up a 'Closed' sign in
the window. And just as everything was set to record, Mister
Grocer had an attack of nerves. So he had another rehearsal.
The oldtimer was right-on with his replies, while Mister Grocer
fluffed his.

'I must take a tranquilliser,' he said and swallowed a pill. He
had worked himself up into such a state that I was ready to suggest that I interview the oldtimer.

Then the interview started. And once he began, the voice
that spoke into the microphone was authoritative, distinct, and
without a trace of anxiety. It was the anonymous 'interview
voice' that radio and television have made familiar. As soon as
he finished he relaxed. And you could see he was no longer
interested in the oldtimer, in mining, in this part of Cornwall.
All he wanted to do was to get away from here.

'That's the start,' he said, walking back to the car. He was full of nervous excitement and kept patting me on the shoulder. 'The hard part is always the start.' I said it was the same in writing. As a parting shot he told the oldtimer the only obvious lie I could detect — that he would let him know when it would be broadcast. But driving on to Land's End he said that he came from a wealthy family just outside Warsaw. That his people were in wood. 'My father had forests.' And when he made a bit more cash in Australia he would go back for a visit. 'I would like to see what the place looks like. We had a magnificent white house — I was born there. We had an Alsatian on a long leash attached to an overhead wire — he patrolled the grounds . . .'

And I didn't believe a word of it.

I could see St Just come out of the midst. And in the town complete silence except for the squawks from the jackdaws and gulls. This is a part of Cornwall not touched by tourists. Instead of 'Bed and Breakfast' the signs here said 'House for Sale'. Empty square, large Wesleyan chapel, squat church. And right beside them small fields with cows and horses, barns and dung. A gull flew low down a wide empty street and the mist lay on the surrounding hilltops with stooks of corn on the slopes. Around the perimeter: abandoned tin-mine chimneys and the Atlantic.

We went to the Western Hotel — I had once met the owner. Mister Grocer had me rehearse with him before we came to St Just all the facts about St Just that I thought he ought to know, until he had memorised them word-perfect — he might have been an actor learning a part. And, for a few minutes, he did talk intelligently about St Just with the hotel owner. He rehearsed the interview. Then again went into a flap. I was posted outside to keep guard. Doors were locked. And just as soon as the interview was over he wanted to get away from here. It was as if he had done something he knew he shouldn't and was afraid of being found out.

By the end of the second day I was beginning to have doubts whether this little holiday trip would last the week. I was convinced that Mister Grocer was on the verge of a nervous breakdown. He turned up around ten that night at the door of the cottage with his bags and portable equipment, sweat on his face. 'William, I'd like to move.'

'What's wrong?'

'Nothing's wrong. But the place — it's not for me.'

My wife gave me a knowing glance. She was brought up in a London suburb and doesn't approve of the mild bohemian life that flickers here in the summer.

'Why don't you take him to Mrs Richards?' she said.

I walked him over to Mrs Richards, helped carry his stuff. On the way down he suddenly stopped, put his bags on the road. I thought he was tired. 'William, I forgot to pay at the last place. Could you, for me?' And he took out a couple of pounds.

'Sure,' I said.

'Tell them I had to go to London, unexpectedly. And didn't have time to pay or say goodbye.'

I left him at Mrs Richards and went to the other place and saw Leo — one of the owners.

'Leo. Al Grocer had to go to London. Here's what he owes.'

'*Grocer*. That friend of yours is some character.'

'What's up?'

'He came into my room last night, said he had Angst. Said he wanted to tuck me in and kiss me goodnight.'

Next morning when I got to the car park he was putting away *The Times* and his notebook in the dashboard compartment.

'Is Mrs Richards' place OK?'

'Fine William,' he said cheerfully. 'It's healthy the food here — I've broken out in pimples.'

We drove out. The rain had stopped. And there was a fresh morning smell to the air. He suddenly became concerned about my welfare. 'You must get out of Cornwall — the place is too slow. You have been spoiled living here. You won't be able to survive in a city. I'm not joking. And the longer you live here the harder it will be. Come to Australia. With your education you could make money over there — like mud.'

He watched me smoke a cigarette, with disapproval. Finally, he said. 'You smoke your cigarettes too much. You must throw more of a cigarette away. You sell yourself cheap . . .'

We headed for the south coast in sunshine. Over the car radio a crooner was singing.

> *Tear a star from out the sky*
> *And the sky feels blue . . .*

In Falmouth he interviewed three housewives and got their recipe for making a pasty. In Helston he got the mayor to talk about the Flora dance. Then came cursing out of a public lavatory.

'England's finished — there's no reason for a civilised country to have *such* toilet paper.'

In Bodmin he saw, at a magazine stall, that Daphne du Maurier lived in Cornwall. He bought one of her books. Read about a dozen pages while we were having tea. 'She's a very good writer. I wish I had time to go to a library and get some background reading on Daphne du Maurier. She interests me very much.' And he went to the hotel's phone and rang her up. But she wouldn't see him. As we drove across Bodmin Moor, he tossed her book out of the window.

A couple of miles later the car broke down. The clutch burnt out. We left the car, on the side of the road, on the moor. Hitch-hiked to the nearest phone, and rang up the garage. Then got a lift to St Erth and walked over to the station. Al Grocer wanted to go in a first-class compartment. I told him on these one track lines they were exactly the same. Anyway, we had bought a second-class ticket. But he wanted first. He had a stubborn streak in him.

And just when it seemed I had enough of him (he pocketed my change when I paid for lunch; he would never buy a round when we stopped off at a pub; and I began to think of the whole thing as a fiasco) I began to like him. I can't explain why. But I found I was looking forward to seeing him again the next day, and being in his company. Perhaps it was no more than knowing he was going away. Or maybe because neither of us belonged here, and we had come a long way to be thrown together. Or maybe the explanation was even simpler: certain things had now happened to both of us — we had a past in common. I told this to my wife. She thought I was crazy. She said she didn't want Al Grocer around any more and wouldn't care if she never saw him again.

He came to the door on his last night. A face made sad by the large bulging eyes. Neatly dressed in a grey suit, and very apologetic. '. . . you mind William if we have a few drinks?' He held up a bottle of whisky. And for my wife he brought a miniature cherry brandy. She relented.

As he entered he said excitedly. 'I've taken a room for my last night here — bet you won't guess —?'

'The Tregenna Castle?'

'No, not quite. The Porthminster.'

It wasn't a bad evening. He was very good at telling a story, especially against himself. Near the end he began to get introspective. 'I wonder why I feel insulted after a day interviewing people — I meet people all the time — but I've never got to know anyone — you know what I'm getting at?'

'It's a job,' I said.

'— there's something about the business — it makes you lose something of yourself as a human being — something of your dignity.'

But he had drunk too much and went upstairs and was sick. It was past midnight when I suggested that we'd better call it a day. He said he enjoyed his stay in Cornwall and enjoyed meeting both of us very much.

'Now, could you get me a taxi.'

I told him it was only a three-minute walk to the Porthminster, and I would walk him back. He insisted on a taxi. I didn't think anyone would bother to come at this time for such a short distance — and I was right. But he wouldn't have it. 'I'll get a taxi,' he said defiantly, and walked unsteadily out of the room to the phone. I could hear him putting on his interview voice.

'You know who I am. I'm *Al Grocer — Al Grocer —*'

'He says Al Grocer,' my wife said, 'the way other people say

Happy Christmas.'

'— *Al Grocer* will put Cornwall on the map — All *Al Grocer* wants is a taxi — to take him to your Porthminster Hotel — where he's staying —' He must have tried a half-dozen places, going through the same routine. Finally a taxi agreed to come. And he came back to the front room. 'I had to throw a bit of that personality stuff around,' he said deprecatingly, 'it comes in useful,' and sank back into one of the chairs. I could see headlights sweeping the dark street. So I went and hailed the taxi. The taximan had got out of bed and all he had on was a coat over his pyjamas and slippers. He apologised — with one hand by his mouth — for not having time to put in his false teeth.

But Al decided he didn't want to go. I helped him up and steered him to the door. He kept on about 'dignity'. Then, with great effort, he pulled himself together and said very precisely.

'Come up tomorrow morning, William, and have breakfast with me at the Porthminster.'

I did go up next morning. He was back to the navy blue blazer, grey flannels, and those large black sunglasses.

'You know, William, I've put something of yours in my quotation book.' He turned some pages. 'I got it from your novel. *I don't want to get to know anyone too well,*' he read slowly, '*when I do I don't like them.*'

I was going to explain that it was just a character talking — but he didn't give me a chance.

'It's very true,' he said quietly. 'Sad isn't it.'

Then he asked me if I would carry his bags down to the station while he carried the portable recording equipment. I didn't mind, but as we walked down the slope I couldn't help feeling that the reason I was asked up for breakfast was to carry his bags down for him. And immediately I was annoyed with myself for thinking this. To make up for it, at the station, I went over to the paper-kiosk and bought him a copy of the morning's *Times*.

'Business can wait,' he said with a laugh. And with a grand gesture flung the paper to the corner of the compartment. And shook my hand a long time. Large black sunglasses on a pale face, leaning out of the train, was the last I saw of him.

Ten weeks later I received a glossy picture post-card from Sydney. On the front was a coloured photograph of its most expensive hotel. On the back he had written:

> *I am resting up here after a very rough ocean voyage. I have a few ideas for 1968. How would you like to come over and do a journey through the Outback. Will write again and send address.*
>
> *Cordially, Al.*

# A Writer's Story

At the beginning of 1952 we were married. And in the spring
we left London (two uncomfortable rooms in a cold house in a
northern suburb) for the south of Cornwall. And rented a
granite house on the lower slope of a hill. It had a high walled
garden with palms, bamboos, copper beech, and hydrangeas.
Wild roses were on a frame bent over to form an arch. Blackberries grew on top of the wall. And between two trees was a
hammock.

The house was once a schoolhouse. And in the front room,
where we would eat and sit in the evenings, there was a long
table with fixed benches on either side. And cut in the dark var-
nished wood were generations of children's names.

I worked in a large building attached to the house. The only
furniture was a small stove where I burned wood in winter, a
chaise longue where I read the landlord's little magazines
(*Blast, Tyro, Horizon*) and the novels of Henry Green that were
in a bookcase against the white wall. And a table where I
wrote. The building must have been the gym or the assembly
hall for there was a raised platform at one end. And it had a
high ceiling and large windows.

From a window overlooking the road I could hear the stream that went by outside and see, in the field opposite, a light pink house surrounded by trees with white blossoms. And further away the small green fields, separated by irregular hedges, sloping gently upwards. And in the distance a farmhouse.

From a window on the other wall I could see — over the garden and over the slate roofs and chimneys of the village — the water in the bay, the long sweep of the far shore. At dusk the land was often coloured purple. And we could hear the curlews as they flew back to the rocks at the sea's edge. And hear them again the first thing in the morning when we were still in bed. That gentle melancholy sound of a curlew flying over the house on the way to the fields above.

Sam, our landlord, looked like a Tolstoyan farmer. He always wore baggy trousers, worn shirts, a wide leather belt, and large working-men's shoes. He was tall and broad but he had a small head and a close-cropped ginger beard. For such a big man he had a gentle voice. And he spoke well and smiled easily.

He lived with his wife in a cottage on the moors. They believed in the simple life, in living off the land, in natural foods. They had these handsome blonde children running around in bare feet. And because I had an MA and because he wanted something better for his kids than the local school, I signed a form that said I would look after their education. But it was my wife who taught them how to read and write.

By the time we knew him, he must have been in his middle forties, I had a feeling that he had lived quite a different kind of life before coming here. It was his voice which told it all. Years later someone told me that Sam was an Old Etonian. That's part of Sam's story that I don't know.

I only know that he was kind to us. He would arrive, on a bicycle, in the morning. His lunch in a brown paper bag. He always brought something for my wife: endive, new potatoes, a cabbage, a cauliflower, duck eggs or honey that he collected. We would all have coffee in the front room. Then he would go into the back of the gym which was partitioned off and quite separate from where I worked. And here he would do his paintings. 'My pot boilers,' he said with a smile. But he was still hopeful that he would make a breakthrough and become known. When he did show me twenty or thirty canvases — it looked like a class at an art school — every picture was painted in a different style.

If Sam, dressed like a peasant farmer, was getting away from his past, so was I. The navy blue blazer with nickel-plated buttons, the grey flannels, the pipe — they belonged to the last four years at university and to three previous years, in uniform, in the war. But behind them were the streets of Lower Town, the houses with stables in the back. A working class community of French Canadians and immigrant Europeans that I was running away from. I just had a first novel accepted and thought of myself as a writer. I expected being a writer would be a continuation of the life I knew at university: where I edited the literary magazine, had poems and stories on the Montreal radio, and wrote the novel in my final year. Things appeared to follow one another, and fall naturally into place, without my having to try very hard. The war . . . university . . . novel accepted . . . getting married. And now coming here to write the next book.

But for the first few weeks we took it easy. The early spring days were warm and sunny. Few people were about. The place had an air of nothing happening, of people gently living out their lives. Rooks and gulls flew slowly by. It was so quiet. And full of colour. The sea. The sky. The yellow sand beaches. Things growing in the fields and in the hedgerows.

Around ten in the morning Charlie would come up the granite steps to bring me *The Times*. He thought I was a painter. And if the back pages of *The Times* had a photograph of some disaster (like the Lynmouth flood, an air crash or a fire) he would open the door, grin, and say.

'This make good picture.'

'Yes, Charlie.'

Later I found out that Charlie, though in his thirties, couldn't read.

Or else Sam would come in to tell me some story he heard in the village. 'You can write about that,' he said.

I tried to write.

I spent hours at the wooden table in the large high room. And I didn't know what to write about. That's the trouble with going to university, I thought. I didn't have to try hard enough. The results for a little effort were too immediate and too great. You think you're a writer because those at university say so and make a fuss. But now that I was on my own —?

'You must write,' I told myself. 'It will come if you write.'

But what to write about. I didn't know.

I thought at first that, at twenty-seven, I had run out of material. But as the weeks went by I realized it wasn't that at all. I didn't know what my material was.

I sat at the table, smoked (the pipe kept going out), read the little magazines, went to the windows.

What a pleasant place to be idle in.

I decided to take a notebook and go out. I walked to the sea's edge. And made notes. 'The way the sun appears on the water on a hot summer's day. The blue water sparkles. Then it seems as if it is raining sundrops. They are hitting the water — slanting down — golden moving streaks — just like rain.'

'I walk by the tideline,' I wrote, 'and I can see my footsteps behind me. But a little while later the footsteps disappear in the moist sand leaving no trace.'

Then I sat on the granite pier and tried to describe the colours of the sea, the changing colours of the land as the clouds passed over.

When my wife asked me at lunch. 'How's the writing going?'

'Fine,' I said.

On Sundays we went for walks in the country. She knew all the wild flowers. She would tell me their names. And I would repeat. But when we went out the following Sunday, I had forgotten. So she would name them again.

'What did you do as a child?' she asked.

What did I do, I wondered.

'We had other flowers,' I said.

We passed a field with chickens. Horses in another. It was so still. So quiet.

'See the mole-hills,' my wife said.

I didn't know they were mole-hills.

'That's buddleia,' my wife said, 'butterflies like it.'

She was right. There were butterflies resting on this bush.
The sun caught them. Some with their wings spread, others
drawn up. I counted twenty. And there were more.

'Those are Red Admirals,' she said. 'That's Tortoiseshell.
That's a Peacock —'

But on Monday morning I was back in the large high room
by the wooden table. It was much better when I was out looking at things.

That is how I met Mrs Burroughs.

I was out with my notebook. And she was standing by her
front gate with a letter in her hand.

'Are you going to the post office?' she said. 'Will you take
this for me?'

After three more times taking letters for her she invited me
into her house.

We walked along the gravel path with the garden on one
side. Mrs Burroughs' ankles were swollen and she had difficulty in walking. She used a cane. She was a large woman,
slightly bent, with grey hair combed tight to her head and in a
bun at the back. She had a large face, almost like a man's, thin
lips, a strong jaw with loose skin under it. But her china-blue
eyes were delicate. They slanted upwards.

'I don't go out much,' she said quietly.

It was dark when we came into the house. I thought, at first,
it was because we came in from the sunlight. But the walls of
the rooms were painted brown. And they had dark Victorian
oil paintings on them. Cows by a stream. Trees in a field. In
front of the fireplace was a highly polished copper screen. And
hammered out in the copper was a sailing ship. On a dark
wooden side-table, in a glass case, were three exotic stuffed
birds with long tails. Their feathers were blue and green. But
the colours had faded. The brightest things in the room were
various glass bottles, glass vases, on the window sills. They
were all the same ruby colour but with different designs.

'Sit down,' Mrs Burroughs said. 'I heard you are at the old

schoolhouse. And you're a writer. What are you writing?'

'I have a novel coming out,' I said.

The phone rang. She didn't appear to hear it.

'The phone is ringing,' I said.

'Oh,' she said. And quickly went out of the room. I could hear her shouting from the next room. When she came back she sat down in her chair and said.

'What are you writing *now*?'

'Nothing.'

'Why not?'

'I don't know.'

She looked puzzled.

'You mean you don't know any stories?'

I didn't know what to say.

'I know lots,' she said. 'I'll tell you.'

And she did.

Every time I came up to see her she would show me into the front room, ask me to sit down, and tell me something else from her past.

It began eighty-one years ago. Her father was a farmer. She was a teacher and taught in a country school. Then she married Mr Burroughs who had a timber business. They moved into Penzance and had two daughters and a son. She packed up the teaching and ran the accounts. As they made money they put the money into land and houses. They had properties all over Cornwall. When her husband died her son ran the business. Then the youngest daughter, Shirley, died when she was in her thirties. And Mrs Burroughs didn't go out of the house after that. She didn't get on with her older daughter, Brenda.

'I don't go to see her often,' Brenda told me, when I met her a few months later. 'When I do, Mam begins to cry and says: why aren't you Shirley?'

I would sit in the darkened room with the Victorian paintings and watch how the light from the windows caught the ruby glass. While Mrs Burroughs talked.

'Last year,' she said, 'I went to Jean's — my granddaughter's — wedding. One of Jean's girlfriends had a quarrel

with her boyfriend. They split up. And she didn't have anyone
to take her to the wedding. So she hired a boy from an agency.
Someone she had never seen before — to take her. At the wedding I saw this woman. I remembered her when she was a
child. Her father and mother — they had their own farm —
were devoted to each other. But they didn't have children.
Then when she was in her forties she got pregnant. The baby
was born. But the mother died in childbirth. The father was
out in the fields. When he heard he went and shot himself. And
there was this child, now a woman and married, at the
wedding. Isn't that a good story for you to write?'

'Yes,' I said.

'I have a cousin,' Mrs Burroughs said. 'She was going out
with this boy. He worked as an accountant. Very neat. But the
family didn't think he was good enough. So there was opposi-
tion to the wedding. But they did get married. Then the war
came along. The Second World War. The man was called up.
And he cut his throat because he was frightened of being killed
in the war.'

I'd go and see Mrs Burroughs on Saturday mornings
because her grandson came in from Penzance to play the piano
for her. They were old tunes, mostly waltzes.

'It reminds her of the time when she was a girl,' he told me.

I'd be in the front room looking out over her garden, the
sounds from the piano came from the other room, while Mrs
Burroughs talked.

'My daughter's husband is called Jack,' she said. 'His
grandmother — when she was a girl — fell in love with Mr
Doo. Mr Doo was an artist. But he was poor. So she married
Mr Wilsher. He was very rich and old. They lived together for
seven years. And then Mr Wilsher died. And she then went
and married Mr Doo. And they lived happily. Then Mr Doo
died. And Mrs Doo lived in that pink house opposite you. She
had butlers and gardeners and servants and cooks. All these
people to wait on her. And all she could talk about was her
darling Mr Doo.

'Her daughter was brought up as a lady. And when she was
getting on she fell in love with a young man — he was thirteen

years younger. He worked on a farm. They married. And after they married — the daughter began to look more and more like a gypsy. And the young man dressed and behaved like a gentleman.'

'That's a good story,' I said.

'I have lots more,' Mrs Burroughs said.

It was at Mrs Burroughs that I met Mr Oppenheimer. A neat man, about five foot two, bald, and with glasses. He was dressed in a hand-stitched tweed suit, a handmade shirt, and a woollen tie. Mrs Burroughs told him I was a writer.

'I've met a lot of writers here,' Mr Oppenheimer said. 'I used to visit D.H. Lawrence and Frieda on Sundays when they lived at Zennor.'

'How was Lawrence?'

'*D.H.*' Mr Oppenheimer raised his voice. 'He was a gentleman. One time I rode over on a horse. It was a hot day. And the horse gave me a rough ride. When I got there I must have said some swear words. *D.H.* got angry. "No need to say words like that here, Oppenheimer. There is no need." '

'Arthur, my gardener,' Mrs Burroughs said, 'also thought Lawrence a gentleman. Because when he went out there with a pony and trap to deliver a loaf of bread, Lawrence always gave him a shilling tip.'

'After *D.H.*,' Oppenheimer said, 'there was Harris. And after him, another writer, Johnson. He was always talking about money. He stayed only a year. How long are you staying?'

'I don't know,' I said.

I walked back with Mr Oppenheimer to his cottage.

'I've known Mrs Burroughs for over forty years,' he said. 'Very tight with her money. Never gives anything away.'

How could I tell him that she was giving me all these things from her past.

'She can't hear very well,' Oppenheimer said. 'But if you start talking about money. She'll say wait — I'll just get my hearing aid. She had a grand-niece getting married in Canada. She told me she sent her a pound as a wedding present. *A pound.* Come inside and have a drink. I start the day with a small glass of brandy. The doctor told me to take it. It warms the system up.'

His cottage was small and untidy. There was a dog, a terrier, also old, sitting by the electric fire. There were papers, magazines, and books piled everywhere. Often when I would come down to visit Mr Oppenheimer I would look in at the window to see if he was in. The place was in a mess, plates and cups still on the table. And Mr Oppenheimer, sitting in a chair with his feet up, reading a book.

He told me why he came here. His family owned freighters in Wales. He began to work in the Cardiff office. Then he got a spot on one lung. 'The doctor told me to go to a warmer climate. Or else I wouldn't make old bones. I'm seventy-six,' he said proudly. 'I started a restaurant here just after the First World War. But I don't have anything to do with that now. I still have my office there. Come and see me.'

I did go.

His office, above the restaurant, was as untidy as the cottage.

'Augustus John sat where you are sitting and drank a half bottle of whisky. And little Stanley Spencer — he came up to here.' Mr Oppenheimer stood up and put his hand under his chin. 'I don't think he changed his collar once in the three months he was here. Have you heard of Guy Gibson. During the war?'

'Yes,' I said.

'I gave Guy Gibson piggybacks on the sand,' Mr Oppenheimer said. 'He used to come here as a child. Have some more brandy.'

His hand shook as he poured. But it was because of arthritis in his fingers. It was painful for him to shake hands.

'Tell me about D.H. Lawrence,' I said.

'*D.H.* He had a red beard. He worked at night. In the day *D.H.* went for walks on the moors. He was very good with his hands. He fixed things in the cottage. Why don't you come and see my house in the country. I've got a lot of land around it.'

I said I would. But as he had bought the house for his

daughter Mary and her husband George — and only went there, reluctantly, on week-ends — I never did go to see the place.

But on Monday afternoons I would go to see him at his cottage. I'd say.

'How are things Mr Oppenheimer?'

And he would say. 'Have some more brandy.'

This time he began to laugh. 'I shouldn't laugh,' he said. 'But George had something else go wrong. George decided to cut some of the old trees — I shouldn't laugh — There are fourteen acres. He got the wood.' And Mr Oppenheimer began to laugh again. 'I shouldn't laugh,' he said, tears in his eyes. 'He got the wood and started to cut it. And phlewt — half of his finger flew off. I shouldn't laugh at this. But he couldn't find the piece that flew off.'

'What happened,' I said. I wondered why I was laughing.

'Mary got the ambulance. They rushed him to Penzance hospital. But it was too late. They couldn't sew the two pieces together.'

Next morning, sitting at the wooden table in the high room, I though how rich Mr Oppenheimer's talk was and Mrs Burroughs' talk. Compared to Sam's and mine. Sam never once talked about his Old Etonian past. Just as I didn't talk or even refer to my past. I was like Sam. We were both trying to cut out our pasts, to cover them up. And it made us boring.

The next time I saw Mr Oppenheimer he said, 'I don't have the dog any more. I took him out for his walk. We went along the harbour. The dog always peed against the railing. This time he went on the wrong side of the railing. There was no rail. He flipped over. Fell into the harbour. The tide was out. He broke his back.'

Besides visiting Mrs Burroughs and Mr Oppenheimer, I also found two places that I would make for on my walks. One was in the country, just off the road. It had a broken-down gate. Then, a slope up, a field of green grass. And at the top of the slope this house. An ugly house. With two dormer windows downstairs and two upstairs. And a white door that was always half-open. All the paint was peeling. The curtains were grey, half-drawn, and falling to bits. But there was something marvellous about a broken-down place with a sign at the front gate that said *Venton Vision*. No one lived in the house now except the animals: a goose, some cows, chickens.

Then, in December, with a mist closing in, in grey light, I found this field of anemones. The flowers were not very high above the ground. But the colours stood out. There were blues, purples, deep reds, light reds, and whites and pinks. Low colours, rising from the green, moving from side to side in the wind. Some were wide open with their dark centres. Others in bud, others opening. Very delicate colours, in the grey light, the mist closing in. And here and there a tall dead stalk from last summer's thistles. A lovely field. And no one picked them.

And I couldn't get over seeing the anemones, and the surrounding green fields, because it was December. I think of December as snow, ice, double-doors double-windows, and skating on frozen rivers. I would come here just to look at this field. And wish I was back to the snow, the crisp air, the harsh glare on sunny days.

I went to see Mrs Burroughs to tell her about the field of anemones. I found her crying.

'What's the matter Mrs Burroughs?'

'I'm remembering the happy times,' she said.

She was holding a photograph of herself, before she was married, as a teacher with her class.

Meanwhile the problem was getting clear. How was I to earn a living if I couldn't write my next book? I started to make lists. Of the people I grew up with in Ottawa. Of the popular songs I knew when I was at school. Of the streets, the streetcar lines, the market, the library, the parks. But the money was running out. The novel was due in two months. It was time to leave.

I went to see Mr Oppenheimer. The door of his cottage was locked. I looked through the window. Things were just as I last saw them. The newspapers, the magazines, the books.

On Saturday morning the taxi came to take us to Penzance station. we said goodbye to Sam. He still dressed like a

Tolstoyan farmer, smiled easily, and talked of his pot boilers.

We wished each other luck.

I told the taxidriver to go to Mrs Burroughs. As I went along the walk I could hear her grandson playing the piano. And as soon as I came in she said. 'You haven't been up for a couple of weeks. Sit down. I have another story for you.'

'I can't stay Mrs Burroughs.'

But she interrupted or else she didn't hear what I said.

'You know the farm that you can see from where you are? That farm was run by Mr and Mrs Brill. She died when she was fifty-five. And six months later Mr Brill had a heart attack. And he died. The relatives were saying how sad it was. How he tried and couldn't live without her.

'When the relatives came to divide the valuables they found a camera with a half-used film in it. They had the film developed. And it was full of pictures of Mr Brill and his girlfriend — she was someone else's wife. There were pictures of this woman in his wife's kitchen. In her favourite chair. And Mr Brill had made plans for them to go away to London. *Now* the relatives were saying the heart attack was the best thing that could have happened.'

'What has happened to Mr Oppenheimer,' I said. 'He's not at his cottage.'

'He fell in the street,' Mrs Burroughs said. 'He is gone to live with his daughter in the country. We won't see him again. That's what happens. The family takes over and the friends don't see you any more. When that happens to me, I'll have to go and live with my daughter Brenda. Then no one will see me.'

'Oh, you've got lots of time yet Mrs Burroughs.'

'I don't know,' she said quietly.

'I came to say goodbye,' I said.

'Where are you going?'

'To London.'

'When?'

'Now.'

I could hear her grandson playing *Morgenbläter*. Since living here I had learnt the names of a lot of things.

'Do you like my red glass?' Mrs Burroughs asked.

'Yes.'

'Take the one you like.'

'I couldn't do that.'

'Why not. They will only fight over it when I'm gone. Do you like this one?'

And she gave me a red glass vase with a pair of cockerels etched in it.

I returned to the taxi with the red glass.

'Look what Mrs Burroughs gave me,' I said to my wife.

'It's beautiful,' she said.

But she was looking out of the window as the taxi drove along the coastal road. On one side — the earth with the small green fields, the yellow gorse, a stone church with old grave-stones. And on the other — an immense sky against the thin flatness of the sea.

My wife took my hand.

'I'm glad we are leaving,' she said. 'Now things will begin.'

# Class of 1949

The end of January is quiet and empty in this seaside town. Martha is away at university in Manchester. A nine-hour train ride from here, on the fastest train. She has just phoned, as she always does on Friday evening. Ella has come back tired from school. She is doing A levels but buys magazines in order to read: 'I was pregnant at 15' . . . 'Are my kisses a match for his' . . . 'My husband beats me'. She has gone up the stairs to her room and put on a Joni Mitchell record. For I can hear

> The wind is in from Africa
> Last night I couldn't sleep
> Oh, you know it sure is hard to leave here
> But it's really not my home

I am sitting in a comfortable chair, by the side of the open fire, waiting for the news to come on the television. Emily is on the settee, in front of the fireplace, knitting a red sweater for Ella. The black kitten is chasing a shallot as if it was a ball, knocking it from one paw to another.

The phone rings. 'I'll go,' said Emily.

'Who was it?' I said as she came back into the room.

'Someone wanting the old people's home. That's the second

time today. If it's not someone wanting matron then it's
Linda's the hairdresser.' She took up her knitting. I listened to
the clock on the mantel above the fireplace.

  *Maybe I'll go to Amsterdam*
  *Maybe I'll go to Rome*

The phone rang again. Emily went quickly out of the room. I
could hear her voice becoming louder. She came back excited.

 'It's Victor,' she said.

 'Victor. Here?'

 'Yes. He's at the Sheaf. I told him you'll go down and bring
him back.'

 'I guess there is no way I can get out of this,' I said as I put
on my coat.

 But as I walked down the slope in the light rain — past the
terraced houses, a few had lights on in the front rooms; by the
closed post office, the closed summer restaurants — I remembered it was Victor who was responsible for my coming here in
the first place.

I met Victor in 1946 in Montreal while going to McGill. We
were two from the thousands of returning servicemen and
women who went to university just after the Second World
War. I remember that winter looking out from the top window
of an apartment opposite the campus. It was snowing. And
bundled-up young men and women in blue and mustard and
black overcoats were walking to and from a lecture. Furthest
away, through the dark trees — the Arts Building, the
Engineering, the Library — bits of light, bits of orange. There
was no sound. Just the snow falling. And the moving great-
coats.

 Victor would have got to McGill war or no war. But a lot of
the others depended on the Veterans Act — fees paid by the
government and sixty dollars a month to live on. When Victor
came in his car to pick me up for dinner with his parents and
saw the basement room I had by the boiler on Dorchester next
to the railway tracks, he put it down to some eccentricity on my
part. Then he drove through wide streets with trees and lawns
and elegant houses. To the paintings on the wall of Emily Carr,

the first editions in the bookcase, the butler bringing in the drinks. It was through Victor that I met the rich and powerful English families of Westmount and Outremont. In those days I was attracted by the rich — their houses, their possessions, the way they lived. Perhaps this is what I found interesting in Victor.

But there was something else. We both wanted to be writers. And we were convinced that the first step was to get out of Canada and go over to England. To get over I needed money. That meant putting in for a fellowship. I said I would do a thesis on 'The Decay of Absolute Values in Modern Society'. And got five thousand dollars spread over two years. Victor got his father to give him a chunk of capital in the form of Bell Telephone shares, Canada Packers, Canadian Pacific, and Dominion Tar.

I am trying to be as brief and accurate as I can of those early postwar years. The girls wore their skirts and dresses long and our jackets had padded shoulders. We had youth and high spirits — but they were held in check. When we graduated, in May 1949, the principal made a speech saying what a fine generation we were, how we fought the enemy of civilization and made the world safe for democracy, and now we would take our place as useful citizens. The person they thought most suitable to give the convocation address was the Chief of the Boy Scouts — I cannot remember a thing he said.

Next day, Victor flew to England. Two weeks later I took a freighter to Newcastle. We met up in London. Victor had rented a cottage in Cornwall for us both. London, he said, would be too hot in July and August. It was a marvellous summer. The wartime restraint suddenly went. And in its place I felt an exhilarating sense of personal freedom.

In September we went up to London. To a flat in Swiss Cottage. We were both writing first novels in different rooms on typewriters. The house was broken-up into flats. In the others were middle-aged European refugees. And workmen were still repairing the bomb-damage. We went to Soho, to the pubs, the drinking clubs, the small restaurants. We met painters, writers, editors. It was very pleasant.

Now and then Victor would say we were invited for the week-end to some large country house. (They were relations or acquaintances of his family.) And I would rent tails from Moss Bros. and we would go by train into the country. To the lengthy meals with many courses and wines and the mothers complaining that England was dull, that their daughters were not having the time they had. Then the Hunt Ball, champagne, dancing all night to the Harry Lime theme. And back to the seedy flat. To ration books and queues at Sainsbury's for the small egg, the Irish sausage, the cube of butter, the bit of cheese and meat. While the pile of typewritten pages for our novels increased. We both knew we had two years to live like this and finish our books. Then get them published and go on as writers — or else return to Canada.

The Sheaf was ahead. There was one room with a light. From the window I could see an open coal-fire. Two people by a table. The rest of the room was empty.

As I walked in Victor called my name, got up, and smiled. We shook hands. He continued smiling. I saw that his once white teeth were discoloured. That his blond hair was grey. And I wondered what changes he could see in my face.

'This is Abdullah,' Victor said. And introduced a small young Arab, very fine features with a dark moustache, neatly dressed in a brown suit.

'When did you get here?'

'Late this afternoon,' Victor said.

'Will you have the same? Is it draught?'

'Yes.'

I went to the bar and ordered three draught Guinness. Abdullah came up. 'I'll bring them back for you,' he said. I returned to the table and sat down opposite Victor.

'I didn't think you would still be here,' he said. 'I thought you would have gone back to Canada.'

'We've been waiting for the kids to finish school. Martha is at university in Manchester. Ella is in her last year here. So we'll be able to move soon. What made you come down?'

'I thought Abdullah ought to see a bit of Europe. We've

been in London the last two weeks. Going to art galleries, plays, movies, walking around —'

'It was very tiring, all that walking,' Abdullah said.

'I decided to take us away from London for the weekend. We took a train to Truro, hired a car, and drove here.'

'Where are you staying?'

'At the first hotel that had a car-park opposite.'

'That would be the Porthminster,' I said. 'Did you remember it?'

'No,' Victor said.

He took out a package of cigars and gave me one. Then brought out a gold lighter and we both lit up. He seemed reluctant to talk. So I said. 'My hair is a bit longer than it was.'

'At least,' he said, 'it's the same colour.'

'Emily and the kids wanted me to have it like this. So I let it grow. I didn't like it at first. In summer some of the places here have signs in their windows, ''no undesirables''. It means boys and girls with long hair who do not have much money to spend. I began to feel I might be undesirable. Abdullah, have you been to England before?'

'No. This is the first time for me out of Morocco.'

'How long will you stay here?'

'Just the weekend,' Victor said. 'We leave Monday for London then fly to Amsterdam for a few days. Then a couple of weeks in Paris. He learned English himself,' Victor said proudly. 'In three months.'

'You speak very well,' I said. 'What do you do in Morocco?'

'I register births and deaths,' Abdullah said. 'I begin when I get back. It will be my first job. As assistant.'

We finished the draught Guinness.

'Let's go back to the house,' I said. 'Emily is waiting to see you.'

We went out of the pub. The tide was out. The widely separated lights along the front and the pier were reflected in the shallows. Up ahead, in the dark, were clusters of lights from the houses above the harbour. It felt damp and cold.

'I walked around with Abdullah earlier,' Victor said. 'A shame the boats are gone.'

'It's become a tourist town,' I said. 'You're seeing it at the best time of the year. In summer you can hardly walk.'

We went along a dark street. I stopped beside a cottage.

'Pop Short lived here,' I said. 'Remember him?'

Victor was silent.

'He let you read a first edition of *Lady Chatterley*. He used to ask after you. He told me there was a White Russian colony here after the First World War. Like we were after the Second. And I guess there will be others like us later on. Pop showed me a Fabergé egg that he got from the White Russians. He died last year. He was ninety.'

We walked along a bit further on the wet cobblestones. I stopped beside a street light. There was an opening with stone steps going up.

'Do you remember this?'

'No,' Victor said.

'It's where we had our first cottage, halfway up the steps. We were charged two pounds a week for it. At that time we didn't know we were overcharged a pound because we were Canadians. The rooms were damp. The gaslight came from small wire baskets. The toilet was outside in the courtyard.'

'I remember that,' Victor said hesitantly.

We walked a little further along. 'This used to be Maskell's. He would put aside cigarettes for us. The cigarette paper had a thin pin stripe, like on a shirt. He died some years ago. And the Gay Viking? Here. We would go for coffee in the morning. Meet other people and have long talks. The Saint and Elsa ran it. They're both dead.'

'I don't remember,' Victor said.

'Victor's here,' I shouted as soon as I got into the hall. Emily came out of the dining-room, smiling. Victor was also smiling. He opened his arms.

'Emily.'

'Victor.'

They embraced and kissed.

'What a surprise,' Emily said. 'Here we are thinking no one comes to see us. And here you are.'

'You haven't changed,' Victor said.

'You've got taller,' she said.

'It's these new shoes. They have thick heels. It's the latest fashion. This is Abdullah.'

We introduced Ella.

'You remember Victor?'

She stood there smiling.

'How could she,' Emily said. 'She wasn't born.'

I took their winter coats and hung them up. And we went into the kitchen where Emily had laid out the table.

'Someone gave us this pâté for Christmas,' I said. 'We were waiting for an occasion to open it. Do you know what it is?'

'It's pork,' Abdullah said, chewing it slowly. 'In my country I'm not supposed to eat it.'

'It's very good,' Victor said.

I helped myself to a hard-boiled egg.

'Do you remember Tom Slater? We met him in one of the Soho pubs. He wrote short stories —'

'I don't remember him,' Victor said.

'He died nine years ago. He was thirty-six. He used to come down with his wife to see us. He knew I liked sardines. So he would bring a different tin of sardines every time he came down. He said he told a friend of his about my liking sardines. ''That used to be the way you could tell a gourmet,'' the friend said. ''Now, it's hard-boiled eggs.'' '

Abdullah laughed.

'Aren't these plums good. Have some more,' I said to Abdullah.

'As you see, Victor, we are still here,' Emily said. 'We seem to sit here waiting for something to happen.'

'We'll get out soon,' I said quietly.

'I've heard that before,' Emily said.

'We have a chance. Now that the kids have grown up. Ella finishes school this year. Then we'll be able to go.'

'But where will we go *to* —?' Emily asked.

'You two sound like characters in a Beckett play,' Victor said.

No one spoke. Then Emily said sharply.

'How *could* you come back here, Victor?'

He didn't answer. He went on eating, looking not at all at ease.

'Do you remember Keith Haydon,' I said. 'He came over a few years after us and became an authority on nuclear strategy. He used to write articles, appear on television. He died last year in Venice.'

'That's a shame,' Victor said.

'And remember Len Mason? One time the three of us were walking along Sherbrooke Street after a late lecture. It was winter. Lots of snow on the ground. We told him we were going to be writers. And he said he was going to be an actor. So we said we would write plays for him. Len did become an actor. He acted in Canada and over here and in the States. He was killed two years ago while driving a car on a highway.'

'I'm sorry to hear that,' Victor said.

'How do you live in Morocco?' Emily said changing the subject.

'I have a house in an Arab quarter. I designed the inside of the house. Also had my own furniture made up. It's got lots of rooms. Now and then I have some European friends staying with me. But most of the time I only see Moroccans.'

'What do you do in the morning?' I said.

'I go shopping. Buy food.'

'Do you still cook?'

'Yes. But I have a cook and a houseboy.'

'Is it hot there?'

'It can be during the day,' Abdullah said. 'But at night it freezes.'

'What do you wear?' Emily asked.

'He wears a silken —' Abdullah smiled mischievously at Victor.

'It's something I got in Japan,' Victor said nervously. 'A karate suit.'

'It's like the old men wear,' Abdullah said, still smiling.

We went into the other room. I put more coal on the fire. Emily came in with the coffee. I brought in some whisky and brandy and began to pour the drinks. Victor took out the package of small cigars and offered me one. 'I used to smoke one cigarette after another,' he said. 'Now I smoke one cigar after another.'

'What do you work at, Victor?' I said.

'I'm a dilettante,' he said lightly, 'I do several things. But as an amateur.'

'Then you're a professional dilettante, Victor,' Emily said.

'No,' Victor said. 'I'm not professional at anything.'

'But you could cook — very well,' I said.

'He is doing a cook book,' Abdullah said proudly.

'I'm supposed to be doing one,' Victor said. 'But I don't think I will. Just putting down one recipe after another would be boring. I paint most of the time.'

'What kind of paintings do you do?' said Emily.

'Landscapes.'

'Like what painter that we would know?'

'Like Corot.'

'That's a name to conjure with,' Emily said.

'I like being an amateur,' Victor said. 'The good painters and writers I know — they lead such miserable lives. I was going through immigration at London Airport. And the official looked at my passport and asked me. What do you do? I said writer — I still say that sometimes. What have you written, he asked. *Nothing*, I said.'

We all laughed.

'He let me through.'

And for a moment he was like the Victor I knew. The one who used to make me laugh. But just as quickly he went back into his shell of not talking freely and looking uneasy. A few minutes later he stood up. 'I think it's time we went to the hotel.'

'I'll walk you there,' I said.

Back with Emily in bed. She said. 'I was looking out of the window. And I saw three people coming up. And I thought, supposing Victor's married. And he's bringing his wife . . . Do you think Abdullah is his boyfriend?'

'I didn't ask. But I guess so.'

'I thought he liked girls?'

'He did,' I said. 'I knew of three at McGill and one over here. Just before I met you he began to see a lot of this girl. I don't remember her name. She was a Canadian in London from the same background as Victor. About your height, only very dark hair, high cheekbones, a nice smile. She looked a bit like Claudette Colbert. *Very* sympathetic. One night he came to the flat I had in Notting Hill Gate (Victor was then living in Chelsea) to tell me that he had just left this girl. And she told him she was pregnant. He didn't know what to do. He said he would marry her. Victor has a great sense of doing the right thing. "The trouble is," he said, "I have enough income from my capital for one person to live. But with two — I'll have to get a job." So he went and signed up as a salesman to sell encyclopedias. He did that for a month. Didn't like it. Then the girl told him it was a false alarm. And that was the end of that.'

We lay in bed for a while not speaking.

'He's not giving much away,' I said.

'Maybe he knows what writers do,' Emily said.

'I don't think so,' I said. 'I remember when he finished the novel and showed me the typescript. The characters were lifeless. I asked him why didn't he write about people he knew. About his family, about Montreal, his private school, McGill. He said he didn't want anything to do with Canada or anything connected with it. I don't know anyone who hates Canada so much. And how can you be a writer if you reject your past? Seeing Victor, I can see the person I was.'

'Yes,' Emily said. 'He can tell little lies. He said we haven't changed. I know we have. It's the kind of small talk you used to make. Why say things you don't mean?'

'It's a form of politeness,' I said . . . 'I wonder what would have happened to Victor if that dark haired girl was pregnant?'

'But he's happy with his life,' Emily said. ' "The nice thing about these trips," he told me, "is that at the end I can go back home to Morocco. To my house and my Arab friends." I think he's very lucky to live in a place he likes.'

I didn't reply. I expected her to go on and say: we're about the only ones who live in a place they don't like. Instead she said, 'I think Victor disapproves of me. Every time he looked at me, I felt it.'

'I also think he disapproves of me now,' I said. 'For not living better — for not getting on.'

'Well you have written a few books since you last saw him.'

'But he's not curious about our life at all,' I said. 'He hasn't asked me one question as to what I've been doing these past twenty years. It's as if he looks at the way we live — and doesn't want to know. And he has forgotten a lot. I walked down the street with him showing where we had the cottage that first summer — where Pop Short lived — Maskell's — The Gay Viking. All he said was: I don't remember. I don't remember.'

'Perhaps that's why he was able to come down here,' Emily said. 'He doesn't have much to lose.'

Next day, Saturday, they didn't arrive until noon.

'I've been walking up and down the street,' Victor said. 'I couldn't find the house. All the houses look so much the same.'

'I've found Morocco in Ella's Atlas book,' Emily said. And showed Abdullah the map. 'Are you anywhere near the coast?'

'We are about three hundred miles from the coast. Beside the mountains.'

From the window I could see the sky was still overcast. 'I hope you'll get a bit of sun while you're here,' I said to Abdullah. 'Then you'll be able to see the colours.'

'I like the way it is,' Abdullah said. 'I have never seen anything like this.'

'Why don't we go for a drive across the moors,' Victor said. 'Stop at a few pubs. Then I'll take you and Emily out to a meal.'

I got in front with Victor. Emily was in the back with Abdullah. And in a matter of minutes we were on the moors. The small green fields with the grey broken-stone hedges. The hedges with gorse and hawthorn on both sides of the road. Last year's bracken a light rust colour. Some deserted tin mine chimneys.

'In Morocco,' Victor said, 'you have these wild flowers. One day they are all yellow. Next day they are all pink.'

'I suppose you find this drab.'

'No,' he said. 'I wouldn't mind getting out here and doing some painting.'

I can hear Abdullah telling Emily, 'My father has two dozen head of cows, some chickens and sheep.'

'If a Moroccan sheep saw this green grass,' Victor said, 'it would go ga-ga.'

We drive along the turning road. There is a drop to the green fields below us on the right while the moors go up on the left.

I can hear Emily with Abdullah in the back. 'Have you any brothers and sisters?' 'I have thirteen brothers and sisters. My father has fifteen wives. But only four at a time. When my father comes in and tells the women to start cleaning and cooking — I know he is getting a new wife.'

'He has written an autobiography,' Victor told me. 'That's all in it.'

I hear Emily say. 'Why have you written your autobiography?' And Abdullah saying: 'Because I have had a very interesting life. I find life much more interesting than fiction.'

'How old are you?' I asked Abdullah, turning my head.

'Twenty-three.'

'How long have you and Victor known each other?'

'Five years.'

We come to Zennor and Victor stops the car by the Tinner's Arms and we get out and see the old squat church. No clock but a sundial. Inside the Tinner's we stand and drink Guinness and take in the atmosphere. On the wall there is a painting of a stallion.

'It's an Arab,' Abdullah said.

'How can you be so sure,' Emily said.

'See the smooth lines. Your English horses are more heavy in the stomach.'

A group of young people sit at the far end where a fire is going. I recognize one as the son of a painter Emily and Victor and I knew twenty years ago.

'Are you one of the Sparks?' I asked him.

'Yes,' he said standing up and saying my name. We shake hands. He is the same age as Abdullah and twice as tall.

'Your mother and father,' I said, 'brought you over to see us when we lived in Mousehole.'

'When I was in diapers,' Sparks said laughing.

I introduce him to Abdullah. 'He's from Morocco.'

'I was there last summer,' Sparks said. 'I was thrown in jail. My friend the chief of police got me out and then I was in even worse trouble.'

There is an immediate rapport between the small Arab and the tall country-faced young man.

While Abdullah is talking to Emily, Sparks tells me: 'Abdullah — it's like Fred over there. You see all these mothers come running out of their houses calling: ''Come here Abdullah you naughty boy.'' '

'He's just like his father,' I said when we were getting back in the car, 'outgoing — giving of himself.'

'He tried to say goodbye to me in Arabic,' Abdullah said.

We drive over to Mousehole. (We are covering old ground that Victor knew.) We came here just after Emily and I married. Lived for a year in a large granite house on the side of a hill. It had a nice garden with bamboos, copper beech and palm trees. In the morning, when we were still in bed, we could hear the melancholy sound of curlews flying over to the fields above. And again at dusk when they flew back to the rocks at the sea's edge. Victor was living in St Ives and he would come on Friday night for meals that Emily made. Our novels were finished and were making the rounds of the publishers . . .

Now, we look through the bare hedge at the granite house in silence. Emily wants to get away. 'Some things are best left undisturbed,' she tells me. Victor shows no interest at all.

'Let's go,' he said, 'and have a meal.'

The little village is very clean, the colours as fresh as paint, the streets deserted. But we are too late for lunch.

We drive into Penzance. The restaurants are shut. Finally we find one open in Market Jew Street. It is packed. Every seat taken. People are standing up. I see stairs. I suggest we go up the stairs. Here it is all empty. The tables nicely set with white table-cloths and facing a wall-window overlooking Market Jew Street.

'I see the advantage of a university education,' Emily said.

'Now,' Victor said, 'we'll have a feast.'

The menu was brought to us by a stocky middle-aged waitress. She had white shoes on. And gave the impression that there was still lots of life in her yet. We all agree to have soup and scampi.

The waitress came carrying the bowls of soup close to her breasts. And she was singing. *Isn't It Romantic —'*

The soup was terrible. The scampi wasn't very good either. But we were hungry.

The waitress came back with a bottle of standard fish sauce. Her hips swaying.

'Let's try some of this exotic sauce,' Victor said, putting his knife into the bottle.

'I'll have some too,' I said.

*Isn't It Romantic —'* she sang.

Abdullah didn't like the scampi. The waitress went back and sat down by another table. I guess she had her eye on Abdullah. But Abdullah was looking out into Market Jew Street.

'In Morocco,' he said to Emily, 'the people would be on the road and the cars on the pavement.'

An old man came up and sat down at a table.

'Hullo, my handsome,' the waitress said loudly. And went over carrying a cup of tea.

That night in bed Emily said. 'Yesterday, early Friday, it was raining. And you know how it is here sometimes. You think it's all coming down on you. I just wanted to talk to someone. And there was Mr Care outside his nice pink house with a broom. And I said, You're not going to change the colour? No, he said, I've been away for a few days. I'm just tidying up. Where did you go? To Brighton. My son is a vicar there. He is the vicar for the crematorium. And I remembered our neighbour with her obsession about the dead. It was all getting me down. Then

Victor phones to say he's here. And the next day I am out driving in a car across the moors and there were the green fields and this very English landscape. And sitting beside me is a dark little Arab. Suddenly life seems to have all sorts of possibilities. If this can happen — there's hope. I was so excited I was almost jumping up in the back seat. Thank God for Abdullah. Victor is too glum for me. And his talk is so superficial. I don't suppose you would have anything to do with him now if you met him.'

'I don't suppose either of us would,' I said. 'He didn't expect to find us here when he came. I don't think we'll even exchange post-cards when he gets back.'

'That happens all the time,' Emily said. 'People who know each other when they are young drift apart. Are they coming tomorrow for lunch?'

'Yes,' I said.

'I'll do a roast chicken and make a nice dessert.'

'Fine,' I said. 'And I'll get some wine.'

Soon after they arrived at noon I brought them upstairs to this room. It seemed necessary, for me, that Victor should see what I had done with all those years. I showed him the books. For twenty years they seemed so few. But I tried to make it look better by showing him the various editions. Knowing his predilection for the exotic I showed him an article on some of the books in *The Bangkok Post* of 2 August, 1970.

'This is nice,' Victor said as he read it.

'Do many people come to see you?' Abdullah asked.

'A few.'

'What do they want?'

'I think they want something to happen to them. Then they go home.'

'Do you write about them?'

'Sometimes,' I said. 'People are very generous. They let you into their lives. So you don't want to hurt them by what you write. In any case I write about people I like or have liked. And only about people I know. Their visit is only the tip of an iceberg.'

The meal went all right. Victor kept touching his chin when he talked. Abdullah was much more at ease. He told us that he was circumcised when he was six, that the Jews and Arabs were cousins, and what was all this stupid fighting for.

After lunch I took them both for a walk. 'That's Emily's garden,' I said. 'There used to be a greenhouse but the storm blew it down. Underneath the pear tree there is a little cemetery of children's animals — part of Martha's and Ella's childhood — two cats, one kitten, two hamsters, a goldfish.'

I walked them through the twisting back streets and around the harbour. 'You have seen the small stone cottages,' I said to Abdullah, 'and the kind of terrace houses we live in. Now I'll show you how other people live here.'

We got in the car and I told Victor to drive out of the place. Then down a road with trees. And through a wide gate. And there were the fine lawns with the large house at the end. The sides with trees. And a sheer slope down to the sand and the water of the bay. Abdullah could not contain his excitement. 'Shall I take some pictures?' he asked Victor.

'I don't think the light is good enough,' Victor said woodenly.

And I wondered why Victor hadn't taken any pictures of where we lived or of Emily, Ella, or myself.

'You might remember Henry Nicolle,' I said to Victor as we walked towards the house. 'He was a painter. We went to his first show in London in 1949. His widow still lives here.'

But Victor didn't remember.

The front door was shut. I looked inside the front room with the paintings on the wall, the antique furniture. 'I guess no one's in,' I said.

But Victor had already gone back to the car. He looked impatient to get away. Did it remind him of the house in Westmount, of summers in Murray Bay, St Andrew's Ball, Sherbrooke Street, McGill? I didn't know. When we got in the car he said. 'I'll drive back to say goodbye to Emily.'

For a while Victor and Emily looked at each other in the hallway. Neither knew what to say. Then they embraced and kissed. 'If you are ever in Morocco,' Victor said. And Emily laughed. 'Yes, Victor —'

I went out to walk them back to the car-park. It was dusk.
Most of the houses were in darkness.

'You'll be able to get back to work,' Victor said.

'The importance of work is highly exaggerated,' I said.
'Sometimes I think it is just another con trick.' I didn't know if
I believed this or not. Or was I trying to tell him that I understood his life. 'It's probably just another way of passing the
time.'

He didn't reply.

When we got to the car, Victor turned and said. 'It's been
fun.'

He said this with something of the gaiety that I remembered.
I shook hands with both of them. And walked quickly away.

For the next three days I came up here and tried to get on with
some work but couldn't. Victor's visit had made me
dissatisfied with the sort of life I was living. Why am I chained
to this desk, I asked myself. What's so important about
writing? Victor was living a much freer life. He had travelled
and continues to travel all over the world. But when I make a
trip it is back to Canada — to keep in touch with the past.
Another chain. I deliberately remain uninvolved with things
here because I don't want to lose the past — to put too many
layers between. While Victor —? I suddenly envied his life. I
don't mean living in Morocco or his house or Abdullah — I
envied him his freedom. Chains and freedom, I thought.
Chains and freedom.

But on the fourth day the visit began to fade. Things here
were getting back to the way they were before. Emily came up
at ten-thirty in the morning with a cup of coffee and a biscuit.
And I began to go on with the writing where I left off.

A week later I had a letter from Montreal, from the
Graduates Society of McGill, letting me know that this year
was our silver anniversary. 'Dear Classmate,' it began. 'Yes
indeed it is hard to believe that a group as young as we are
graduated from the old Alma Mater 25 years ago! But that's
the way it is!'

# By a Frozen River

In the winter of 1965 I decided to go for a few months to a small town in northern Ontario. It didn't have a railway station — just one of those brown railway sidings, on the outskirts, with a small wooden building to send telegrams, buy tickets, and to get on and get off. A taxi was there meeting the train. I asked the driver to take me to a hotel. There was only one he would recommend, The Adanac. I must have looked puzzled. For he said,

'It's Canada spelled backwards.'

He drove slowly through snow-covered streets. The snow-banks by the sidewalk were so high that you couldn't see anyone walking. Just the trees. He drove alongside a frozen river with a green bridge across it. Then we were out for a while in the country. The snow here had drifted so that the tops of the telegraph poles were protruding like fence posts. Then we came to the town — a wide main street with other streets going off it.

The Adanac was a three-storey wooden hotel on the corner of King and Queen. It had seen better times. Its grey-painted wooden verandah, with icicles on the edges, looked old and fragile. But the woodwork had hand-carved designs, and the white windows had rounded tops. Beside it was a new beer parlour.

Fifty years ago it was the height of fashion to stay at the hotel. It was then called the George. The resident manager told me this, in his office, after I paid a month's rent in advance. His name was Savage. A short, overweight man in his sixties, with a slow speaking voice, as if he was thinking what he was going to say. He sat, neatly dressed, behind a desk, his grey hair crew-cut, and looked out of the large window at the snow-covered street. The sun was shining.

'Well,' he said slowly. 'It's an elegant day.'

His wife was a thin, tall woman with delicate features. She also hardly spoke. But would come into the office and sit, very upright, in a rocking chair near Mr Savage and look out of the window. The office connected with their three-room flat. It was filled with their possessions. A small, bronze crucifix was on the wall. Over the piano a large picture of the Pope. There were a few coloured photographs: a boy in uniform, children, and a sunset over a lake.

I rented the flat above. I had a room to sleep in, a room to write and read, and a kitchen with an electric stove and fridge. To get to them I would go up worn steps, along a wide, badly lit corridor — large tin pipes carried heat along the ceiling. But inside the rooms it was warm. They had radiators and double windows.

I unpacked. Then went to the supermarket, by the frozen river, and came back with various tins, fruit, and cheap cigars that said they were dipped in wine. I made myself some coffee, lit one of the thin cigars, and relaxed.

I saw a wooden radio on the side-table in the sitting-room. A battered thing. I had to put twenty-five cents in the back. That, according to a metal sign, gave me two hours' playing time. But that was only a formality. For the back was all exposed, and the twenty-five cents kept falling out for me to put through again.

Listening to the radio — I could only get the local station — the town sounded a noisy, busy place, full of people buying and selling and with things going on. But when I walked out, the first thing I noticed was the silence. The frozen, shabby side-streets. Hardly anything moving. It wasn't like what the radio made out at all. There was a feeling of apathy. The place seemed stunned by the snow piled everywhere.

I quickly established a routine. After breakfast I went out and walked. And came back, made some coffee, and wrote down whatever things I happened to notice.

This morning it was the way trees creak in the cold. I had walked by a large elm when I heard it. I thought it was the crunching sound my shoes made on the hard-packed snow. So I stopped. There was no wind, the branches were not moving, yet the tree was creaking.

In the late afternoon, I made another expedition outside. Just before it got dark, I found a small square. It began to snow. The few trees on the perimeter were black. The few bundled-up people walking slowly through the snow were black. And from behind curtained windows a bit of light, a bit of orange. There was no sound. Just the snow falling. I expected horses and sleighs to appear, and felt the isolation.

That evening I had company. A mouse. I saw it just before it saw me. I tried to hit it with a newspaper, but I missed. And as it ran it slipped and slithered on the linoleum. I was laughing. It ran behind the radiator. I looked and saw it between the radiator grooves where the dust had gathered. It had made a nest out of bits of fluff. I left food out for it. And in the evenings it would come out and run around the perimeter of the sitting-room, then go back behind the radiator.

Birds woke me in the morning. It seemed odd to see so much snow and ice and hear birds singing. I opened the wooden slot in the outside window and threw out some bread. Though I could hear the birds, I couldn't see them. Then they came — sparrows. They seemed to fly into their shadows as they landed on the snow. Then three pigeons. I went and got some more bread.

On the fourth day I met my neighbour across the hall. He rented the two rooms opposite. He wore a red lumberjack shirt and black lumberjack boots with the laces going high up. He was medium height, in his forties, with pleasant features. And he had short, red hair.

'Hi,' he said. And asked me what I was doing.

'Writing a book,' I said.

'Are you really writing a book?'

'Yes.'

'That must be very nice,' he said.

And invited me into his flat. It was the same as mine, except he didn't have a sitting-room. The same second-hand furniture, the used electric stove, the large fridge, the wooden radio.

I asked him what he did.

'I work in a small factory. Just my brother and me. We make canoes. Do you like cheese?'

'Yes,' I said.

He opened his fridge. It was filled with large hunks of an orange cheese.

'I get it sent from Toronto. Here, have some.'

I met the new occupants of the three rooms behind me next morning. I was going to the toilet. (There was one toilet, with bath, for all of us on the first floor. It was in the hall at the top of the stairs.) I opened the door and saw a woman sitting on the toilet, smoking a cigarette. She wasn't young. Her legs were close together. She said, 'Oh.' I said sorry and closed the door quickly. 'I'm sorry,' I said again, this time louder, as I walked away.

A couple of days later she knocked on my door and said she was Mrs Labelle and she was Jewish. She heard from Savage that I had a Jewish name. Was I Jewish? I said I was. She invited me back to meet her husband.

The people who rented these rooms usually didn't stay very long. So there was no pride in trying to do anything to change them. But Mrs Labelle had her room spotless. She had put up bright yellow curtains to hide the shabby window blinds. She had plastic flowers in a bowl on the table. And everything looked neat, and washed, even though the furniture was the same as I had.

Her husband, Hubert, was much younger. He looked very
dapper. Tall, dark hair brushed back, neatly dressed in a dark
suit and tie and a clean white shirt. He had a tripod in his hand
and said he was going out to work.

'Savage told us you were a writer. I have started to write my
life story — What the photographer saw — I tell all. You
wouldn't believe the things that have happened to me.'

His wife said that the mayor was trying to get them out of
town. 'He told the police that we need a licence. It's because he
owns the only photograph store here. He's afraid of the com-
petition. We're not doing anything illegal. I knock on people's
doors and ask them if they want their picture taken at home.
He's very good,' she said, 'especially with children.'

After that Mrs Labelle came to the door every day. She knew
all the other occupants. And would tell me little things about
them. 'He's a very hard worker,' she said about the man who
made canoes. 'He doesn't drink at all.' Then she told me about
the cleaning woman, Mabel. 'She only gets fifteen dollars a
week. Her husband's an alcoholic. She's got a sixteen-year-old
daughter — she's pregnant. I'm going to see her this afternoon
and see if I can help. Be careful of Savage. He looks quiet, but I
saw him using a blackjack on a drunk from the beer parlour
who tried to get into the hotel at night. He threw him out in the
snow. Dragged him by the feet. And Mrs Savage helped.' She
complained of the noise at night. 'There's three young
waitresses. Just above me. They have boys at all hours. I don't
blame them. But I can't sleep. I can't wash my face. It's
nerves,' she said.

Then I began to hear Mr Labelle shouting at her. 'God
damn you. Leave me alone. Just leave me alone.' It went on
past midnight.

Next day, at noon, she knocked on the door. She was smiling.

'I found a place where you can get Jewish food.'

'Where?'

'Morris Bischofswerder. He's a furrier. Up on the main
street.'

I went to the furrier. He had some skins hanging on the

walls. And others were piled in a heap on the floor.

'Do you sell food?' I said.

'What kind of food?'

'Jewish food.'

He looked me over.

He was below middle height, stocky, with a protruding belly. A dark moustache, almost bald, but dark hair on the sides. He was neatly dressed in a brown suit with a gold watch chain in his vest pocket. He was quite a handsome man, full lips and dark eyes. And from those eyes I had a feeling that he had a sense of fun.

'Where are you from?' he asked. 'The West?'

'No, from England.'

'All right, come.'

He led me through a doorway into the back and there into his kitchen. And immediately there was a familiar food smell, something that belonged to my childhood. A lot of dried mushrooms, on a string, like a necklace, hung on several nails. He showed me two whole salamis and some loose hot dogs.

'I can let you have a couple pounds of salami and some hot dogs until the next delivery. I have it flown in once a month from Montreal.' He smiled. 'I also like this food. Where are you staying?'

'At the Adanac.'

His wife came in. She was the same size as Mr Bischofswerder but thinner, with grey hair, a longish thin nose, deep-set very dark eyes, the hollows were in permanent shadow, and prominent top teeth.

'He's from England,' he told her.

'I come from Canada,' I said quickly. 'But I live in England. The place I live in England doesn't have snow in winter. So I've come back for a while.'

'You came all the way from England for the snow?'

'Yes.'

They both looked puzzled.

'I like winters with snow,' I said.

'What have you got in England?'

'Where I live — rain.'

'Have you got a family?' Mr Bischofswerder said, changing the subject. 'Is your mother and father alive?'

'My mother and father lived in Ottawa, but they moved to California eight years ago.'

'I bet they don't miss Canadian winters,' Mrs Bischofswerder said.

'We have a married daughter in Montreal and five grand-children,' he said proudly, 'four boys and one girl.'

'Sit down,' Mrs Bischofswerder said. 'I was just going to make some tea.'

And she brought in a chocolate cake, some pastry that had poppy seeds on top, and some light egg cookies.

'It's very good, isn't it?' she said.

'I haven't had food like this since I was a boy,' I said.

'Why are you so thin?' she said. '*Eat, Eat.*' And pushed more cookies in my direction.

'I wonder if you would come to *shul* next Friday,' Mr Bischofswerder said.

My immediate reaction was to say no. For I haven't been in a synagogue for over twenty years. But sitting in this warm kitchen with the snow outside. Eating the food. Mrs Bischofswerder making a fuss. It brought back memories of my childhood. And people I once knew.

'I'll come,' I said.

'Fine,' he said. 'If you come here around four o'clock, we'll go together. It gets dark quickly.'

That night the Labelles quarrelled until after two. Next day, at noon, Mrs Labelle knocked on the door. 'He didn't turn up. This woman was holding her children all dressed up. I told her to send them to school.'

'Is this the first time?'

'No. It's only got bad now. He's an alcoholic.'

She began to weep. I asked her inside. She was neatly dressed in dark slacks and a small fur jacket. 'My sisters won't have me. They say I've sown my wild oats.'

'Would you like some coffee?'

'Thanks. We had a house in Toronto. I have in storage lots

of furniture — a fur coat — real shoes — not shoes like this. And where would you see a woman of my age going around knocking on doors? I'm sure I'm going to be killed. He calls me a witch. I found a piece of paper with a phone number. And a name — Hattie. I called up and said to leave my husband alone. I found another piece of paper. It said Shirley. They're all over him. He's a good-looking guy. And when he's working — these women are alone with him. You know —'

That afternoon, while I was writing, the phone went. It was Mrs Labelle.

'I'm in someone's house waiting for him to come and take the picture. Can you see if he's in. He hasn't turned up.'

I knocked on their door. Mr Labelle was sitting on the settee with a middle-aged man in a tartan shirt, and they were both drinking beer out of small bottles.

I said she was on the phone.

'Say you haven't seen me,' he said.

'Yes,' the other man said. 'Say you haven't seen him.'

But Labelle came after me and stood by the open door. 'Why don't you just say hello?' I said.

He went in and I could hear him saying, 'I'm not drunk. I'm coming over.' He hung up and closed the door.

'I'll tell you,' he said. 'Man to man. I'll be forty-one next month. And she's fifty-eight. We've been married fifteen years. I didn't know how old she was when we married. Then she was seven months in a mental home. I used to see her every day. At two. I had to get my job all changed around. But I'll tell you what. I knocked up a woman two years ago. And she heard about it. The child died. She can't have children. She won't give me some rein. I've had her for fifteen years. Don't worry,' he said. 'I won't leave her. You may hear us at night. I shout. I'm French Canadian. But I'll look after her.'

He went back and got his camera and tripod. And he and the other man went down the stairs.

Ten minutes later she rang up again.

'Is he gone?'

'Yes,' I said.

That evening around nine, there was a gentle knock at the

door. It was Mrs Labelle, in a red dressing-gown. 'He's asleep,' she said. 'Thank you very much. He hasn't eaten anything. I make special things. But he won't eat.'

It was quiet until eleven that night. I could hear them talking. Then he began to raise his voice. 'Shut up. God damn it. Leave me alone. You should have married a Jewish businessman. You would have been happy.'

On Friday afternoon I put on a clean white shirt and tie and a suit. And went to call on Mr Bischofswerder. He was dressed, neatly, in a dark winter coat and a fur hat. We walked about four blocks. Then he led me into what I thought was a private house but turned out to be the synagogue. It was very small. Around twenty-four feet square and twenty feet high. But though it was small, it was exact in the way the synagogues were that I remembered. There was a wooden ark between a pair of tall windows in the east wall. A few steps, with wooden rails, led to the ark. The Ten Commandments, in Hebrew, were above it. A low gallery extended around the two sides. In the centre of the ceiling hung a candelabra with lights over the reading desk. There were wooden bench seats. Mr Bischofswerder raised one, took out a prayer book, and gave the prayer book to me.

'Shall we start?' he said.

'Aren't we going to wait for the others?'

'There are no others,' he said.

And he began to say the prayers to himself. Now and then he would run the words out aloud so I could hear, in a kind of sing-song that I remembered my father doing. I followed with my eyes the words. And now and then I would say something so he would hear.

I had long forgotten the service, the order of the service. So I followed him. I got up when he did. I took the three steps backwards when he did. But most of the time we were both silent. Just reading the prayers.

Then it was over. And he said.

'Good Shabbus.'

'Good Shabbus,' I said.

On the way back, through the snow-covered streets, it was freezing. Mr Bischofswerder was full of enthusiasm.

'Do you realize,' he said 'this is the first time I've had someone in the *shul* with me at Friday night for over three years.'

For the next seven Friday nights and Satuday mornings I went with Mr Bischofswerder to the synagogue. We said our prayers in silence.

Then I went back with him to his warm house. And to the enormous Sabbath meal that Mrs Bischofswerder had cooked. Of gefilte fish with chrane, chicken soup with mandlen, chicken with tzimmes, compote, tea with cookies. And we talked. They wanted to know about England. I told them about the English climate, about English money, English society, about London, Fleet Street, the parks, the pubs. How I lived by the sea and a beautiful bay but hardly any trees.

And he told me how the trappers brought him skins that he sent on to Montreal. That he was getting a bit old for it now. 'Thank God I can still make a living.' He told me of the small Jewish community that was once here. 'In 1920 when we came there were ten families. By the end of the last war it was down to three. No new recruits came to take the place of those who died or moved away. When we go,' said Mr Bischofswerder, 'all that will be left will be a small cemetery.'

'Have some more cookies,' his wife said, pushing a plateful towards me. 'You have hardly touched them. You won't get fat. They're light. They're called nothings.'

Mrs Labelle knocked on my door. She looked excited. 'I'm selling tickets,' she said. 'The town's running a sweepstake — when will the frozen river start to move? Everyone's talking about it. I've already sold three books. Will you have one? You can win five hundred dollars.'

'How much are they?'

'Fifty cents.'

'I'll have one,' I said.

'Next time you go to the supermarket,' she said, 'you'll see a clock in the window. There's a wire from the clock to the ice in the river. As soon as the ice starts to move — the clock stops. And the nearest ticket wins.'

She gave me my ticket.

'Good luck,' she said. And kissed me lightly on a cheek.

She looked, I thought, the happiest I had seen her. My ticket said: March 26th, 08: 16: 03.

That night I noticed the mouse had gone. No sign of it anywhere. It was raining. The streets were slushy and slippery. But later that night the water froze. And next morning when the sun came out it was slush again. The snow had started to shrink on the roofs; underneath the edges I could see water moving. I walked down to the river. It was still frozen, but I saw patches of blue where before it was all white. Crows were flapping over the ice with bits of straw in their beaks. The top crust of the river had buckled in places. And large pieces creaked as they rubbed against each other. Things were beginning to break up. It did feel like something was coming to an end here.

Next day, just before noon, Mrs Labelle came to the door. She looked worried. 'Savage told us we have to leave. I went to see him with our week's rent in advance. But he said he didn't want it. He said we were making too much noise at night. The waitresses make noise, but he doesn't mind them. I don't know where we'll go. We've been in Sudbury, in Timmins, in North Bay —'

It's OK,' Mr Labelle said, coming to the door. 'We'll be all right,' he said to her gently. And started to walk her back toward their door. Then he called out to me. 'If we don't see you, fellah, good luck.'

'Same to you,' I said.

'But where will we go Hubert?' Mrs Labelle said, looking up to his face.

'There's lots of places,' he answered. 'Now we got some packing to do.'

After the Labelles had gone, it was very quiet. I had got the reminders I wanted of a Canadian winter. I had filled up three notebooks. It was time that I left. I went down to the office and told this to Mr Savage. He suggested that I stay until the ice started to move.

But I left before it did.

I took a light plane, from the snow-covered field with a short runway. From the air, for a while, I could see the small town. But soon it was lost in a wilderness of snow, trees, and frozen lakes.

# The Girl Next Door

In October 1976 I came back to Ottawa and rented three rooms in an old house on Cobourg Street just below Rideau. It wasn't anything — plain bare rooms with brightly coloured wallpaper — but the windows looked out over a small park. And that made all the difference.

For the first two days — apart from going out to buy some small cigars and groceries — I stayed in and looked at the park.

It's a lovely little park . . . made for the human scale . . . people look right when they are in it. The two Lombardy poplars. One, at the edge of the park, by the sidewalk, in front of the window. The other, towards the middle of the park but off centre, raised, where the earth formed a mound. And on top of the mound, on a small plateau, a gazebo. And beside the gazebo — with its open arches, its sloping brick coloured roof — this other, very tall, Lombardy poplar.

I could tell a wind's direction not only by the arrow on top of the gazebo but, from the near poplar's leaves showing their light green underside, I could also tell its strength. Elsewhere there were maple trees — young and old — their leaves, in autumn colours, some lying thick, underneath, on the grass.

I was quite happy to stay by a window. There was always
something moving. A leaf from a maple, people walking, grey
and black squirrels, boys throwing passes or kicking a rugby
ball, others rolling from the gazebo down the slope. Pigeons,
sparrows, and the occasional gull flying slowly over.

I watched until the park lights came on. Then it was too dark
to see. That's when I switched on a small radio and listened to
the news (the local, national, international), the sports, the
time, the temperature, the weather forecast, and the commercials in between.

On the third day I woke up, drew back the curtain, and there
was snow. It was the first snow I had seen in years. I made
some coffee, lit up an Old Port cigarillo, and watched a man
dressed in black with a black umbrella above his head walk
through the all white park. The wind picked up some loose
leaves and moved them swiftly on top of the snow. Fascinating
to see fallen leaves lifted then carried by the wind across the
snow. They look like small birds. They are small birds.

I decided to go out. I had no destination. I walked along
Rideau to the Chateau Laurier. In the lobby I took off my coat
and sat down in a leather chair, as if I was waiting for someone.
There were others also sitting down and watching.

I left the lobby as the bell in the Peace Tower was ringing ten
and walked across Confederation Square, down Elgin, to the
National Gallery. And found this Monet.

There was a Renoir to the left, of a mother and child. And a
Braque to the right of the Port of Antwerp. And elsewhere in
the room: a red landscape of Vlaminck, a red nude of
Duchamp, a Derain, a Leger, an Epstein, some Cezannes,
Pissarros, Sisleys, and Gauguins, several Degas, and a Van
Gogh of some irises.

But it was this Monet, *Waterloo Bridge — The Sun in a Fog,
1903*, that I kept coming back to see.

When I was close to it it was just paint. But when I went
back, about ten feet, the sun was round at the top coming
faintly through the fog. The sun was orange on the water in the
front and, further away, on the water through an arch of the
bridge. While the darker shapes, of the bridge, the barges,

came visibly through.

At the end of the second week Lynn moved into the apartment next door. I had pulled back the curtain and saw that the little park was almost hidden by fog. Only the gazebo — the arches filled with fog — and the near poplar and the near maples were visible. The rest was fog and the sun trying to come through. When a taxi drove up. A slim girl with long hair that almost hid her face came out. She was about five foot six or seven, dressed in jeans, a black sweater, and a black duffle coat. The taxi driver helped bring in her few things.

Next evening I knocked on her door.

'I saw you move in yesterday. I live in the next apartment.'

'Come in,' she said quietly.

The room was like mine. But she had put up art posters of Chagall and Picasso. And a Snoopy poster that said:

*No problem is*
*So big that you*
*Can't run away*
*From it.*

There were picture post-cards and a row of paperbacks by the wall. There was a small wooden table and two wooden chairs.

'I haven't had time to do this right. Would you like coffee? It won't take long.'

She filled an electric kettle and plugged it in. I noticed that she was left-handed.

'How long have you been here?'

'Two weeks.'

'Will you stay?'

'I don't know. How about you?'

'I've got to sort myself out,' she said.

I saw Jung's *Modern Man in Search of a Soul*, Sylvia Plath's *The Bell Jar*, books on psychology, poetry, philosophy. And art books on Klee, Magritte, Kandinsky, Munch.

'I go to the National Gallery,' I said. 'They have a lovely Monet.'

'I like Monet,' she said.

'Where are you from?'

'From New Brunswick,' she said, 'near Fredericton, in the country.'

'I've been to Fredericton,' I said, 'about ten or eleven years ago. I deliberately go to places — some I know some I don't — and isolate myself because I want to work. Why don't we go to my apartment. I have a bottle of wine and some records.'

I put on Bix Beiderbecke and Sydney Bechet. And she took off her shoes and began to dance in heavy white woollen socks. She danced, for a while, by herself. Then she came over and stretched out her hands.

'Dance.'

I got up and we danced. She was very firm, no fat at all.

After that we would see each other every day.

She had dark straight hair that she parted in the middle that almost hid her face. Now and then I caught a glimpse of her blue eyes, the longish straight nose, a small mouth and, occasionally, a shy smile. When she smiled she also seemed to look amused. I liked her from the start.

After I told her I was a writer she would turn up at the door with a piece of paper and say. 'Do you know this?'

*When Spring comes round*
*If I should be dead,*
*Flowers will bloom just the same,*
*And trees will be no less green than they were last Spring,*
*Reality doesn't need me.*

She wouldn't read it aloud. But give me the paper that she had written it on. It was through Lynn that I got to know the poetry of Pessoa and Osip Mandelstam. She also gave me several paperbacks of Hermann Hesse. I think he was her favourite. But I didn't get very far with Hesse. I didn't try. I don't read much when I'm writing. And I was working on a long story, a novella, and I was often thinking of that even when I wasn't writing.

She would come to see me in the morning, in bare feet, a

Hudson Bay blanket draped around her shoulders.

'Walking in bare feet,' I said, 'that's the quickest way to get a cold.'

'It's the way I grew up,' she said.

She would light a cigarette and we would have coffee together and talk about writers, books, painters, movies, music, the weather . . .

After the coffee she would go out shopping. She always asked me if I wanted anything. About twice a week I would ask her to get some apples, grapes, tins of soup, salmon, coffee, rye bread (if she was passing Rideau Bakery), or nuts, if she was going near the mall. She always came back with a small white paper bag full of warm nuts from the Nut House. That's another thing we had in common. We both liked nuts.

She also went out every day for walks. And she would come back and tell me what she saw. She didn't tell me right away. There was this reserve — the silences — the shy smile — then she would say:

'I saw some gulls. Against the snow they looked dirty.'

Or else I would have to guess what took place when she said.

'I went to the cafeteria at the National Gallery to have a cup of coffee and listened to the conversations around me. People talk a lot of nonsense — don't they?'

'Do you know anyone in Ottawa?'

'Only you,' she said.

'Why did you come here, Lynn?'

'I had a quarrel with my boyfriend. He's white. But he works for a black revolutionary organization in Africa. We were together nearly a year. I let my heart rule my head. Because I was in love with him I became interested in politics. Then we had a quarrel. And he left.'

'What did you do before?'

'I went to college for a while. Then to Art School. I was trying the wrong things. I left Art School after two years. They were all on an ego trip.'

'Can't you go home?'

'There's only my father. We don't get on. He wanted boys. But he got three girls. I'm the eldest.'

'How old are you?'

'Twenty-three.'

'You're young,' I said. 'You still have your life ahead of you.'

'I don't know,' she said. 'There are times when I don't see any point —'

I thought, if I was twenty years younger it would be different.

'I'm the wrong person for you,' I said.

She didn't say anything. But she appeared at the door more often. And now I found that she began to stay too long. Her visits became more like interruptions. I would say.

'Yes, come in Lynn. But you can't stay too long. I have to do some work.'

Finally I said. 'I'm sorry Lynn — I'm busy.'

She went away. But the next time I became annoyed.

'Lynn — I can't see you. I'm working.'

'Work. Work. That's all you do. What's so important about work?'

'Without my work,' I said, 'I'm nothing.'

She walked away, slamming the door.

I didn't see her next morning. But in the afternoon the phone rang.

'Hello.'

Silence.

'Hello,' I said. 'Hello —'

I thought I heard a voice but far away.

' — is that you Lynn?'

Silence.

Then quickly she said. 'I'm going to kill myself.'

'Where are you?'

'In a phone box — by the Chateau Laurier.'

'Stay there. I'll be right over.'

I got a taxi on Rideau and saw Lynn inside the phone booth, leaning in a corner with her head down. Her hair hiding her face. I put my arm around her and brought her to the taxi.

'I'm sorry,' she said when we were inside her apartment. 'I'm all right now. I feel tired. I'll lie down. You can go now.'

Next morning she came around for coffee — in her bare feet, the Hudson Bay blanket around her — and we talked as if nothing happened. She asked me if she could do any shopping. Was there anything I wanted mailed.

'No thanks,' I said.

When she came back that afternoon from her walk she came back with a small present, a jar of honey, that she wrapped up very neatly in Snoopy wrapping paper.

She left me alone, but not for long. The following day she came around and wanted to talk. We did for a while. Then I had to say. 'You'll have to go now. I must get back to work.'

She went out. A few minutes later a piece of paper was pushed underneath the door. On it she had written. 'I'm going — and I won't come back.'

That afternoon I found myself going to the window, looking out to see if I could see her.

She did come back as the light in the park was fading.

'Where did you go?'

'To the Chateau Laurier,' she said. 'I sat in the lobby and watched people. I did that for an hour. Then I went to the National Gallery and looked at the Monet. Then I walked. I walked until I got cold. So I went into department stores to keep warm. What's wrong with me?'

'Nothing,' I said. 'Just wait. Time has to go by. Things have to happen.'

'You're lucky,' she said. 'You are doing what you want to do. I don't know what I want to do. I like going out for walks. I like looking at things — paintings, reading books.' Tears appeared in her eyes. 'Isn't there a place for someone like me?'

I went over and kissed her.

'Yes,' she said quietly. 'There's always that.'

For the next three days it went more or less all right. She still went out for her walks. But instead of telling me about them when she came back, she showed me sketches that she did. Of the market, and people in the market, of people crossing near the cenotaph, of the mall, the frozen Rideau River with the snow, the trees, and the white Minto bridges.

On Friday she came in, around noon, with her sketch-book

and a pencil. She wrote something on the paper, tore the piece off, and gave it to me. It said.

'I can't talk.'

'Of course you can,' I replied.

'No,' she wrote. 'I woke this morning and I wanted to speak but I couldn't.'

'It will come back,' I said.

Silence.

'Has this ever happened before?'

'No,' she wrote.

Silence.

'I had a letter from my boyfriend,' she wrote. 'He wants me to come to Toronto.'

'Why don't you go.'

'Do you think I should,' she wrote.

'Yes,' I said.

She must have packed before she came to see me for when I saw her again, a half-hour later, she was ready to leave.

'Thanks for talking to me,' she said. 'You don't know how much all those talks we had meant to me.'

And I felt bad. All I could think of was how abrupt I was with her. How little I did give of myself.

I watched her go with her few belongings into a taxi.

A month later I walked to the National Gallery to see the Monet again. And as it was a particularly cold day I decided to go to the Lord Elgin, into Murray's, to have a cup of coffee. The large room was crowded with civil servants having their morning break. I found a seat by a table in a corner. It was pleasantly warm. The coffee was hot. I sat and smoked a small cigar and looked at the lights near the ceiling. They were set in round wooden circles, like wooden crowns. When I noticed a lively group of boys and girls come in. They were talking and joking together. They all looked excited, handsome. Lynn was one of them. Her hair was short. She wore a bright yellow sweater. A tall young man was beside her. And like the others she smiled and laughed a lot.

# To Blisland

Sunday morning on a hot warm August day. And we were in a train that was going to London. Two hours later, at Bodmin Road, we got off in the country. A long outside platform with upward sloping green fields, trees, and hedges. The sun shining on them.

We crossed the tracks, to the other side, by the covered wooden bridge. And to a waiting small green bus.

Marie carried a carrier bag. I another. Hers had a carton of six eggs that she had boiled with onion skins to make the shells dark brown, a jar of gooseberries that she had cooked the night before, some panties, socks, soap, and writing paper with envelopes and stamps. I had several comics, grapes, apples, bars of chocolate, a paperback, and a kite.

It was warm in the bus. We were the only passengers. After twenty minutes it drove along a country road, then a small bridge, over a narrow river, and onto the main road.

Fifteen minutes later we came to the town. It was deserted. The bus went, slowly, up the rising main street. (The houses, the buildings, looked as if they had resisted change.) At the top, at crossroads, we got out and began to walk along a straight wide road.

On the side we were walking were small houses with small front gardens and, at the back, farmers' fields.

On the other side was a continuous brick wall. Behind the brick wall, cut grass lawns and, further away, Victorian brick buildings. The brick buildings had many windows and fire escapes — an institution, looking stark against all the greenery around it.

About a quarter of a mile down the road the brick wall had a gap. A drive went from this gap, down a short slope, to a small new bungalow-like building.

Carol was sitting outside on a wooden bench.

She saw us.

We both began to walk quickly towards one another.

'Hullo love. Happy birthday.'

Tears appeared in her eyes.

'You both look so handsome,' she said quietly.

Marie wore a light blue summer dress with short sleeves. I had a light grey summer suit with a dark blue sport shirt open at the neck. Carol was all in black — black trousers and a long black sweater. Her black hair almost hid her face.

'We got some things for you —'

I took the kite. It was made and painted to look like a red butterfly.

'I don't think we can fly it today. There's not enough wind,' I said.

'We brought a picnic,' Marie said. 'Shall we leave the other things in your room and tell Mister Patrick. Is he on today?'

'Yes,' said Carol.

We went into the bungalow-like building, into the corridor. It was dark. A door was open, the office, and an outgoing young man in a white coat was sitting behind a desk. He was medium sized, stocky, with dark hair.

Marie went with Carol further along the corridor to her room.

I went into the office.

'We thought of taking Carol out for a picnic.'

'It's a good day for it.'

'Can you suggest anywhere?'

'Have you been to Lanhydrock?'

'We were there a few weeks ago.'

'Altarnun — ?'

'We have been there as well.'

'There's a nice spot — just down the road — you can walk it from here. Down a hill. Go to the railway tracks. Then walk along the tracks. No trains run there on Sunday. And you will get to a river. It will be cool by the river.'

'How is she?'

'Some weeks there is a step forward. Others not. At least she hasn't gone back.'

Marie appeared with Carol.

'What time do you want her back?'

'Not later than five,' Mr Patrick said.

'Could you order us a taxi for five?'

'I'll do that,' he said. 'Have a nice time.'

Carol didn't say a word.

We walked along the short drive, to the opening, then along the main road. On the horizon, the white grey hills of China clay.

'Have you been down this way?'

'No,' Carol said.

'They've made a poster for Carol,' Marie said. 'They put it on the inside of her door. It says Happy Birthday. Everyone signed it. I remember my eighteenth birthday. My mother made a large party, invited all my relatives, and I didn't like it at all.'

'Have you still the room to yourself ?'

'No,' Carol said. 'They put someone in with me on Tuesday.'

'How old is she?'

'Seventeen.'

We walked along the side of the road, down the slope, in silence.

'Someone else came in on Tuesday —' Carol said. 'His name is George. He sits beside me at the table when we eat. He did the poster.'

'Mrs Smith asked after you,' Marie said. 'So did Flossie. And the woman in the paper place always asks how you are getting on.'

Where the road levelled out we came to the railway tracks. We left the main road and walked between the tracks. There were trees on either side and overgrown grass. After a while the trees became thicker and the earth sloped more steeply down. There was a path near the top of the slope. We walked on the path, between the trees. It began to get dark. And we could see water.

It was a strange light. The sun (not able to come through the trees except for a shaft here and another some way along) left the top parts of the trees a bright yellow-green. Halfway between the tops of the trees and the river the light changed from bright to dark. The river was dark — dark green, dark blue, with large rocks in it. Sounds carried. We could hear boys and girls talking and splashing somewhere ahead. A dog barking. It was very still. We were walking in the dark light while above was this bright light-yellow and light-green. And all the colours seemed softened.

We sat on the trunk of a fallen tree, on the slope, where we could see the river. And had a picnic from the hard-boiled eggs, apples, grapes, and bars of chocolate.

'You look better,' I said.

'I don't take the pills.'

And she brought out, from her trouser pocket, some small red pills.

'They give them to me. I put them in my mouth, but I don't swallow. If they find out I will be in trouble.'

'I'll take them,' I said. 'And get rid of them. If they get to know about this they may not let you go out.'

'What's the girl like that is in the room with you?' Marie asked.

'She lies on her bed most of the time,' Carol said. 'They brought her in because she took an overdose.'

'What's wrong with George?' I asked.

'He broke all the clocks in the house. Then the mirrors. Then the windows . . . How's Min?'

'She had kittens,' Marie said. 'In the cupboard under the stairs. Five this time. Four ginger and one black and white.'

'I miss Min,' Carol said quietly.

'We painted your room,' I said changing the subject.

'I don't know,' she said. 'Sometimes I think home is my room here.'

We got up and walked by the river stepping over rocks and fallen branches and smelling the mud. The river turned. And as we came around the turn the sun had come through a gap in the trees ahead and we could see, in the shaft of light, a boy, two girls, and a dog. The boy was splashing in the water with the dog. While the others sat on the rock. They were in bright sunlight. The water, near them, a light bright blue. While all around it was dark.

We clambered up the slope to the railway tracks and into the sunlight. And walked farther along the tracks until we came to a road. The fields, on either side, were lush with grass and wheat. We came to an avenue of trees. They led to wide lawns and banks of flowers. And behind them, slightly raised, a large stone house with farm buildings. We walked on the lawns, picked some flowers. There was a small bridge over a stream. When we crossed the bridge we dropped the white and light pink flowers in the water.

Then we walked towards the farm buildings. They looked very old and used. A large pile of cut wood was neatly stacked by a barn. Others had machinery. In a stable a white horse with blue eyes had his head out of the stable door. He stood there not moving.

There was no one about.

We walked to the house. From the front it had a magnificent view over the lawns, over the trees, and onto a valley with the higher fields and trees on either side. The house was dark. It looked tatty, as if it had been lived in a long time.

'It looks so feudal,' Marie said.

We crossed the lawn to go out on the far side. And crossing the stream we saw the flowers that we had dropped at the start, passing by, carried on the slow moving water.

Some way down the road were two neat cottages.

'My grandma worked on an estate like this,' Marie said. 'She was a teacher on the Royal Estate at Windsor. But that was nearly a hundred years ago.'

'I would like a small cottage in the country, near here,' Carol said. 'I'd have a goat and a cat or a dog. I would grow my own vegetables. And I'd get better, if I can be left alone for a while. If no one bothers me. If there is no noise . . . I looked in an estate office window in Bodmin. There are cottages at two thousand pounds. When I'm twenty-one, I'll be getting five hundred pounds from the policy — maybe they will take that as a deposit —'

'Yes,' I said. 'That's a good idea.'

We came to crossroads. One sign said to Bodmin, the other said to Blisland.

'Let's go to Blisland,' Carol said.

It's too late,' I said looking at my watch. 'We have to get you back by five.'

'I don't want to go back.'

'We'll go to Blisland another time,' Marie said.

By the time we came back to the town we were all tired.

I tried to find a restaurant or a cafe. But all of them were closed. I saw a filling station open. Part of it had a small room with several tables with plastic tops.

We went in. We all had coffee in silence.

Then two motorbikes drove up. And four young people in white crash helmets and black leather jackets and jeans came in. When they took their helmets off I could see they were two young boys and two young girls. They talked loudly and laughed a lot. They had soft drinks standing at the counter. One of the girls went to the juke box and put some money in. The music came out loud and clear.

*Nothing's gonna change my world*
*Nothing's gonna change my world*

We remained sitting not saying a word. Marie and I finishing our coffee. Carol hunched over looking down at the table.

'What's wrong love,' I asked Carol.

'It's the noise,' she said. 'I can't stand it.'

*Nothing's gonna change my world*
*Nothing's gonna change my world*

I got up and awkwardly we left.

Outside it was warm. I started to walk briskly. I was first, then Marie, then Carol. And Carol became further and further away. I stopped to wait for her.

'I don't want to go back there,' she said.

'You can't come home yet.'

'I'll never come home,' she said.

We were approaching the hospital when I saw Carol leave the side of the road and start to walk towards the middle.

A car, coming from the opposite direction, blew its horn.

'Carol,' Marie shouted.

I ran over to Carol to try to make her come to the side of the road. But she shrugged me off.

More cars were coming at speed. They blew their horns. They took evasive action. One angry driver leaned out and shouted.

'Do you want to get killed.'

We were near the opening in the wall that led to the short drive and the bungalow-like building. The taxi was there. We waited for Carol. She came, slowly, away from the centre of the road and walked through the opening.

'I'm sorry,' she said quietly.

'Thanks for all the nice things. I had a lovely time. Will you come next week?'

'Yes,' we both said.

'You better go in love,' I said.

We kissed outside the door.

She stood there with a plastic bag that had the remains of the hard-boiled eggs and the apples.

We went into the taxi that would take us to the railway station. As it drove away we waved.

And she went inside.

# Why Do You Live
# So Far Away?

'Why don't you go out?' Emily said. 'Do you know it's over a week that you haven't been out of the house?'

'I went out on Tuesday to the post office.'

'I meet people in the street. They all ask. And how is Joseph? What can I say? He's working. He's up in his room. He's busy. Why don't you go out and see people?'

'It costs money to see people,' I said. 'If I meet anyone they say let's go in for a drink. I'm too old to go bumming.'

'So what do we do? Play cards, read newspapers and watch television. I'm tired watching television.'

'You're tired when we go to bed.'

'You expect me to be excited just because we're going to bed? Why don't you go out for a walk now? You'll feel better. Walk around the harbour, or through the town, go to the library.'

'I hate this place,' I said. 'All I can think of is how to get us out. I've got a sign up on the wall of my room, *You've got to get out of here*, facing me all the time. I don't want to end my life in this cut-off seaside joint.'

The phone rang.

'You answer it.'

'Now you don't even want to answer the phone,' she said and went out of the room to the kitchen.

I went up to this room, looked at the collection of picture post-cards stuck on the large mirror. (When I look in the mirror, to see myself, the post-cards give a 3-D effect.) They were from people scattered over North America, Africa, and Europe. I've stuck them on with sellotape with spaces of glass in between. I even have a post-card of Carnbray in with the others. A summer's day . . . palm trees . . . the sea a shade darker blue than the sky . . . a large green-and-white yacht in the harbour . . . people on a sand beach . . .

As a post-card, I thought, I could like this place.

I went to my desk and looked at the pieces of paper listing what payments I expected to come in. They added up to £325. But I had learned not to count too much on other people paying when they said they would.

Next morning Emily had a letter from her mother in London, and with it came a money order for ten pounds for Christmas.

I got a small tree and put it up in the front room. I went and got some ivy and Emily put it around the room, on the walls near the ceiling. Cards began to come in. And I went out and had a drink in a pub with people I hadn't seen for several months.

On the evening of December 23rd we were waiting in the front room, which looked very nice and warm. We had the fire going in the fireplace. There were some coloured balls hanging from the lights. There was this nice fitting red carpet. It's a splendid room with a large bay window and we only use it when people come, or perhaps in summer, for it's too cold. Emily had made some sandwiches and I got a bottle of sherry and wrapped it in coloured paper, and bought some extra glasses. We were waiting for the people Emily had been evacuated to during the war. They lived near Truro. Since our marriage they've sent a chicken for Christmas and I've given them a bottle of sherry. We sat in the large second-hand chairs with the scratched sides where the cat sharpened its claws, waiting for them to come. It was past seven. I thought they were late.

'They have to put the cows away,' Emily said, 'and do a lot of things before they can leave.'

A few minutes later we heard sounds outside the front door.

'No,' I said, without knowing why. And it wasn't.

It was a wizened, hunched-up little woman, determined, thrusting her face toward. It was not a pretty face, although it had new blondish curls.

'Does Joseph Grand live here?'

It wasn't so much a question as an assertion. And it was said by my sister Mona from Meridian. I hadn't seen her for ten years.

Afterwards, she said I just stood there not saying anything but shaking my head.

I went outside and saw Oscar. He looked like a gentle wrestler. A squat little man with sleepy eyes, a hat on, a camera around his neck, a brand-new black coat and black gloves.

I shook Oscar's hand.

'Why didn't you write or phone or send a telegram?'

'I wanted to,' Oscar said, 'but your sister didn't let me.'

I looked into the taxi, half-expected to see my father and mother inside.

'I bet you're surprised,' Mona said excitedly when we were inside with the bags and hung up their coats. Oscar kept his hat on.

'Why didn't you let me know when you got to London?'

'We didn't want you to go to any trouble,' Mona said.

Oscar said: 'I've got a movie-camera — I wanted to record the expression on your face when you saw your sister.'

I steered them into the front room. Mona lit a cigarette.

'You don't look like your pictures, Emily,' Mona said. 'You've lost weight,' she said to me. 'It suits you. The last time I saw you, you were fat. I thought you had heart trouble.'

Then the kids were introduced.

'This is Martha — this is Ella — this is Rebecca —'

'They're like dolls,' Mona said.

'— this is your Uncle Oscar and your Auntie Mona. They've come all the way from Meridian in Canada. How was the trip?'

'Terrible,' Oscar said. 'We had to change twice on the train. You know it took longer to come down here from London than to fly from Montreal over to England. Why do you live so far away?'

'If you sent a telegram or phoned,' I said, 'I would have told you what train to get. You wouldn't have had to change —'

'I told her,' Oscar said.

'I didn't want to put you to any trouble — shall we give them the presents?'

They brought their new bags into the front room and brought out gay bunny pyjamas for the kids. They gave Emily a Norwegian ski sweater.

'He always wears black,' Mona said. 'Why, I don't know. So I thought I'd get him a white sweater.'

It was a splendid sweater with a turtle-neck.

'You smoke?' Oscar said. And gave me several red-and-white flat tins of duty-free cigarettes.

'Thanks. Why didn't you write from Canada?'

'We didn't know if we were coming or not. You know your sister. She was terrified of flying.'

'Everyone told us to go to Miami,' Mona said. 'At this time of the year England, they said, would be full of smog, fog, accidents.'

'It was a toss-up,' Oscar said, 'whether to go to Disneyland or to come here.'

'Didn't you know *something* was in the air when I didn't write?' Mona said.

I didn't say anything to that. I couldn't remember when she last wrote.

'Here,' Oscar said to the children, taking out his wallet from his back buttoned-down pocket. 'From your Grannie and Grandpa in Canada — your Chanukah gelt.' And he gave them two pounds each. Our kids never had so much money.

My sister looked at the Christmas tree, the decorations, the cards.

'Do they know about Chanukah?'

The kids were silent.

'Your Daddy will tell you.' Then back to me in the same low disapproving voice.

'You celebrate Christmas?'

'We sort of have a tree — and I give out the presents on Christmas Day.'

'I always say, how you want to live your life that is your business,' Mona said.

The kids went upstairs to their rooms to try on their pyjamas.

'What would you like to drink?' I said confidently. It was the first time that year I had so much drink in the house. 'Scotch, gin, sherry, beer —'

'You have no rye?' Mona asked.

'No.'

'I won't bother.'

'Oscar. What'll you have?'

'I don't care for the stuff.'

'Won't anyone join me in a drink?'

'I'll have some sherry,' Emily said.

'Let me taste,' my sister said. 'It's not bad. I'll have a drop.'

'How's Maw and Paw?' I said.

'The same,' she said. 'Maw still works at the hospital.' Then suddenly brightening up. 'If they could only see the kids — Paw's got to go in for a check-up when we get back. You should see how nervous he was when we told him we were flying.'

I remembered the last time I saw him. We were waiting for the taxi to take me to the station. He was in his shirt. A towel around his head. He was in the middle of shaving. 'I hope I'll still be here next time you come,' he said and began to weep. 'Sure Pop,' I said. How pathetic and kind he looked. Then we saw each other in the hall mirror. He pointed to his weeping face in the glass. 'I look like a Chinaman.'

I suggested to Emily that Mona and Oscar might like to have some coffee.

Mona hunted in one of their bags and came out with a jar of instant coffee and gave it to Emily.

'We drink a lot of coffee, and I heard you can't get good coffee over here.'

'We've got instant coffee,' Emily said.

'Oh, you have,' Mona said, puzzled. 'Well, we like it strong.'

As soon as Emily was out of the room, my sister said:

'I thought you said she was *half* Jewish.'

'I said that long ago, because of Maw. She asked me where did I get married? Who was the rabbi? Now she knows. I know she knows. She said if this happened in her time the family would be sitting Shiva.'

'I always say, the way you live your life that's your business,' Mona said.

Emily came back with the coffee, and she also had some hamburgers in buns that she made earlier and heated up.

'Gee, these taste good,' Oscar said.

'They're like we make them,' Mona said, somewhat surprised.

I was surprised how she had aged. I knew she was two years younger. But she looked in her forties. Except for her body, which was very slim. She sat hunched, her back curved, jaw thrust forward, smoking one cigarette after another.

I heard a car go up. We live on the side of a hill. Mona stopped eating.

'What was that?'

I told her.

She heard a rail outside the house rattle. People hold onto it for support as they walk up the hill. But it was loose.

'And what was *that*?'

We were all quiet.

'I heard something — it's upstairs,' she said.

I went upstairs.

'Nothing,' I said.

'Are you sure?'

'I've got to do this every night,' Oscar said. 'You should see the locks on our doors. And the bolts. And the chains. When I go away after breakfast she locks the double doors with double locks — they're special locks. Then the chains. And then the bolts. She even has a gun and a dog.'

'But what for?' I said.

'I don't know,' Mona said quietly.

'You weren't like that,' I said.

'Let me tell you,' Oscar said, with a sleepy grin. 'You're got some sister.'

Just before nine the farmer and his wife came. And it became a small party. They drank several gins too quickly. They gave us a chicken and pressed tongue. I gave them the bottle of sherry. They left presents for the kids under the tree. They thought it was marvellous to come and find people who had only twenty hours before been in Canada. The farmer's wife — bright faced, plump — and Mona found something to talk about.

'— I also had my gallstones out.'

'Mine burst,' Mona said, 'as the surgeon was putting it on the tray.'

But they couldn't stay as they had to get back to the farm.

Though the room had become much warmer, Oscar had not taken his hat off all evening. He had removed his suit-jacket, sweater, and tie. With his hat on his head he went to sleep in the chair by the fireplace.

As soon as Mona saw that Oscar was asleep she said:

'What do you do about teaching the children religion?'

'We don't,' I said.

'Our kids celebrate Chanukah. They all wear Mogen Davids around their necks — *This* is the Star of David, Emily,' Mona said, showing her the thin gold chain around her neck. 'In my home I have two sets of dishes. I light the candles on Shabbus. We eat bacon — but outside, in someone else's house. You might think that was hypocritical. Do you light the candles on Friday night?'

'If I did that, Mona, I'd feel hypocritical.'

'Who did you name Rebecca after?' Mona quickly changed the subject.

'After Aunt Rocheh,' I said. 'You may not remember her. She's the one that never married. I think she died when we were kids. How did you get Francine?'

'After Fruma — Oscar's grandmother.'

'Fruma is Frieda or Fanny,' I said.

'No,' she said. 'You can take anything from the F's. . .'

'But why just the F's . . .?' I said.

'Well, it's got to be *like* Fruma — you can have Faith, Felicity, Fawn.'

'They don't sound like Fruma to me.'

'They don't have to sound, long as the first letter's the same. For instance, your Rebecca is after Auntie Rocheh. Then you could have had Roxana, Roxy. . .'

'That's the name of a cinema,' I said. 'Who's Lance after?'

'He's after Oscar's grandfather Laybel — he could have been Lawrence, Lorne . . .'

'What about Lou or Lionel?'

'They're old-fashioned.'

Mona stubbed out her cigarette and immediately lit up another. I had noticed earlier the area of nicotine on her finger, but it was while I gave her a light that I noticed her hand was shaking.

'We don't let Francine go out with any English boys in Meridian. We send her away to Montreal during the holidays. She also learns Hebrew.'

'Girls in Canada,' I said, 'learn Hebrew?'

'Why not?' Mona said aggressively. 'I believe in God. Don't you?'

'No.'

'Don't *say* that,' Mona said. 'You must *never* say that.'

'Don't believe him,' Emily said, trying to calm her down.

'I believe in fate,' Mona said, 'that between Rosh Hoshannah and Yom Kippur your fate for the year is decided.'

'I don't go along with that,' I said.

No one spoke.

Then Mona chuckled. 'It's a good thing Oscar's asleep, otherwise he'd never forgive me for talking like this.'

We gave them our bedroom. We slept on a mattress in my office with coats over us. This arrangement was all right for tonight. But tomorrow we'd have to try and get some sheets and blankets from the woman next door.

Emily and I were trying to get to sleep. Our eyes seemed level with the gap at the bottom of the door that showed the light from the hall.

'She must have been saving that up for a long time,' Emily said. 'I wanted to like her.'

'I know,' I said. 'I've never felt terribly close to my sister.'

Fifteen years ago, in Montreal, I was asked to leave the middle of an English 10 class.

'Someone to see you,' the Dean's secretary said.

And there in the dark cool hall, under the Arts building clock, was my mother. A bit frightened but dressed nicely in a small blue hat, a new black coat, and dark gloves. She had come up, on her own, from Ottawa to try and make me change my mind about coming to Mona's wedding. I don't know what excuses I gave for not going. And I don't know why I chose my sister's wedding to make a stand.

My mother took me out for a meal, in a small restaurant on St. Lawrence Main, which I enjoyed. It wasn't as good as her cooking, but it seemed ages since I had Jewish food. And the signed photographs on the wall of Max Baer, Al Jolson; her, all dressed up, across the table — the food — brought back my childhood on Murray Street; the stillness of the house on the Sabbath, with my mother, a handsome woman, sitting out the afternoons by the window. She wept — she may even have given me a few dollars — and I said I would come.

At the wedding I remember my father coming down the aisle with Mona. He was abut the same size as Mona, but looked smaller. In a double-breasted blue serge suit which was cut down to fit him from one of my uncle's discarded suits. His lips pressed tight, near to tears, a little frightened. Away from the house he always looked lost.

Then the reception downstairs in the vestry rooms. There was something like three hundred guests. Most of them I didn't know. Perhaps I had, even then, gone further away from home than I thought. (The way the waiters were openly helping themselves to the booze — the way the people were stuffing themselves.) It seemed to me — at university because of the Veteran's Act, $60 a month, which meant eating peanuts in the last week — that my mother, who had cleaned out her bank account for this wedding, was feeding a lot of strangers.

I remember the young rabbi sitting in front of me, eyes moving continuously. He was new, 'from outa town.' And ate very quickly. Then he got up to make his speech. He talked of Mona, whom he had never seen before.

'Mona, today you are a Princess. Oscar, you are a Prince.'

Earlier that week Princess Elizabeth and the Duke of Edinburgh had got married.

Then he sat down, mumbled quickly and indistinctly his after-eating prayers, gave a few little shakes of his body, and vanished.

Next morning Emily and I and the kids were up early. The kids were very excited. Oscar and Mona came down after ten. Said they slept well. Didn't eat very much but drank endless cups of coffee that Emily kept making and smoked cigarettes.

It was the coldest winter England had for over a century. And though there have been Christmases in this resort where I have been able to walk out without a coat, this time we had fires going in every room. Fortunately our lavatories didn't freeze, though the neighbours' did.

Oscar became a great favourite with the kids. He had a way with children. He sat two of them on one of his knees. He told them stories about Canada and their summer cottage by a lake.

'. . . we've also got a speedboat and we go through the lakes. You could come up and stay at the cottage with us and have some of Mona's blueberry pie and see the animals. You've never seen a skunk. They come right up to the cottage window . . .'

He spoke in a sleepy, genial way. The kids loved him.

'Why don't you go back?' he said.

'We'll see — maybe next year.'

'You owe it to the kids,' he said.

Mona began to speak in Yiddish. 'Was it a question of money?' Emily and the kids just looked on, puzzled.

'It's a bit more complicated,' I said in English.

'How about if we take the kids back with us?' Oscar said. 'We'll take Martha and Ella. We'll look after them and they can go and stay with us in the summer at the cottage.'

Martha and Ella were hugging Oscar.

I didn't think for a minute he was serious.

'Look,' Oscar said. 'We can take them back for nothing on our tickets. We'll feed them, look after them. It's not a question of adopting them. They're yours.'

'We'll see,' I said to the two excited kids. It hurt the way they were so willing to go away from us.

Whenever Mona didn't want the kids to understand something she began to talk in Yiddish. Until I finally decided to send the kids into the other room. Only to have Rebecca come back upset.

'They're whispering,' she said. 'They've got secrets.'

It was nearly noon and we hadn't left the kitchen table. I suggested I might take them out, show them the place, and get some fresh air, so as to give Emily a chance to clean up and do some shopping.

It was freezing outside. There was no one out. The puddles in the narrow streets were frozen. The long fine sand beaches were empty. The water in the bay was grey. No boats in the harbour, only a few gulls were huddled together at the harbour's entrance, facing the wind.

'You should see it in the summer,' I said.

'I can imagine,' Mona said, huddled up in her Persian lamb coat. 'It sure is a nice-looking place.'

Oscar took coloured moving pictures of Mona and myself and the kids. And of the empty streets, the empty restaurants, the empty beaches, and boarded-up shops. Then we came back with rosy cheeks and sat around the fire in the dining-room.

'It's healthy the fire here,' Mona said, lighting up a cigarette. 'Not like our place — so stuffy.'

I went outside in the courtyard with the coal-bucket and came back with it full to the top.

'You know what you remind me,' Mona said, 'you coming in like that — with the pail of coal?'

'I know,' I said. 'Paw.'

There were times when I went out to get the coal from the shed in the courtyard that I remembered my father coming up from the cellar in the house on Murray Street, with a bucketful of coal for the Quebec stove in the hall. Just as there were times, upstairs in my room, when I was making out a list of payments to come, and remembered him and his black book with his list of people owing him money.

'Do you remember you telling me. Don't let boys touch you between *here*,' she drew a line across her neck. 'And *there*.' Another line at the knees. 'And you remember when you were at university and I saw you in Montreal. You had written that song. When you met me you gave me twenty dollars. I said no. What, you said, it's not enough. And gave me another twenty.'

I didn't remember either of these.

Instead, I remembered when she was about eight or nine. When she was hit with a stone from a slingshot. It cut her head. They had to shave her head. And she wore a beret. She wore it in school. And the kids made fun of her.

'And you remember my wedding?' Mona said. 'You remember Betty's fiancé, Sam? He was supposed to take a movie of the reception. But all he took was pictures of Betty . . .'

I didn't remember that either. I remembered Mona being sick. The doctor came to examine her. He gave her a large bar of chocolate for being a good girl. She gave me some. And we went upstairs and ate it in her room. Later, I watched the long, thin white-yellow worms come out of her mouth and lie slowly twisting on the floor.

Mona and Oscar had never seen Christmas before except in the movies. So I briefed them.

'This is the way it's going to be tomorrow. We wake up in the morning. We say Happy Christmas to each other. Then the kids come down. We have breakfast. Then go into the front room. And I read out the names and give out the presents.'

When they heard this they went out and came back loaded with presents that they wrapped up in their room and put under the tree.

'I arranged for a taxi to come on Boxing Day,' I said. 'We'll drive around and see some of the country around here.'

'I thought you told Maw you had a jalopy.'

'I might have said that,' I said, 'for Maw's sake.'

In the evening we sat around and watched television.

'They've got the same programs here,' Mona said, 'as we've got in Meridian.'

'They're American shows,' I said.

We watched a quiz for children. 'Your TV is so much better than ours,' Mona said. 'It's so educational.'

But they were mainly interested in the commercials.

After the news I switched off and we sat around the fire, drank coffee, and smoked cigarettes.

'Why don't you go back to Canada?' Oscar said.

'It takes money to get out of here,' I said. 'And maybe, now, I've lived too long away.'

'With your education you could have been a doctor,' Mona said.

'It's true,' she said to Emily.

'But I'm a writer,' I said. 'How many doctors has Canada got — thousands. How many writers? A handful. It's easier to be a doctor than a writer.'

'Yeh, I know,' Mona said sadly. 'But it's hard.'

I went and got some whisky — no one joined me.

'In a year's time I figure I'll make enough money to retire,' Oscar said.

'Talk, talk,' Mona said. 'That's easy.'

'You'll see if I don't,' Oscar said. 'I'd be half way there if it wasn't for her operations. You know, she's had half a dozen already.'

'It's true,' Mona said.

Oscar I knew was in the scrap-metal business. But he bought anything that he could sell at a profit. He would fill up his warehouse and then load up a truck and drive the stuff to Montreal or Toronto and sell it.

'I've got to ring her up *every* night,' Oscar said, 'when I'm away from Meridian.'

'We've got a system where we don't have to pay,' Mona

said. 'If we don't want to talk just let the other one know that
he arrived in Montreal or Toronto — Oscar asks person-to-
person and makes up some name like Johnson. "May I speak
to Mr. Johnson," he says. And I say, "I'm sorry Mr. Johnson
is not in." And I know he got there all right.'

'You think *that's* something,' Oscar said. 'We know a
woman who rings up Montreal long distance to get her kosher
meat. She'd call up the butcher and say. "Is Chuck in?" And
of course the man would say that Chuck wasn't in. But he
knew that meant she wanted chuck that week.'

'We've got three properties in Meridian,' Mona said. 'So
you could come and stay there. I know it's a small out-of-the-
way place. But until you find your feet.'

'Thanks,' I said.

But I didn't see much point in exchanging one small town
for another. I desperately wanted to get out of this seaside town
and live in London again. It's a cosmopolitan city that I miss. I
try to go to London as often as I can, but it's expensive. Even
so, a few days in London and I come back as if I had a shot in
the arm. I feel sharper in London. I go through the streets and
feel like singing. I do sing. I go to bed in London feeling slim
and not the way I feel here, as if I'm carrying a large body with
lots of weight and deadness.

'I've got to get us out,' I told them. 'There are times I've
just got to take myself away from here. So I take a train to
Plymouth. And just to walk down straight streets again. Until
about noon it's fine. After that, I know I've got to come back to
this place.'

'Do you miss London, Emily?' Mona said.

'It's my home town. There are days here when I feel life is
going by — day after day the same — and you're waiting for
something to happen.'

'Like us coming,' Oscar said.

And we all laughed.


On Christmas morning the kids were up early. Emily had filled
up their stockings by their beds when they were asleep. And by
the time we all came down for breakfast the kids were excited

and some of that excitement went over to us. We all said Happy Christmas. And after some coffee we went in the front room. It looked cold outside, no snow but the puddles were frozen. Emily had the large open fire blazing away in each room.

I began to call out the presents. The children's first.

'This is for Rebecca from Uncle Oscar and Auntie Mona — I wonder what it is?' And the excited child undid the parcel and showered Mona and Oscar with kisses. ''Who's this for —?'

Martha, just over nine, got a toilet set from them. There were things for cleaning her nails, plucking her eyebrows, putting on nail polish, and some perfume. The others got the most expensive dolls in the place. I know, I saw them in the store window. It embarrassed Emily more than it did me. There were boxes of candies from Emily's relations, reading-books, and colouring-books for the children, toys, bits of jewellery, and soap and lots of handkerchiefs.

Around two we sat around the table in the dining-room, all seven of us, for dinner. Emily brought in the turkey. 'It's nearly twelve pounds,' I said. And all the kids said Ah and looked excited.

'You think that's big,' Oscar said to the kids. 'If you come to Canada you'll have turkeys twice that size. You remember,' he said to Mona, 'the turkeys we had that time?'

'Canadian turkeys are a little bigger,' Mona said politely.

On the last night we were sitting around the fire, watching some play on television. I decided to switch off. I went out to get some more coal in the bucket. When I came back Oscar was saying:

'. . . one thing we got for sure. A place in the ground. It's six feet long, three feet wide.' He moved his hand as if he was measuring. 'And six feet deep.'

I noticed Emily getting flushed. She turned her head away from Oscar. 'Stop it. Stop it,' she said quietly.

'It's all the same,' Oscar went on taking no notice. 'We'll all have it in the end.'

Emily turned her head away from us all. 'I'm sorry,' she

said. And, weeping, got up and went out of the room.

Mona and Oscar looked astonished.

'Is she upset?' Mona said.

'No,' I said, sarcastically.

'She's got to accept this, you know,' Oscar said. 'It's no use running away.'

'She doesn't accept it,' I said.

'But we all got to die,' my sister said.

'I think,' I said, 'you brought back her father.'

'So?' Oscar said. 'I buried my mother.'

'Maybe you better go and speak to her,' Mona said.

I went back. Emily had stopped crying, although her face looked as if she hadn't. I put my arms around her and kissed her.

'I'm sorry,' she said. And I kissed her again.

'It was a lot of things. It was suddenly as if I realized that she, they, being a Jew. As if I was an outsider and we weren't close, man and woman, like we are when she goes on talking Jewish. This is my house she's in and I suddenly felt we'll die and they are able to believe in something — that you are part of, and I'm not. And there isn't anything I could do about it.'

I kissed her again. 'Let's go back in.'

We did.

'I'm sorry,' Emily said.

'He's going to put us all in a story,' Mona said, 'just watch.'

'I don't care,' Oscar said. Then turning to me. 'If you can make a buck out of it — that's OK with me.'

I phoned up London and fixed them up with a room in the Strand Palace. 'It's so much with a bath and so much without,' I said.

'We'll have without,' Mona said.

They were going to London because Oscar wanted to do a round-up of some of the places he knew when he was a soldier over here in the war.

'I'll cry when I say goodbye,' Mona said. 'I don't know why. I'm not like him. I'm like Paw. I cry.'

We had to wait for the train at the station. Mona looked at

Oscar. And Oscar put out his hand to shake mine.

I felt a piece of paper in my palm. I looked and saw it was a five-pound note.

'Thanks,' I said, and gave it back to him. Since two of the kids were with us there was no scene.

'My pocket is deeper than yours,' Oscar said, still holding the note out for me.

I put my hand in my coat pocket. Then put my hand in his pocket.

'It *is* deeper,' I said.

Then the train came. I went in with their luggage and got them an empty compartment and kissed my sister. She wept, without a sound, her face screwed up. And I thought how like my father she looked. I shook hands and embraced Oscar.

They rang up that night to say they got in OK and the room was fine, the hotel was fine, and a blizzard was on. I told them to go to Blooms in Whitechapel for a meal.

Next night Mona spoke to Emily. They decided to go back tomorrow morning. London they found was expensive. ('There are no bargains.') The weather was miserable. And they missed their kids.

On the morning they were to take off, we returned the bedding to our neighbour, cleared the rooms. Nothing had really changed. And again that feeling of being cut off, and the need to get out of here. Luckily one of the payments came through. So I took myself off to Plymouth. Went to see the new books and the new magazines at W.H. Smiths. Had some coffee and doughnuts at Joe Lyons. Saw a bad movie. Had a meal. And came back. On the following Monday we got a letter from Mona. On page two she said:

. . . Dad was operated on this morning and it's a good job they did as both doctors said he wouldn't have lasted four months. I never saw such a big stone that he had in his bladder. The doctor said he got through better than average. We saw and spoke to him but he was in pain and got his hypo so thought we had better leave so he could rest. Poor Mom she looks terrible and it's taking a lot out of her. As soon as I hear anymore will let you know.

On January 22nd came another letter.

It has been sometime since we heard from you and hope all is well. Saw Dad yesterday afternoon and he got his stitches out and is looking better. I saw the doctor and asked him how he is getting along and he said as well as can be expected. Dad seems confused at times though. We brought the children yesterday and he was happy to see them. He's well looked after.

February 2nd, Meridian.

Hope all is well with you. Haven't been down to see Dad the last while and everytime I spoke to Mom she seemed upset so yesterday afternoon I got the cleaning woman to watch the children and went down to see him. I also saw the doctor. He says Dad is coming along but is confused and that he doesn't know if he'll get better. He wants to put him in a rest home if he can get him in. The other day he went out in his pyjamas and it was below zero. I don't think he realizes he is in hospital. He recognizes us all but talks as if we were still living on Murray Street and gets confused.

February 25th, Meridian.

Dad was moved to the nursing home on Friday and went down yesterday to see him. He seems much happier and I don't know if he realizes where he is or not. At night they put a restrainer on him so he won't get out. Thursday morning at the hospital they found him outside at the Parking Lot. It was his fourth time out.

March 10th, Meridian.

Hope all is well and what's the matter I haven't heard from you? Saw Dad on Thursday and he was so happy to see me. Apparently he got out again so when I was there the Director of the Nursing Home spoke to me and asked me to tell him not to go out and he got angry with me and said how can I get out as you see I'm lying here.

April 6th, Meridian.

Last week he got out with just his clothes and slippers and the Nursing Home is past the exhibition grounds and he walked to Bank Street and went in a restaurant (he had no money) they gave him a cup of coffee and phoned the Nursing Home and an orderly came with a taxi and got him.

'For some reason he wants to get out,' I said to Emily. 'But once out he doesn't know what to do. It's at the opposite end of town from where we live. He doesn't know how to get home from there. I don't know why, but I'm proud of him running away like this . . .' Tears were coming to my eyes. And with Mona's letter I went upstairs to my room. There was the sign, *You've got to get out of here*, facing me on the wall. The mirror with the post-cards.

I went to the window. It overlooked a small valley of cottages. There was a funeral taking place in the street immediately below. The hearse with the glass sides had driven up outside a small stone cottage. Men in black brought out the light wood coffin. And heaped it with bright yellow flowers in the hearse. The mourners walked behind it. They seemed to walk like mechanical toys.

I stood at the window, over to the side, so they couldn't see me, and watched them go by.

From this window I have now watched several funerals. They were all of people I didn't know.

# A Visit

The phone woke us.

We let it ring. And looked anxiously at one another.

'Answer it,' Emily said urgently.

I got out of bed and ran up the stairs to the office in the attic. At this time of night it could mean only one thing, someone was calling from Canada.

'I have a call for you,' the operator said. 'Go ahead.'

'Gordon,' an excited woman's voice said. 'It's Mona.'

'Hullo Mona.'

'Did I get you out of bed?'

'Yes, It's after three in the morning.'

'I'm sorry,' she said. 'Nothing's wrong. But I thought I'd ring to let you know that I'm coming over with Ma on Wednesday. We're flying from Montreal.'

'I thought Ma was to come on her own?'

'It's the first time for her in an airplane. She asked me if I could go with her. Is that OK?''

'We can put Ma up,' I said. 'But there's no more room.'

'I don't mind where you find me a place,' she said. 'I thought I'd bring Chuck as well. It will probably be the only chance he'll have.'

'July is the height of the season,' I said. 'It will be difficult to find a place.'

Suddenly I felt cold in the almost dark attic room. The only bit of light, moonlight, came from the uncurtained windows. And I could see the slate of the roofs glistening, the stars.

'I don't mind where you put us up,' she said. 'Any hotel will do, Gordon. As long as it's near you. Is that OK?'

'Yeh,' I said. 'That's great.'

'Are you sure?'

'Yes,' I said. 'That's fine. What time have you got?'

'After ten — I'm sorry I got you out of bed. You're sure it's OK?'

'It's fine,' I said.

Back in bed I said to Emily. 'You heard the conversation. My mother is coming over with my sister on Wednesday. I told her to spend the first day in London and come down the next so they won't be too tired. Mona is bringing her boy.'

'I could hear you say fine, fine,' Emily said. 'And I knew you didn't think it was fine at all.'

We lay on our backs unable to sleep. I didn't know what Emily was thinking. But I guessed she was as anxious about this visit as I was. For neither she nor the kids had met my mother. All these years, I thought, I managed to keep the two sides of the family apart.

'Where do you think we'll get them in?' Emily asked.

'We can try Miss Benson down the road. It's only for a couple of weeks.'

'Remember when your sister came with her husband? They walked in from Canada unannounced.'

'I remember.'

'You don't think they will do something like that again?'

'No,' I said. 'I told Mona to stay Wednesday in London. They won't be here until late Thursday afternoon.'

But I was wrong.


They arrived on Wednesday. No one to meet them. They opened the door and stood in the hall looking tired and nervous. Mona grey in the face, Chuck vacant, mother neat and

self-contained in her navy blue suit. As I came further down
the stairs, I called out to Emily who was in the kitchen. There
was some kissing and tears from mother, Emily, Mona, and
the children. I paid the taxi-driver. We moved into the front
room. And they sat down exhausted.

'Why didn't you stay the day in London?' I asked Mona.

'We couldn't get into a hotel.'

'How many did you try?'

'One,' she said. 'Then they told us at the air terminal that if
we rushed we might get the train for down here. You should
have seen how fast that taxi went. We got to the station. No
time to get tickets. We ran to get on the train. It's been like that
since we left Montreal.'

Mona lit another cigarette.

'I was told back home not to go Air Canada. That BOAC
was better. *She* got the tickets. She said we're going first class. I
told her, no. Our tickets were economy. She insisted they were
first. At Dorval the British plane had engine trouble. Another
scramble. I was going around getting nervous, while she goes
on as if she has all the time in the world. When they said we *had*
to go Air Canada — I just stood there and laughed.'

'It was a very good flight,' mother said. 'I enjoyed it. She
looks like a Raport,' she said about our eldest girl, Martha.
'Except the Raports are dark and she is blonde. Kate must look
like your side of the family, Emily. Judith looks like one of us.'

They brought out their presents. Emily made tea. And, on
the quiet, sent out Martha to get some fish for supper. Mother
said she wouldn't eat meat, it wasn't kosher, only fish. I got
Chuck and Mona into Miss Benson's. And they went there
after supper. Mother had our bedroom. Emily and I would
sleep on the mattress in the attic-office. I thought I'd better see
if mother had settled in.

I saw her, sitting up in bed, giving candies to the kids. She
looked refreshed and excited. She was patting the bed around
her and saying:

'Come, sit down. And I'll tell you —'

Next morning when I went to open the front door to get the
milk there was Mona and Chuck.

'Hi,' Mona said. 'We've been up early. I couldn't sleep. Neither could he. He came and sat outside my door until I got up.'

Mother came down. She said she slept well. And while Emily was making breakfast she and Mona opened their purses, gave the kids five pounds each and ten pounds to Emily and me.

'Where is the nearest bank,' Mona said. 'I need to cash some traveller's cheques.'

'Me too,' mother said.

When they came back they had bags filled with grapes, peaches, apples, oranges, cherries, bananas, pears. I don't remember having so much fruit in the house — not since I lived in Canada.

'People live differently over here,' mother said. 'It's more slow. I like it.'

She was curious about British money. And in no time she was doing sums in her head faster than any of us. They had bought post-cards — showing the harbour, the beaches, the bay — to send to people in Canada. Mother insisted that Mona write hers for her since she wrote English phonetically. (I remember her criticism of my last book: 'Why do you always write about bed people.' Or the time after father died she wrote: 'He was not used to go out with the hearse' — meaning horse.) And they soon got into an argument. Mona wanted to write the same message on each card. Mother wanted each one to be different. You would think they disliked each other the way they were talking.

'That's a lot of cards,' I said in an attempt to break up the squabble.

'I've sent twenty-five,' mother said. 'And I'm not finished. Everybody likes me. All my friends are millionaires.'

'That must be comforting,' I said.

'It's true,' mother said.

'I stayed at the Queen Elizabeth,' Mona said. '$31.75 a night. Hamburgers and chips cost $3.75.'

'The way you do your washing,' mother said to Emily who had come in from the courtyard, 'and hang it on the line and pull it up. It's just like the old country.' And when she saw the enamel casserole with the purple-blue cover. 'I haven't seen one like that since I left Poland.' We looked at the bottom. It said Made in Poland.

But I remember in Canada when I asked her why did she leave Poland. She wouldn't say except something about taxes being high. When I said I'd like to go to Poland and see where she and Pa lived, she said, 'It would be better if you didn't go. If you could do without.'

And here she was excited because of seeing washing on a line, an enamel casserole, and narrow cobblestone streets.

The kids took them to the beach. They stayed there until late afternoon. Mona swam and lay on the sand. Mother walked by the tideline and picked small delicate pink shells that she brought back to her room. In a few days they looked much better, especially Mona, more relaxed. And they had caught the sun.

'We met this couple on the beach,' Mona said. 'They're on holiday from Scotland. They pay forty pounds a week rent for a house here. He earns fifty pounds a week — he must save up. They have a car — it cost them twelve hundred pounds — is that a lot?'

'Guess how much this tan is costing me?' mother interrupted.

'I don't know,' I said.

'Take a guess.'

'Five hundred dollars?'

'Seven hundred and fifty,' she said with pride.

Chuck was left with us. He didn't like to go outside. He was frightened of steps, of a hill, and the beach. The first time he saw the sand he couldn't understand why we didn't fall through it. And when he was left on his own he would talk in these two voices. One was high, the other low. He would talk rapidly, in a sing-song. High. Low. I couldn't make out what he was saying. The first time I heard him I asked.

'What are you doing?'

'Talking to myself,' he said quietly.

He liked to watch television. The Americans were sending two men to land on the moon. And Chuck knew all the astronauts' names and what they had to do. He knew every stage of the journey into space. He rushed in.

'Halfway — moon gravity —'

He would stand in front of the television, only a few feet away. When he became excited he would bring his hands up by the side of his face, fingers wide apart, and they would quiver.

On days that it rained we sat around the breakfast table listening to the noise on the roof while Mona told the kids' fortunes in their tea leaves. She had complete faith in doctors and tea leaves. And mother asked Emily for the recipes of some of the things she had baked — cakes and desserts — so that she could make them for her Golden Age club when she got back. She showed us photographs. They were of elderly ladies sitting, all dressed up, by long tables with white table-cloths.

On the fourth morning it was drizzling. I was coming down the stairs. There was a nice smell of cooking from the kitchen. I saw Chuck at the bottom.

'You're *fame-us*,' he said to me as I came down. 'Me see you on TV. *Fame-us*.' Then he looked at his face in the hall-mirror and said to himself. 'Fame-us. Fame-us.'

Inside the front room Mona continued to chain-smoke. Mother was in a chair by the window looking out. She looked at the valley of granite cottages, the houses on the other side of the hill.

'I like this,' she said.

It was a summer light rain. It gave the slate roofs of the cottages a blue colour.

'Could you live here?' I asked her.

'It's nice. But not for me. I'm used to a different life.'

She looked around the room, at the shabby furniture, the damp walls, the shelves of books, the worn red carpet.

'Did you ever think of changing your job?'

'And do what?'

'You could work yourself up and become a journalist.'

'Journalists come down to interview me.'

'But what have you got?' she said. 'No home of your own. No new furniture. Children need nice clothes. Appearance *is* important.'

I didn't think it mattered much. But perhaps it mattered more than I ever admitted. Else why did I always meet people who came from Canada, to see me, in a pub. Then take them for a conducted tour of this seaside town, ending with a call on a rich acquaintance who had a large granite house with a drive, wide lawns and gardens, above the bay. So they could go back with that. Was that so different from what she was saying?

'You remember Lionel?' mother said.

I said nothing.

'I betcha he makes thirty thousand dollars a year. Maybe more. And his brother, Jackie, the one you played ball with. He makes forty thousand dollars, at least.'

And Mona said. 'Cousin Lily's daughter got married. You should see what they got. They have black leather Mediterranean chairs and settee. They have a new sports car. They pay two hundred dollars a month and they have a swimming pool. And it's so nice. Music comes in all the rooms — all the day.'

'It's wonderful,' mother said. 'I'm telling you — it's wonderful.'

Emily had come in to join us. I wanted to change the subject. Mona had put out a cigarette and lit up yet another.

'Why don't you ease up on the smoking,' I said to her.

'I tried. But I can't. It's my nerves. I need a cigarette. I tried candies but they don't work. What can I do?'

'Many men smoke,' I said. 'But Fu Manchu.'

Only Emily laughed.

'You should go and see Israel,' mother said. 'It's wonderful. For three hundred and fifty dollars you stay at the David Hotel. You have a table full of fish. You take what fish you want. You pay no more. No tips. Nothing. It's wonderful.'

'But you haven't been there,' I said.

'People who have tell me,' she said quietly.

I went out of the room and when I came back mother was

saying: 'I have had two proposals so I went and asked the doctor. He said what do you need another man to get sick on you and you have to look after him. I'm sixty-seven but I look sixty-one or sixty-two.'

I didn't expect to be but I was taken back by this.

A few moments later tears appeared in her eyes. 'Next year will be the fiftieth anniversary of my getting married.' She rubbed the back of her hand against her eyes.

'How old is Chuck?' I quickly asked Mona.

'Twenty,' she said.

'What are you going to do when he gets older?' mother said.

'What do you mean?' Mona came back.

'You should get out of Meridian,' mother said. 'Go to Toronto — you might meet someone there. You ought to marry again.'

Chuck came in very excited.

'Landed on moon. Landed.'

Then he went back, to the other room, to watch television.

'What do you and Gordon do, Emily, on Saturday nights?' Mona asked. 'Do you go out?'

'We stay in and watch television.'

'That's just like Chuck and me. That's what we do, every Saturday night.'

Next morning it was bright and sunny. We were sitting around the kitchen table having breakfast. Mother was talking. She was telling the children. '— your grandfather was an architect. He came over to Montreal in 1904. He stayed a couple of years. But he didn't like the life. So he went back to Poland.'

When the phone went.

Emily answered. She spoke quietly, didn't say much, and hung up.

'That was my mother to say Florrie died,' she said and went into the back kitchen.

'I knew someone was going to die,' Mona said. 'Because of the birds. They were so loud this morning. They woke me up.'

'Those are gulls,' I said. 'They are with us all the time.'

'I thought it would be one of us,' she said.

I went to see Emily. She was standing in the sunny courtyard against the whitewashed wall crying.

Mother, Mona, and Chuck went with the kids to the beach.

I remember Florrie. We spent our honeymoon at their farm, about forty miles from here. Emily was evacuated from London during the war. She came to Cornwall with her name on a luggage label around her neck. Florrie picked her out, at the station, from all the other kids because she said she was dressed in a nice fawn coat. She lived the war years with Florrie and her husband Morley. Helped to bring the cows in, helped with the milking. Bicycled and walked around the country roads. The fields with the derelict mine shafts. 'I used to write letters to my parents,' Emily said, 'saying I hate it here, take me away, they make me work. Now I look upon it as one of the happiest times of my life. I was lucky — it's like having a bonus. Now Florrie is dead and something has ended.'

And I remembered Florrie coming every Christmas with our Christmas goose or turkey. 'A dear little family,' she called us. And the last time, when we told her we were all going up to London for a holiday and would be on the Cornish Riviera Express, Florrie said she would come out and wave a white table-cloth. We all stood in the corridor of the train looking out as we came near the place where Emily grew up. And there, in the distance, the white table-cloth moved slowly in the breeze — as we waved our handkerchiefs back.

The funeral on Sunday was in a Methodist chapel. Very plain except for the organ. The chapel was packed. The singing was loud and excellent. And I sang as loud as I could because Florrie was the only one who said I could sing. Everyone else says I can't keep a tune.

Then we went to the cemetery. There was this tall church on top of a hill with the cemetery on the steep grass slope. There were fields with hedges and trees on both sides. As we stood by the open grave, a cow was going across the field opposite us.

Emily saw faces of people she knew twenty-five years ago. And she showed me the gravestones of Florrie's father, of Morley's mother and cousin. Trees, grass, fields. It somehow felt right, here, in the cemetery. And I envied people who knew where they were going to be buried.

When we came back and opened the front door we could hear singing. Mother and Mona were in the courtyard clapping their hands and singing with the kids.

*Oh, how we danced*
*On the night we were wed...*

We didn't want to see them. So we went upstairs to the attic room. Emily went to the window and looked out at the deep blue water in the bay, the stone cottages, the far shore fields.

'I hate the sea,' she said and began to cry. 'I wish I belonged to something. I don't belong to anything. There's your mother, your sister, and yourself — you all belong to something. Even if you have run away from it. And there's Florrie and Morley — they belong to something.'

I thought, where do I belong? Where does Emily? Mother? Mona?

Although it was after six in the evening the light was still bright. The sky had high summer clouds. And they were lit up by greens, light pinks, and orange. A gull was making its honking noise close by. And further away it was answered by another.

I could hear the children, inside, around the piano. They were playing a duet and singing loudly. 'Things ain't what they used to be.'

There was still another week to go but I was marking off the days. I found myself coming up to the attic to get away from the constant talk they kept up. Even the kids no longer listened to what they were told and had stopped being on their best behaviour. Judith had one of her little bursts of temperament and answered Emily back. When Mona heard this she said.

'Judith, you remind me of me. What's the matter honey? You don't look pleased.'

Emily was also becoming edgy. When she asked me to do

something. And I said I would do it later.

'You're like your mother,' she came back sharply. 'You both live as if life goes on forever. But I don't think that way. I know there isn't much time. When a week goes by and I haven't done something, I feel I've squandered a bit of my life. But both of you think you have all the time in the world.'

They could have stayed another week with us. But I told them they ought to see London while they were over here. They didn't want to very much. I said I would phone and get them a room in a hotel. It had to be central as Chuck couldn't get on a bus.

'How about twenty-five dollars a night?' I called from the phone.

Mona agreed.

Mother was against it. 'Twenty-five dollars just to sleep in a bed?'

In the end I got them something cheaper.

'Type me out a list of what to see,' Mona said. 'Put, first, Fiddler on the Roof. And I want to travel on the train first class.'

The last morning came.

'How time flies,' mother said at breakfast. 'It went so quickly.'

Mona came in without Chuck. She seemed to shrink physically in size and become anxious. Except for the tan, she looked like she did when she arrived. 'I can't get Chuck out of bed,' she said. 'He's hiding under the bed-clothes. He doesn't want to get up today. He thinks if he doesn't get up we won't have to go.'

'I'll go and get him,' mother said.

And she did. She came walking back with him holding his arm in a tight grip so that she took most of his weight.

'Look at us,' she called out. 'We are going steady.'

When the taxi came Mona and mother wept as they kissed the kids.

We went with them to the mainline station.

'It's like Europe,' mother said as the taxi drove through the country. 'It looks so nice here, the fields, the trees.'

Mona and Chuck looked lost. I had a feeling, even then, that they were waiting for me to say: why don't you stay the last week here.

But I didn't say it.

At the mainline station we had to wait for the train. I walked up and down the platform. Mother came over.

'You wear your heels down the same way as your father.'

And when I went to kiss her goodbye she offered me her face sideways — just like Kate, I thought.


Coming back in the taxi Emily and I were silent for several miles. Then Emily said.

'She came too late.'

'Yes,' I said.

The hedges, the small green fields, were by us on both sides. Then the first glimpse of the sea and the hovering gulls.

When I opened the front door one of the kids was playing Happy Birthday on the piano. I had forgotten it was Emily's birthday. The kids had set the kitchen table. In the middle there was a chocolate cake with small candles. And birthday cards were on the dresser.

We sat in our places around the table. Emily lit the candles on the cake. Judith pulled the curtain across the window. It was nice by candlelight.

We joined hands and sang Happy Birthday.

Then Emily stood up and took a deep breath.

'Make a wish,' Kate said excitedly.

Emily hesitated. Then blew out the candles.

We all applauded.

Judith moved the curtain and let the daylight back into the room.

Then we began to eat.

# Thin Ice

In the Spring of 1965 a book of mine was published. And it got more notice and sold more copies than all my previous books combined. It was translated into several languages. The CBC and the BBC made half-hour films because of it. It went into paperback. Money began to come in from various places. Someone in Madrid wanted to use extracts in an English for foreigners textbook. Someone in Halifax wanted to make a recording of it for the blind. I was interviewed for British newspapers and magazines. Articles were written. I received a number of invitations: to open a new primary school in Cornwall, to give talks, to give readings. And one invitation came from the head of the English department of a university in the Maritimes offering three months as resident writer beginning in January. As I didn't know the Atlantic provinces and as I wanted to be back in Canada, I decided to go.

I arrived by plane on January 6th. I was met at the airport which consisted almost entirely of fields of snow piled high and long drifts. 'I can't remember when we've had so much snow and such cold weather,' the head of the English department said. 'We're blaming the Russians.'

His face reminded me of an Indian Chief but he smiled easily and was smartly dressed in a black winter coat, a white scarf, and a black Astrakhan hat that he wore tilted to the side. He drove, in a large low car with chains on the tires, to the best hotel in the city and led me to the top floor, to two comfortable rooms.

'Will this be all right?'

'Yes,' I said.

Suddenly the life of a near-recluse that I had lived before changed. I was in demand. I was interviewed for the student newspaper, the town's daily paper, the local radio and TV. I was invited to contribute a regular article to the local monthly magazine. The commercial radio station would phone up and ask what did I think of a particular current topic? And what I said on the phone was taped and then broadcast. There was a display of my books and manuscripts (in glass cases) in the university library. The main bookshop in the place filled a window with my books. I gave talks and readings to a variety of women's and men's clubs. The leading Jewish businessman, Pettigorsky (he owned the largest department store), gave a dinner in my honour at the Jewish community centre. After a filling meal (that included soup and mandlen, chicken, blintzes, and lockshen kugel) and I had made my speech and everyone was standing up and drinking and smoking, Mr Pettigorsky came over.

'It will take you a while to get used to living here,' he said apologetically. 'The first year you'll hate it. The second won't be so bad. After you have lived here three years you won't want to leave.'

But I liked it from the start.

I enjoyed going to the various teas, luncheons, and dinners. I liked being asked to meet visiting VIP's who were passing through. Besides professors and undergraduates, I was also meeting judges, politicians, engineers, surgeons, scientists, army officers, restauranteurs, businessmen.

And I had this warm office in the Arts Building that overlooked the snow-covered campus and the city. I would go to the office, twice a week, and there would be people outside the door waiting to see me. I was like a doctor. Undergraduates would come — possibly with their ailments, but they would express it differently. Girls would say: 'My boyfriend's too shy to come, but I've come,' and say that he was trying to write a novel.

I was the first resident writer the university or this town had. And, after the early hectic weeks, it was mainly people not to do with the university who came to see me.

The first were two Army Officers' wives from the large Army camp some miles outside the city. They told me that they were from Toronto and Vancouver and were only temporarily at the camp. They were going to put on a musical and wanted my approval. They intended to use the tunes of familiar songs — "Somewhere over the Rainbow", "You Made Me Love You", "It's All Right with Me" — but they would put their own words to the tunes. And these words were to be witty comments on local events, especially Army camp gossip.

'We thought of beginning,' said the lady from Toronto, 'by having a voice come over the loudspeaker. It would be a pilot on Air Canada speaking to his passengers. "You are now approaching the Maritimes — please put your clocks back fifty years." '

Most of the others wanted to tell me things.

When I was having a haircut the barber thought I should know the best ways to hunt duck and moose. A scientist, in charge of a unit to help the surrounding farmers improve their productivity, came over after a reading and said.

'This is a true story. I thought I would tell it to you. Perhaps you can use it. There was this priest. He lived in the country near here. He was middle-aged. And he liked women, especially girls. Whenever he went to visit people who were sick in hospital or at home — if they were girls — he put his hand underneath the covers. Things got so bad that the local mothers got together and wrote to the Bishop. Finally the priest was moved. And he was replaced by a much younger man. This young man didn't have the other's habits. But he began to ask for things. He said he needed a new car. The old one was too old. He wanted the house redecorated. Some special food he liked had to be flown in from Montreal. He wanted the best cigars. After a while the people again wrote to the Bishop this time complaining at the money this young priest was costing them.

'Being chaste is expensive, the Bishop wrote back.'

And Peter, the young owner of a Chinese restaurant where I sometimes went to eat, told me that before coming here he attended university in Red China. He thought I should know the best way to steal chickens off a chicken farm.

'You get this candle,' Peter said. 'It only comes from China. When you light it it gives off smoke. And you let the wind blow this smoke over to where the chickens are. You do it at night. One whiff and the dogs go to sleep for twenty minutes. So do all the chickens. They just lie down and go to sleep. You get a handkerchief and put it around your mouth and pick up these sleeping chickens and put them in your truck. Twenty minutes later, when they wake up, you are miles away —'

I listened to the strangest confessions, humiliations, suffering. And, as if to balance them, an amazing endurance.

By the beginning of February I was so well-known in the town that strangers in the street would smile and say hello. A tall blonde woman with glasses came up to me: 'I saw your picture in the paper — it looks like you.' Kids stopped throwing snowballs to call out. 'I know you Mister — you write books.' When I went into a restaurant heads would turn.

Meanwhile the invitations kept coming in.

One of the early ones was from the Professor of English at St Vincent's — a teacher's college which was affiliated to the university. But as it was a hundred and sixty miles away, I kept putting it off. Until the head of the English department told me that St Vincent's was after him to get me to come.

'It will be the usual thing,' he said. 'A small dinner before. Then you give your reading at the college hall. And there will be a party afterwards.'

I agreed to go next Friday.

Four days later in the faculty club he came over. 'I've just got back from St Vincent's. They're very excited about you coming. They've got posters stuck all over the place. There is a piece about you in their local paper. And they have put you up at the best hotel.'

He ordered coffee and doughnuts for both of us.

'The Board of Governors asked me to tell you that you can be resident writer with us for as long as you like.'

'That's very nice,' I said.

I was to fly to St Vincent's at noon. But fog came on Friday morning. The planes were grounded. The train no longer ran although the tracks were still there.

I took a small green bus from the bus station. Four other passengers were on the bus at the start, but they got off at the small towns on the way. For the first hour the roads were clear. Then it began to snow. The wind increased. It turned into a blizzard. Fewer cars and trucks were coming from the opposite direction and more were abandoned by the sides of the road. The driver kept stopping to wipe the windshield. The snow was coming down so fast and thick that the wipers were not clearing it. Then he stopped at a filling station to get a tow-truck.

'We'll never get to St Vincent's today,' he told me.

'But I'm supposed to give a reading —'

'It's impossible. I can't get through.'

I rang St Vincent's, told the Professor of English the position. He said he understood, that the weather was bad there as well, and it would be best to postpone it.

I went back to the bus and sat inside.

'How about going back?'

'Nothing is getting through *either* way,' the driver said.

The tow-truck towed us for about an hour and a half — where I don't know — as I couldn't see for the falling snow. Finally we arrived in a small town. The street lights were on but there was hardly anyone in the street — snow covered everything.

I asked the driver when he would go back.

'Soon as the roads are open. There will be an inspection tomorrow morning at nine.'

I said I would be there.

I went to look for a hotel but as soon as I stepped off the main road I sank to my knees in snow. I walked that way until I came to cross streets — the road was covered with freshly fallen snow but it was hard-packed underneath. I finally found a sign on a drab looking wooden building that said it was a hotel.

'Can I have a room for the night?' I asked the man.

'It's eight dollars a night,' he said.

'OK,' I replied. And waited for him to give me the room key.

'Is that all your luggage?'

'Yes,' I said holding on to my attache case.

'If that is all your luggage you will have to pay in advance.'

'I'm the resident writer at the university and I was on my way to St Vincent's to give a reading when the blizzard came —'

'Is your car outside?'

'No. I came by bus.'

'And that is all your luggage?'

'Yes.'

'You will have to pay in advance — eight dollars.'

I paid him the eight dollars. It seemed a long time since I was treated this way. I took the key and went up the creaky stairs to Room 2 on the first floor.

It was a small gloomy room — the kind I used to have in my early days when I was poor. A bare light hung from the ceiling. And I needed it on all the time. There was an iron bed, a rickety wooden dresser. No chair. A cracked enamel sink with only one tap working. And every time I turned on the tap it made a wailing noise. The wallpaper was stained. I felt cold. I went over to the thin green-painted radiator. No heat. There were two grey blankets at the foot of the bed and a disinfectant smell when I pulled back the covers.

I felt hungry and tired. I looked in my attache case and took out the toothbrush, the toothpaste, the shaving lather and razor, and the copy of my book that I brought for the reading. But in my rush, or absentmindedness, I had forgotten to take my cheque book. Not that I would have had any luck cashing a cheque here.

I took out all the money I had and counted it. It came to

nineteen dollars and some change. If I'm stuck here another night that's another eight dollars. The ticket back is ten dollars. That left me a dollar and the change. I counted the change — thirty-seven cents. No need to worry, I said, I might be able to get away tomorrow. What I need now is food (I had been five hours on that bus) and a good night's sleep.

I went out to find a restaurant. It was still snowing. I went to the main street. The stores were on one side. The other side consisted of open fields covered in snow and some trees that were almost hidden. I went into a small supermarket and bought a loaf of bread, a tin of sardines, and two apples. That left me forty cents to spare.

I came back to the room. I ate the bread and the sardines sitting on the bed with my coat on. Then I dipped pieces of bread in the sardine oil. And washed it down with an apple.

I lay on the bed with the coat and the grey blankets over me. I thought that now that I was earning my living from writing and giving readings I was past things like this.

I went to sleep. And when I woke I was hungry. I ate the rest of the bread with the last apple. I remembered from my hard-up days that it was important to have something to keep up morale. I went out, found a small restaurant, had a cup of hot coffee and asked the woman if she sold any cigars singly.

'These,' she said, 'are twenty-five cents each.'

I looked at it wondering if I had enough.

'This one is fifteen cents.'

I took the fifteen cents cigar, smoked it slowly. The tobacco was kind of green. I took a long time over the coffee. Then went back to the room in the hotel to lie down. Instead I went to sleep.

Next morning when I woke up I was cold. I brushed my teeth and shaved in cold water and went out. The snow was still falling but it wasn't so thick. I walked to the bus station. The bus was in the garage. I found the driver — a different driver — in a stand-up eating place next to the bus depot. He was finishing his breakfast.

'No — no buses today,' he said. 'Next inspection tomorrow.'

'What time?'

'Around nine in the morning.'

'I know the ticket back costs ten dollars,' I said. 'Could you give me a ticket. And I'll pay when we get back?'

'We don't run the company on those lines,' he said.

I felt hungry and light-headed.

'I'll buy you a cup of coffee.'

'Thanks.'

He paid for his breakfast and handed me the saucer with the cup of coffee.

'I'll see you tomorrow,' I said.

When he had gone — in my nervousness — I spilled half of the coffee before I had my first sip.

I went back to the hotel.

'I'll stay another night,' I told the man.

'That will be eight dollars.'

I paid him.

All I had left was the ten dollar bill. I put it in my back buttoned-down pocket.

'How cold is it?' I asked the man.

'Thirteen below. But near here it's been thirty-five below.'

Saturday morning, I thought I'll go to *shul*. It will be warm. There might be a Bar-Mitzvah or some kind of Kiddish afterwards.

'Is there a synagogue here?'

'No,' he said looking suspiciously at me.

'Where's the nearest church?'

He gave me directions.

It was a wooden church painted grey in a snow-covered field. There was a narrow path freshly cleared to the door. A few cars and a few trucks were sunk in the snow by it.

As I opened the door a man in an ill-fitting blue suit said.

'Bride or groom?'

I must have looked puzzled. For he said.

'What side are you? Bride or groom?'

'Bride,' I said.

'— to your left.'

I went to the left side and sat down on the wooden bench at the back beside the Quebec stove that had large tin pipes going up and across near the ceiling. I don't know what kind of church it was but it was very plain, very austere. There weren't any religious figures or stained glass windows. About thirty people were separated by a wide aisle. Those on one side looked at those on the other. We all had our coats on. Up ahead, slightly raised, were the bride and groom. And the preacher in a plain grey suit. There was a small wooden organ to the right where a woman was playing.

The wedding ceremony didn't last long.

Afterwards the guests walked in ones and twos along the snow-covered street, icicles hung from the boarded-up houses, down a turning to the main street and to a better hotel. And at the top of the stairs, in the centre of a large room, the bride and groom were sitting, side by side, on chairs against a wall. The guests came up to them, in ones and twos, with their presents.

I stayed near the door. There was food. A buffet. I guess that friends and relations of the bride thought I belonged to the other side. Just as the other side thought I belonged to the bride.

'Where are you from?' a man asked me.

'Out of town,' I said.

I didn't stay long. Long enough to have three ham sandwiches and two cups of coffee.

Then I went back into the street.

For some reason I couldn't find the hotel where I was staying. The town wasn't that large. If you walked five minutes in one direction on the main street that was it. There were several side-streets to the one main — but I kept getting into places that ended in dead ends.

I managed to get back to the main street. The place was now packed with people walking, people shopping. Outside a music store, over a loudspeaker, someone was singing, 'Everyone's Gone to the Moon'.

I felt like a vagrant.

I saw a bit of ice on the road and with a run I went down it. I was hungry and cold. But when I came back to the room my cheeks were rosy.

I lay down on the bed. Because of these last few years I had forgotten how it was to be poor. Now that I was back in it, I was hungry. All that had happened to me since the last book was published seemed some kind of fraud. I was a writer. In my world nothing is certain. I needed this reminder, I told myself.

Now, I must get myself out of it. I tried to remember what I used to do. I went though the pockets — of my suit, my overcoat. Not a cent. In my hard-up days I always left a coin or two in the pockets. What could I sell? There was the copy of my book from which I was going to read at St Vincent's.

I went out again. I couldn't find a bookstore. But I did find a second-hand place that had a lot of junk (mostly furniture) lying inside in heaps all over the place. There were some battered paperbacks on the floor.

A woman finally came.

'Yes.'

'I'd like to sell you this book,' I said.

She picked it up, turned a few pages. I hoped she wouldn't come across the parts I had marked with a pen that I usually read.

She closed the book. 'Fifty cents.'

'It sells for $5.95. And it is almost new.'

'Take it or leave it.'

I took it.

If I had to stay another night I could try and sell her my watch. But she would never give me eight dollars for it — of that I was certain.

With the fifty cents I went out and got myself a hot dog and a cup of coffee. And wondered what I would do tomorrow if I couldn't go back.

Outside it had stopped snowing. I went to the hotel room. I felt hungry and cold and went to sleep.

Sunday morning I slept in. I looked at my watch — ten to nine. I didn't have time to wash or shave. I walked as quickly as I could to the small bus depot. The bus was outside, its engine running. The door was closed. The driver was not inside.

Two men, also unshaven and unwashed, were standing by

the door.

'Is it going?'

'Yes,' they said.

I went into the office and gave the driver the ten dollar bill. He gave me a ticket.

When I came out the two men asked me if I could buy them a cup of coffee as they hadn't had any breakfast and they were broke.

'Sorry,' I said.

I got back to the University town at noon. That evening I was a guest at a dinner party given in the Army Camp, in the Officer's Mess of The Black Watch. There were fourteen of us, some with wives in evening dress. The young officers wore their dress uniforms. We sat in tall straight-backed chairs around the table. The lighting was by candles. We were waited on by two waiters. There was fish and white wine. Roast beef and Yorkshire pudding with red wine. Then champagne with some exotic dessert.

I looked at the others. They were young, attractive, well-fed, well-dressed. How secure they all appeared. And how certain their world.

But outside I could see the snow, the cold, the acres of emptiness that lay frozen all around.

# Grace & Faigel

In October I was on my way to Ottawa to give a reading at Ottawa U. But when the taxi brought me to Montreal's Central Station I realized something had gone wrong with my watch during the Atlantic flight for I arrived forty minutes early. There was nothing to do but wait. I didn't mind that. There were these small purple-blue lights, and soft music being played, and plenty of room. In the soft light the men and women walking by were well-dressed. They wore bright clothes. They looked carefree. It was very pleasant just to sit, to look and listen. Or to walk along the marble floor. The signs, by the news stand and cafeteria, were in French and English. The public telephones were of the kind that you touched the numbers, no dialling. And when you touched a number, it gave off a delicate plaintive note. It was so different from the run-down English stations I had left behind.

Then on the train, sitting in a soft seat, by the window, looking at the trees. With the sun on them they looked like coloured smoke. How smooth the train moved. How comfortable, I thought. How clean. What luxury.

I am forty-nine. And since I was twenty-five I have been living away from Canada in England. It was in England that I met my wife, had our children, watched them grow up. But every so often I leave wife and children and make these visits to Canada.

In England we live an isolated life. The apathy of a seaside town in Cornwall, out of season, is hard to believe unless you have ever lived in it. So these trips to Canada. They shake up the system. I always come back to England wanting to do things. And for the first two weeks I do phone London, send cables, write letters. But then the life that we live in Cornwall takes over. I begin to feel cut-off. And soon it is as if I have never been away.

I looked at the young woman on the seat across the aisle. She was reading a paperback with a large *L* on the cover. She had a small boy, of about eight, opposite her. He was half-sitting on the seat and standing up. He began to recite, in a rush: 'A Cub Scout always does his best thinks of others before himself and does a good turn every day I promise that I will do my best —'

He stopped. His eyes looked upward. Then he repeated the words just as fast. And stopped in the same place. The woman said something to him. The boy said quickly. 'To do my duty to God to the Queen help other people and keep the Cub Scout law.'

He laughed. And pushed himself back onto the seat, his feet dangling.

She stood up and, from a small travelling bag in the rack above her, took out a book, a pencil, and some pieces of paper. And gave them to the boy.

She was tall, on the thin side. She had blonde short hair close to her face and two wisps curled upwards beneath her ears. She wore a tight green sweater and a Scotch plaid skirt with a large safety pin on its side. She sat down and went back to her book. As she read her mouth twisted into a frown.

I saw that the paperback was Doris Lessing's *The Story of a Non-Marrying Man*.

She caught me staring. She smiled. And her face changed. She looked beautiful.

'Do you like the book?'

'Yes,' she said.

'I met Doris Lessing,' I said. 'She wanted us to have her house one Christmas and New Year because she was going to be away in Scotland. Who else do you like?'

'Graham Greene,' she said.

'Have you read Henry Green?'

'No. What has he written?'

'*Living. Loving. Caught. Back. Concluding.* I hadn't heard of him either until I went to England.'

'Do you live there?'

'Yes,' I said. 'I was in London yesterday.'

'How was London?' And she smiled again. Her face looked radiant.

'It was raining when I left,' I said. 'What's his name?'

'Justin,' she said.

The next thing I knew I left my seat and came over and sat beside her. Justin's large brown eyes stared at me.

'Do you want to see a trick?'

I took his pencil and held it in the middle by my thumb and first finger, and slowly began to move my hand up and down. The pencil appeared to be bending.

'It's in here,' Justin said. And opened his book, turned a few pages, and there it was illustrated.

'He's advanced for his age,' she said.

'You know any other tricks?' Justin asked.

I stared into space. Then I put my two hands together, fingers apart. I slid the middle finger between the opposite fingers, turned one hand right over, and wiggled the two middle fingers, that stuck out, on opposite sides.

She was laughing.

Justin said. 'What do you call *that*?'

'Milking the cow,' I said. 'Why don't you go over to my seat and see if you can see any animals from the window. I'll give you a cent for every cow that you see, two cents for every horse, twenty-five cents for every goat. And a dollar if you see an elephant or a lion.'

'Boy,' he said. And took his pencil and papers and went eagerly to the window on the other side.

I looked at the large safety pin on her tartan skirt.

'I think,' she said, 'it's the weight of the pin that keeps it down. I don't usually talk to people on a train. Not for long. But you have an interesting face. What do you do?'

I said I was a writer.

'Can you tell me your name?'

I told her.

'I'm sorry,' she said. 'I have not heard of you.'

'No reason why you should,' I said. 'What's your name?'

'Grace.'

'What do you do?'

'That's my trouble,' she said. 'I don't do anything well.'

This time I smiled. 'The only other woman who said that to me turned out to have a very strong character.'

'Oh, I'm a bitch,' she said. 'I know it. I'm selfish. I'm difficult to live with. I lived for a year in England. I used to knock around with the jet set in Knightsbridge. They were a bunch of layabouts just preening themselves. I worked in Selfridge's.'

'How old are you?'

'Twenty-nine,' she said. 'I'll soon be thirty. Are you married?'

I said I was.

'Is your wife in England?'

'Yes.'

'I'm getting a divorce,' she said.

We were coming towards Ottawa. I called to Justin. 'How many animals did you see?'

He came over, adding up pencil marks. 'Ten cows,' he said slowly. '*And* six horses.'

I gave him a dollar.

'Wow,' he said to his mother. 'I've now got a dollar and a quarter.'

He carefully folded the dollar and put it into the back pocket of his jeans. Then went back to the window on the opposite side.

'Besides England,' she said, 'I've been to South and Central America.'

'I've only been to England and Canada,' I said. 'Wasn't it a lucky accident for us to meet?'

'I don't think these things are *accidents*,' she said. 'I think we were intended to meet. We have good vibrations,' she said quietly.

'I'm coming here to give a reading — on Tuesday night,' I said. 'I'll be staying with my mother while in Ottawa. Let's meet tomorrow.'

'All right.'

'How about in the morning? In the lobby of the Chateau Laurier. Ten o'clock. Is that too early?'

'I'll be there,' she said. 'I'm here for the weekend to see my parents. It's a kind of duty. They live just out of Ottawa. The last time I saw them was in August.'

She took a piece of Justin's paper and, in pencil, wrote her parents' phone number then her address and phone number in Toronto.

We were coming towards the new Union Station. I took her case. We got out of the train and walked into the clean, all-glass station. It was quite empty.

'Anyone meeting you?'

'No,' she said. 'I'll have to phone my father at the office. He'll come and get me.'

'I'll take a taxi outside. Will you be all right?'

'Yes,' she said and smiled. 'I'll see you tomorrow.'

The taxi went down Rideau to Cobourg and stopped by the small park with the gazebo, the poplars, the maples, and the yellow dead leaves on the grass.

When my mother opened the apartment door I kissed her on the cheek.

'I expected you yesterday,' she said. 'You look tired. Why didn't you phone when you got to Montreal?'

'The plane was late,' I said. 'There were no trains. I had to spend the night in a hotel.'

'Which one?'

'You wouldn't have heard of it,' I said. 'The big ones were full. The room I was in had no heating. I was so cold I couldn't sleep. I put on a heavy sweater, socks, and my coat on the bed, and I was still cold.'

'I have something that will warm you up,' she said.

And brought out a third-full bottle of brandy from her fridge. She keeps everything she can in the fridge. And what she can't she pushes in the cupboards. There were so many tins, jars, bottles, and plastic bags filled with food — it was like a siege.

She poured herself a bit of brandy.

'To life,' she said.

The brandy was cold.

'It will soon warm you up,' she said. '*Watch.*'

'I'm not cold now.'

'How is everyone?' she asked.

'I'll tell you later. How are you?'

'I've got high blood pressure. I've got to take pills every day. But why do we have to talk about unpleasant things?'

Above her head, on the wall, was a photograph of how I looked when I was twenty.

I brought out presents from my bags — English honey, English marmalade, packs of tea — and gave them to her.

'You shouldn't have bothered,' she said. 'Come and sit down and have something to eat.'

'How is Esther?'

'Fine. She rings me every morning at eight to see if I'm still alive. There was an old lady here. She was dead four days before they found her. Since then Esther rings in the morning, after lunch, and at night. Anyway, I've got good neighbours. Mr and Mrs Budnoff — they are on one side. And someone from the Gatineau — on the other. I don't know him. In front there's Mrs Nadolny — We all wear the same suits.'

It was only then I realized that she was talking about the cemetery on Metcalfe Road.

She returned from the kitchen with a large banana. 'I've bought some bananas for you,' she said. 'If you have two or three a week — it's good for the heart and protects you from high blood pressure.'

That night I couldn't sleep — and my mother's apartment was warm. Perhaps it was jet lag. But I kept looking in the

dark, at the electric digits telling the time in the bedside radio
. . . watching the minutes, the hours, change . . . and thinking
of Grace.

Next morning I was in the lobby of the Chateau Laurier ten
minutes early. She didn't come through the doors until twenty
past ten.

'What an early hour.' She was out of breath. 'My mother
drove in.'

'I nearly gave you up.'

'I left word at home in case you telephoned.'

She had on the same clothes as yesterday but wore, on top, a
handknitted woollen jacket. She looked cold.

'Let's go,' I said, 'and have some good hot coffee.'

We crossed the War Memorial (I saw them putting this up, I
told her) and walked down to the Lord Elgin and into
Murray's. We sat at a table by a window and had coffee. Outside it looked cold, blustery, deserted.

'When I was seventeen,' I said, 'I saw the Lord Elgin being
built. I worked in a government building across the road. The
Department of National Defence. It's not there anymore.'

'I didn't come to Ottawa until I was five,' she said. 'I don't
like the place. It depresses me. I went around with the cocktail
crowd at Rockcliffe. They liked me because I was pretty. I
became a revolutionary at university. I met my husband there.
He was a Che Guevara character. He wore a black beret and a
black leather jacket. I was gun-running in South America.
Some of my friends who were caught were tortured.'

'What do you do now?'

'I work in a lawyer's office and go to school at night to learn
Greek.' She smiled. 'I'm learning Greek because of my Greek
workman. But it's so difficult. I'm seriously thinking of marry-
ing him.'

She must have seen an expression in my face for she quickly
said, 'He's not a workman. He's an architect.'

As if that made any difference.

I lit an Old Port cigarillo, drank some coffee, and remained
silent.

'Will you come back to live in Canada?'

'I hope to — in the Spring,' I said. 'I have to go back to England and sort things out.'

'You don't talk about your wife.'

What could I say. 'She's pretty,' I said.

'Is she English?'

'Yes.'

'You're the first Canadian I have liked,' she said. 'All the others have been Europeans. You must meet my friends in Toronto. George and Isabel. They've been very good to me. George was my lover for a while.'

'While he was still with Isabel?'

'Yes.'

'Lucky George,' I said.

'Yes,' she said. 'Lucky George.'

'Do you like sex?'

'I like the power it gives me over a man,' she said.

We came out of Murray's, arm in arm, and went across to the National Gallery. It was enclosed in scaffolding. All the rooms were closed except for a small Matisse exhibition of drawings by the stairs. The best paintings were the picture post-cards on sale downstairs. I got her a Francis Bacon *Pope*. She didn't like it. She preferred Lawren Harris's *Side Street* of old houses in winter.

From there we walked up to the mall.

She was shivering.

'I didn't bring enough warm clothes. I don't like the cold. I have bad circulation.'

She saw Fisher's. She wanted a Scout cap for Justin and she was told she could get it there.

I remembered Fisher's. When I started university I bought a black winter coat from them. But they were on the other side of the street. I'm sure they were —

After she paid I asked the young man who served her. 'Wasn't Fisher's on the other side?'

'That's the old store,' he said, 'before my time.'

We came out.

'Hungry?'

'Yes.'

'Where shall we go?'

'You choose.'

'Let's go to Albert Street,' I said. 'There used to be a couple of Chinese restaurants.'

We went into the first one. We were the only customers. We had soup to warm us up. Then sweet and sour.

'You're under-nourished,' I told her.

'I don't like eating by myself,' she said. 'I've been living an isolated life these last few years in Toronto.'

Halfway through the tea and cookies I leaned over the table and kissed her.

'That's the second time I've been kissed this visit,' she said. 'My father had some people in last night for a drink. And this friend of my father's said. "Are you Grace? How you've grown." And kissed me.'

'Can you come to Montreal next weekend?'

'I'll see if I can. I have a friend in Montreal. I could come and stay with her. But I've got to think of the money.'

By the time we came out of the Chinese restaurant it was twenty past four. The light was fading and it was colder. We walked along the empty street towards a bus stop. The wind lifted loose papers about.

'Do you like Stephane Grappelli,' she said, 'and Django Reinhardt?'

'Yes. I have their record,' I said. I didn't say it was a present from our eldest daughter for our twentieth wedding anniversary. 'Le Jazz Hot —'

'They've made a lot of records,' she said. 'Do you like Alan Stivell?'

'The Celtic Harp. Yes, I have the record.' Again I didn't say it belonged to our youngest daughter.

We walked about twenty yards along Queen Street.

'I can take a bus from here,' she said.

I put my hand in my raincoat pocket and saw that my mother had put in a bus ticket.

'Here,' I said.

'You are prepared for anything.'

'When will I see you again?'

'Tomorrow, I have to be with the family. And I'm going away early on Monday morning —'

'I'll ring you sometime tomorrow,' I said.

She was shivering. I put both arms inside her woollen jacket and drew her closer. We kissed.

'What would people in Ottawa say if they saw you behaving this way in the street?'

'I couldn't care less. Are you still cold?'

'Not now,' she said. 'I'll see if I can arrange things for Montreal.'

Then the bus came. We kissed, awkwardly, goodbye. But I was singing as I walked back to my mother's place.

Next morning, just after breakfast, I phoned her.

'I was going to ring you tonight,' she said quietly.

'Can you come to Montreal?'

'I can't talk freely,' she said, 'the telephone is where my parents can hear every word.'

'I'm the same way,' I said. 'I have taken the phone into the bedroom — but I have to sit on the floor to talk.'

'I won't be coming to Montreal,' she said.

'In that case I can fly to England from Toronto,' I said. 'I'll come to Toronto —'

'But I'm working during the day and going to school at night. I don't think you're thinking clearly. You are living a very isolated life while you are over here. I told you that I'm considering getting married again —'

I didn't say anything.

'Ring me before you fly,' she said. 'And I'll write to you in England. And when you come back I'll see you.'

Later, I thought how silly. But for two days I felt excited and happy. As though I was experiencing something I thought I had lost.

My mother finished another long telephone conversation. 'That was Mr Laroque,' she said. 'He does memorial stones. He phones me every few months and asks: anyone sick — anyone dying? Everybody here is trying to make a living. Have something to warm you up. The lecture isn't until tonight and you're already nervous.'

She brought a bottle of Bristol Cream from the fridge and gave me a glass full.

The reading went all right. Though at the start I was blinded by the lights and my mouth and lips became dry.

When it was over around twenty people — mostly students — came down from their seats and asked me to sign copies of my books.

As I was getting near the end I noticed a plump middle-aged woman, in a brown cloth coat, with glasses and grey hair, standing about ten feet away, and staring. A grey-haired man was beside her. The woman's lips were pressed tight. She didn't move, just stared. Then she said.

'Don't you remember me?'

I thought — I have never seen this woman before.

She said a name. It didn't bring back anything.

I felt awkward. 'I'm sorry,' I said.

Behind her was a small thin woman. The first thing I noticed was her eyes — large dark eyes set in a white face. Then how smart she dressed. She had on a new camel-haired coat with black leather boots. And there was a nervous vitality about her. Although her shape belonged to that of a young girl — she was clearly in her late twenties or early thirties. She had high cheek-bones, a wide mouth, very good teeth. And dark red hair cut close to her head.

As soon as the grey-haired woman and her husband walked away, the small woman with the large eyes came up and said.

'I'm Faigel Shore. I enjoyed this evening very much.'

She spoke with an accent which I couldn't place.

'It's nice of you to say that,' I said.

'I've heard other writers come here and talk,' she said. 'They say how wonderful their work is. But you sounded different. Honest.'

'Aren't you?'

'No,' she said. 'I tell lies.'

'But why?'

'It makes life much more interesting.'

The engineer was turning off the lights. Everyone else had gone.

'Why don't we go and have some coffee,' Faigel said.

'All right. But I can't stay long. I'm expected at a party a professor is giving for me.'

As we were walking through the leafy streets of Sandy Hill, I told Faigel that I knew these streets, that they were part of my childhood.

'But your parents come from Poland?'

'Yes,' I said.

'Then we have a lot in common,' she said. 'I was three when I left Poland after the war. My mother and father fought with the Polish resistance. We all went to Australia then to England before coming to Canada. I went to school in England. We lived there six years — in London — just off the Fulham Road.'

'I know where it is,' I said.

'You know what I miss — from England?'

'No,' I said.

'Kippers. I liked eating them raw — with juice squeezed from a lemon and pepper on top. And with brown bread. It tastes like smoked salmon.'

'I thought I was the only one who did that,' I said.

She put her arm through mine.

'We have a lot in common,' she said.

I expected that we would have coffee in a restaurant on Rideau Street. But she crossed Rideau and began to walk into Lower Town. She stopped in front of a run-down wooden house which was divided into two apartments.

'This is where I live.'

It looked shabby on the outside. The grey wooden steps and grey verandah, with wet fallen leaves, needed repairing and painting. Inside was worse. The wallpaper was peeling, the curtains were old and torn. There were books, magazines, paperbacks, all over the place. Things were in cardboard boxes.

'It's a mess, isn't it?' she said. 'But I can't throw anything away.'

She pushed aside unwashed dishes in the kitchen and put some coffee on a small electric stove. The light was a bare bulb hanging from a wire from the ceiling.

'Come, sit down here,' she said.

It was her bed — a mattress, on the floor, with a patchwork cover full of colour, made-up of small snowflake shapes. Beside it were boxes of matches, burnt-out matches, saucers for ashtrays, candles, and loose change scattered on the bare floor. How it brought back those early years in England after the war. And people I once knew with little money.

Faigel took off her camel-haired coat — she had on a smart black suit — then her leather black boots. And went around in her stocking feet.

When she goes out, I thought, she takes such care to look nice and neat but she lives in such disorder.

'Clothes are very important,' she said as if guessing my thoughts. 'They tell a lot about a person. When I'm depressed — I go and buy something new to wear.'

'Where's your husband?'

'He works all week at a mining camp north of here. I work in a library. We live quite separate lives during the week. He has his women friends. I have my men friends. But he comes home for weekends. We spend our weekends together. I like my husband very much. I can't find any milk or sugar —'

'I have coffee black.'

'Good. So do I.'

She brought the coffee in two cups without handles and lit a cigarette and one for me. She sat, opposite, on the bed, her legs crossed underneath her.

'You write so beautifully,' she said. 'But if I may make one criticism — you never tell enough. Especially with sex. You say people go to bed. Then it's done. I want to know details.'

That would be telling about my wife, I thought. 'I don't know why I don't describe details,' I said.

'You belong to the nineteenth century,' she said. 'What films do you like?'

'Antonioni,' I said, 'and Ray.'

'Have you not seen Jules et Jim?'

'No.'

'You must. What about books. What do you re-read?'

'Turgenev,' I said. 'And you.'

'Proust,' she said. 'I also shop-lift, about once a month. I've taken cocaine. I've slept with my husband and with another woman in the same bed. I'm just going to change into something more comfortable.'

What is she telling me this for, I wondered. Is this the way the younger generation get to know one another? Instant intimacy.

She came back wearing a silk blue blouse with black buttons in front — the top three she left undone. And I could see a lace see-through bra.

'I'm not on the pill,' she said. 'I tried it. But I put on weight.'

'Then what do you do?'

'I'm very cautious,' she said.

*Cautious*, I thought. Shop-lifting, cocaine, three in a bed.

We kissed.

'Do you like large breasts?'

'Yes,' I said. 'But most of the women I have known had small. What are you, 36?'

'No, 34.'

I moistened a finger and ran it lightly over her lips — it was part of my wife's pre-love making.

But Faigel said. 'Are my lips dry? I don't wear lipstick.'

'They are not dry,' I said . . .

'Stop it,' she said. 'You are working me up. We have gone too far already.'

She sat up on the bed and lit another cigarette. 'You haven't told me about your wife.'

I now knew what she meant when she said she had 'men friends'. I had a feeling that when this point was reached — the others told Faigel about their wives. But what was I going to tell her?

'She's attractive,' I said. 'Intelligent.'

'I expected her to be that,' Faigel said. 'What else?'

'She's not well,' I said. 'She had a lump in a breast removed

— about nine months ago. But why should this interest you?'

'I'm *very* interested,' she said. 'My mother died from cancer. I go for check-ups every six months. Does it affect sex?'

I hesitated. 'Yes.'

And to change the subject I said. 'Do you like Stephane Grappelli and Django Reinhardt?

'I don't like jazz,' Faigel said. She looked at her wrist-watch. 'I think you had better go. I have to get up early.'

She left the bed and walked across the room to a cluttered table. It wasn't only the neatness in her dress, the care she took with her appearance, that stood out. But also the style with which she moved in these shabby rooms.

She came back carrying a small diary-like book. 'I can't see you tomorrow,' she said looking in the book. 'I have an appointment tomorrow. It was made a long time ago . . . And my husband flies in on Friday night . . . How about next week on Tuesday? I can see you on Tuesday. Let's have an appointment for Tuesday.'

'I don't like appointments,' I said quietly.

She took no notice. She wrote in the book and said. 'We'll come together on Tuesday. I look forward to that.'

And I left her.

When I came out, to my surprise, I saw that the clock in the Peace Tower said it was almost half-past one in the morning. In any case I had forgotten the address of the professor's house.

For the next three days I enjoyed myself. After living cut off from people — I felt as if I was suddenly thrown into life again. I didn't think anything of going a hundred and twenty-five miles to Montreal for dinner with a film director who was interested in one of my stories and coming back later to Ottawa that night. And I like the Fall — the colours, the trees, the fallen leaves, and the thin veneer of comfort that modern machinery and money give.

My publisher arranged for me to give another reading next week. But on Saturday morning I received a cable from England — sent by our neighbour — to say that my wife was not well, could I come back. The earliest flight I could get on was Sunday.

I didn't phone Grace. But I did try to phone Faigel. I tried several times, even from the airport. But I guess she didn't answer the phone when her husband was home. Or perhaps they had gone away for the weekend.

My wife was in bed when I returned. After three days she was able to get up. But Canada had a mail strike. The mail strike went on for six weeks. And by the time it was over there didn't seem to be any point in writing to either Grace or Faigel. What was there to say.

I remember the Merchant Navy man who joined the train at Truro. He was going to Glasgow. He had just left his ship at Falmouth. His wife didn't know he was coming back today. He hadn't seen her for three months.

'I have her picture on my cabin wall,' he said. 'For the first few days of the voyage she's nice and big. But as the weeks go by — she gets smaller and smaller . . .'

Perhaps, I thought, even when we are with people it's a kind of pretence. Nothing really matters.

But I still want to get us out of here and back to Canada. And it's not so long now to Spring.

# Champagne Barn

I didn't notice the birds until I saw them flying. Red-winged blackbirds. A flutter of black. Then a flash of red on the black. Lovely to see. I'd follow a bird as it came level with the window, then watch it go quickly back and disappear from sight. Then I'd look ahead to pick up the next flutter of black, then the flash of red on the black. And follow that for as long as I could.

I was on a train from Montreal to Ottawa. It was early June.

On the second day in Ottawa the local CBC people came to interview me in the small park opposite to where my mother lives. I was sitting on a park bench talking to the camera.

'That new building. Across the road. It's for Senior Citizens. But when I was a kid it was the terminus of an Ottawa streetcar line called Champagne Barn —'

When a thin old woman came up. She walked right into the film and said to me. 'Aren't you Mrs Snipper's boy?'

'Yes,' I said.

'You look like your mother. I'm a near neighbour of hers in the Senior Citizen building.'

Then she noticed the camera on the tripod, the cameraman

behind it, the sound recordist.

'Who are these people?'

'From television.'

'Have they come to take a picture of our building?'

'No.'

'What are they doing?'

'Interviewing me.'

'*You*. What for?'

'I'm a writer.'

She didn't say anything after that. Just had a good look and walked away.

When the interview was over I went across the road, through the glass doors of the Senior Citizen building, to the elevator. Mr Tessier was also waiting. As we were going up he said, 'I've seen a lot of people die here since I first come five years ago.'

'How many?'

'Sixty-eight,' he said.

I got off at the second floor, where my mother had her apartment, and Mr Tessier went up to his on the third.

'How did it go?' my mother said soon as I came in.

'All right. Except a thin, tall lady came up in the middle of the interview and began talking to me. She said she was a neighbour of yours.'

'That's Mrs Sobcuff. She has to know what's going on. Come, sit down and eat.'

I went to wash my hands in the bathroom.

'I can't eat all that fish.'

'It's delicious,' my mother said.

'But I can't eat two pieces.'

'Try.'

I began to eat a piece of fish with a sliced tomato and sliced cucumber.

'Eat with bread,' she said.

'I'm trying to watch my weight.'

'You're not fat.'

I finished one piece. And began the other.

'Why don't you eat?'

'I had something earlier,' she said. 'I eat a little bit but every two hours.'

And to prove her point she came back with a piece of hot chicken on a plate.

She ate quickly.

'Slow down,' I said.

The phone rang.

She had it beside her on the table.

'We're in the middle of eating,' I said. 'Let it ring.'

'No,' she said. 'Hullo. Yes. Hullo, how are you?'

She walked with the phone into the next room, her bedroom. And I could hear her say: 'Did you go to Rideau Bakery? Did you get bread? What did you get? Rye. Was it sliced?'

She talked like that for twenty minutes while everything got cold.

When she came back she said, 'Without the telephone I don't know how I would go through the day. It takes up three or four hours. That was Esther. She would like to take you out for a meal. She'll pick you up at six.'

'How is Esther?'

'Her health isn't very good. But she phones me every day.'

It had been hot and sticky. A few minutes before six I went down to the entrance of the Senior Citizen building to wait for Esther. And a sudden summer storm. The wind increased. The poplars began to sway and rustle. The sky got darker. And the rain came slanting across the park.

When Esther drove up I ran to get in beside her.

'We need this rain,' she said. 'I know a good place in Eastview. The food is excellent. It's French.'

Esther's my spinster cousin. In her late forties. Around five foot eight and a hundred and fifty pounds. Large, dark eyes, black hair, heavy bones. Her nicest feature is her eyes. She was made a fuss of as a child, as she was the youngest. Then, when she was twelve, her brother Hank was born. And the fuss was all about Hank. Esther worked in the office of my uncle's wholesale fruit and vegetable business in the market. She did the accounts, saw that the drivers had the right load to deliver, checked the money when they cashed in at night.

I liked going to the market and to Uncle's store. It was always a bit dark when I walked in. But there was the immediate smell of rotten fruit and crates lying all over the wooden floor. Hank would throw me apples and oranges until my pockets were full. Esther would give me a hand of large bananas to take back. And, when no one was looking, Uncle would slip me a dollar and say: 'Go and see a movie.'

Uncle died while I was away in England in the war. And two years ago Hank died from cancer. Then Esther sold the business.

'How are things?' I asked her.

'I wish I could have a rain check,' she said. 'I sure would live it differently. I had to go to a doctor for an examination. He said it was the first time he had seen an intact hymen in someone of my age.'

This was the first time Esther had talked to me like this. I guess I was too young before.

'Things have changed,' she said, 'since the business was sold. I don't get up early any more. I go to the library. I take out books. But I can't remember what I read. In the evenings I stay up. I've got some Bristol Cream. I drink that and watch television. I get so involved with what's on. I talk back to it. Throw things at it —'

The rain stopped as we drove into Eastview. The sky got lighter. The grass, the trees, the painted wooden houses, looked full of colour. She parked the car by a small wooden hotel.

The restaurant was on the ground floor. There were round tables with white table-cloths. The two waiters wore some kind of theatrical soldier's uniform. We both ordered steak and mashed potatoes and vegetables.

It arrived covered in gravy.

She tasted hers.

'It's cold,' she said. *'Waiter.'*

I tried mine. It wasn't cold.

A waiter finally came to the table. 'The meat is cold,' Esther said. 'The potatoes are cold. I would like it changed.'

He took our plates away without saying a word.

'Why shouldn't I tell them to take it back?' she said angrily. 'We used to sit like dummies before. Not any more. If you keep quiet and don't make a fuss — you go under.'

After what seemed a while the waiter returned with both plates.

She tasted her steak.

'It's better now,' she said quietly.

I tasted mine. It was just the same.

'Yes,' I said. 'Much better.'


Esther drove me back to the Senior Citizen building. When I came in mother was reading *The Journal*.

'How did it go?'

'Fine,' I said.

'Did you have a good time?'

'Yes.'

'What did you have?'

'Steak, potatoes, and vegetables.'

'Esther will be home now,' she said. 'Why don't you give her a ring and tell her you had a good time.'

'But I just saw her.'

'It won't hurt to ring her up and talk to her.'

'But I only left her fifteen minutes ago. And I was with her a couple of hours before that.'

My mother picked up the receiver and dialled.

'Hullo, Esther. Yes, he said he enjoyed himself very much. Thank you. It's very good of you. All right. We'll talk again tomorrow.'

She hung up.

'The important thing,' she said, 'is for people to think well of you. So they will have good memories of you.'

'They don't remember for very long,' I said.

And to change the subject I asked her. 'Where are my things? Where's the officer's uniform?'

'I gave them away when I moved into here,' she said. 'What's the use of carrying all those things along.'

'I wish you hadn't given away the uniform.'

'But you weren't here,' she said.

The phone went.

'Hullo, Sonia. Yes, he looks fine —'

This time she was on the phone for over half an hour. When she came back she said, 'That was Sonia. I'll be going with her to Toronto for a wedding. Then we'll come back through Montreal. I'll be away about five days. Why don't you move in here instead of staying at the hotel? Why spend all that money just to sleep? You have everything you want. And it's quiet. Here are the keys.'

That's how I came to be living in a Senior Citizen place in Ottawa. I was thirty-eight. Everyone else was over sixty-five. Most were in their seventies and eighties.

Next morning I rang up Harvey Reinhardt.

'Have you had breakfast?'

'No,' I said.

'Let's have breakfast. I'll pick you up in half an hour. OK?'

'That'll be eleven-thirty.'

'Yeh. I'll pick you up and we'll go to Nate's and have breakfast. OK?'

'OK,' I said.

Harvey Reinhardt is the only one left in Ottawa from the old Lower Town gang. Just before eleven-thirty I went down to wait outside the front glass doors. Mr Tessier was also standing there. His shirt sleeves rolled up.

'It's going to be a hot day,' Mr Tessier said. 'It's almost eighty now.'

We looked at the small park opposite, at the still trees, the grass. It was very quiet.

'I played in this park when I was a kid,' I said.

'When I was a kid,' Mr Tessier said, 'it was a cemetery. When they widened the road they dug up skeletons.'

Harvey Reinhardt drove up in a large olive-green car sending a wake of dust behind him.

'When did you get in?'

'A few days ago.'

'You look the same,' he said.

So did he. His straight black hair had thinned. But the stockiness, the grin, were the same.

'How long is it since you were here?'

'Five years,' I said.

'Before we go to Nate's,' he said, 'I want to stop for a minute in Murray Street.'

He drove by Anglesea Square — where Harvey and I used to play touch rugby — by the Bishop's Palace, Brébeuf School, and into Murray Street. One side of the street had all the houses knocked down. The other side still had the houses I knew when we both lived here. But the doors and windows were boarded up. Sparrows flew in and out from the roofs. Harvey's old house had become a store with a plate glass window and REINHARDT FOODS painted on it.

'Are you still in the butcher business?'

'No,' he said. 'I let my brother Albie have it. I set it up for him. He pays me two hundred dollars a week. I realized early on that there was more money to be made out of the by-products than in meat. For a while I made smoked meat, salami, hot dogs — then I got bored with it. I'm in hides. I'll take you out there later.'

And he grinned.

'I'm the biggest hide man in eastern Canada.'

I followed Harvey into Reinhardt Foods. The room was arranged as a supermarket selling only meat and poultry. The brother was not around so Harvey took me into the back. There was a room with carcasses hanging on hooks. Another room had meat in large vats soaking in brine. Sawdust on the floor. But the only activity was coming from another room. Beside thick wooden tables five men were energetically hacking away at hunks of meat. Separating the meat from the bone. They didn't look at us all the time we were there. They just went on attacking the meat.

Back in the supermarket Harvey's brother appeared.

'When did you get back?'

'A few days ago.'

'Staying at the Chateau?'

'No, in a Senior Citizen place.'

He looked puzzled.

'It's where my mother lives. But she's gone for a few days to Toronto.'

He gave Harvey a cheque. As we were going out he said, very proudly, to me, 'We supply the Prime Minister with food. We've got two smoked turkeys in the back. You know the address on Sussex Drive? Go and take a look.'

'I believe you,' I said.

From there we went into Nate's on Rideau Street. It was much cooler inside than in the street. Harvey ordered large plates full of smoked meat, chips, pickles, and rye bread.

'Not bad, uh?' Harvey said eating a forkful of smoked meat.

'Delicious,' I said.

'They get it from us,' he said. 'I never thought you would be a writer. Christ, I thought Gunner would be a writer — not you.'

'How is Gunner?'

'He's a professor at some university. He comes back every winter and we go skiing. We still go to Camp Fortune, Fairy Lake, Ironsides —'

And I remembered the last time I went with them. But that was more than twenty years ago.

'I want my son Henry to go to university,' Harvey said. 'I told him he could learn about literature, art, science, philosophy, economics. But he wants to be a butcher. He likes it all. The blood, the killing, the whole lot. It must be in the blood.'

He brought out two thick cigars, gave me one. And we had second cups of coffee smoking the cigars in the air-conditioned room. A large blown-up photograph of Trudeau was on the wall opposite.

'I'm still a socialist,' Harvey said. 'But you can't be a socialist in a capitalist economy.'

He carefully took out a large wad of bills from his back pocket, paid for our breakfast, then put the money in the back pocket and buttoned it down.

I felt the sticky summer heat as soon as we went out.

'How long are you here for this time?' Harvey asked.

'Just a couple more days.'

'Next time you're here,' he said, 'I'll take you out to see my plant. It's in the country. I built it all myself — the machinery — the conveyor belts — the whole process.'

We got back into his car.

'The government health inspector is after me,' he said mischievously. And grinned. 'I'm a polluter.'

I like Harvey. I like his style.

He drove slowly through the streets of Lower Town. 'Before,' he said, 'the small park, the playground, the streets and houses — all fitted together. Now, they knocked down a lot of wooden houses — left gaps — and put up these high-rises. Suddenly the park is too small. The playground is dwarfed. Nothing seems to fit.'

From Lower Town he drove over the Minto bridges to Rockcliffe and stopped at the lookout. We got out. It was warm and silent. The trees. The grass slopes. A heat haze over the river. Everything here looked so right and in its place.

'I've got a problem,' Harvey said. 'My daughter Clare won't eat. She's a sweet affectionate girl. But if you ask her to eat something — she refuses. If you insist, she gets angry, loses her temper. I don't know how she keeps going. To get her to eat a cracker or a small piece of cheese we have to go through a whole performance — talking and coaxing. And when she finally does have a spoonful of something, I have to behave as if I've just won first prize in a sweepstake . . . We've been butchers for three generations. I love food. And what she's doing is like a personal insult. She told me that she thinks life is pointless. I can understand someone in their thirties or forties or fifties saying that. But a sixteen-year-old girl.'

'When my sister Mona was growing up,' I said, 'she didn't feel like eating either. She kept to her room. She would go and close the door and stay there. Then we tried to get her to come outside. We had this dog kennel in our backyard. And she used to go in that. My mother would leave out some food for her. In front of the kennel. But she didn't touch it. This went on for weeks. Until my mother put a toy blackbird in the grass by the food. Mona began to show some interest in this bird. And from that day she got better. It took a little while, but she began to eat . . . I miss red-winged blackbirds. I don't see them in England.'

'Don't they have blackbirds there?' Harvey asked.

'They have lots,' I said, 'but I haven't seen any with red on their wings.'

We drove for a while in silence. Then Harvey said, 'We ought to spend a few days together. I'll tell you the story of my life. And you can write it. It will be a best-seller. We can go fifty-fifty on it. I'll show this society up for what it really is. I can tell you things. Christ, did you know we were the poorest family in the street? We burned the furniture one winter to keep warm. When the electricity was cut my grandfather got some tallow and made candles, big candles, and we did our homework by this light. Did you know about that?'

'No,' I said.

'And when I started going to high school they gave three things free at the cafeteria: Heinz ketchup, hot water, soda crackers. This combined together made a delicious soup. This was my daily lunch. I'll tell you things that go on in business that you won't believe. Everyone bullshits. *This is the best. That is the best.* It's all bullshit. If you want to get on you either have to screw somebody or charm somebody . . . When the kids were small I advertised for a nanny in England. She gave me the baloney about being an Oxford grad. She came over. She had beautiful manners. She had character. But no money. What's the good of having good manners, talking nicely, if you've got nothing to eat? Christ,' Harvey said, 'why live now in England? That country is on the skids. The last good time they had there was during the war.'

'I'm thinking of coming back here,' I said.

We were now back outside the Senior Citizen building. The heat haze had gone with the afternoon and it felt cooler. Small, pink clouds were in a clear blue sky.

'My mother believed,' Harvey said, 'that there had to be rich people so the poor could live off them. Let me know when you're next in town. Give me a ring. I'll come and get you, show you the plant, and tell you about my life.'

'OK,' I said.

I left Harvey and went into Champagne Barn. It was like going into a quiet residential hotel. I decided to walk up the two flights of stairs to my mother's flat. The carpets in the hall. The copies of *The Citizen, The Journal, Le Droit*, outside the numbered doors. Between the buildings there was a connecting passage with the walls all glass and where some men sat in their shirt-sleeves and played cards. Above their heads, on the wall, were large posters of Betty Grable in a tight sweater and red lips, and another poster of Ann Sheridan.

A woman went by and said, 'Is that all you've got to do, play games?'

Next morning I was sitting by the window looking at the park and thinking (This is what I miss in England — trees. Living, as we do, by the sea and all that stone. It's as if something is missing in the diet. The lack of trees. When I'm with trees I feel better.) when a police car with its flashing light drove up, followed by an ambulance. Men went into the building and came out carrying a woman on a stretcher, an oxygen mask over her face. She looked very grey. She still had her hair in curlers.

Then they drove away.

I went downstairs. I went over to Mr Tessier.

'I was just talking to her,' he said. 'About an hour ago. We were watching them pull down that house. And I said — it sure don't take them long to pull down a house.'

'Have they taken her to hospital?'

'She's dead,' he said.

I went to my mother's flat and made myself a cup of coffee. There were the reminders of the past on the walls and on top of the dresser. I looked through a drawer. And found my logbook from the Air Force. And a pile of unused cards. There were Get Well cards, Deepest Sympathy cards, Happy Birthday cards, Happy Anniversary cards, Speedy Recovery, several said Congratulations on your Success.

Next morning my mother appeared just after six.

'Look what I brought you,' she said.

And excitedly took out pieces of wedding cake and assorted pastry from the reception, as well as salami, smoked meat, smoked salmon, hot dogs, bagel.

'I know you like these things,' she said. 'And what you get in Montreal tastes better than here. *Now* what would you like me to make you for breakfast? Some salami with a couple of eggs?'

'Just coffee,' I said.

'What's wrong? Don't you like this food any more?'

'I do,' I said. 'But I don't want it now.'

After the coffee I thought I would go out. It was my last day here. And mother had started to make cookies for me to take back to England. She's happiest when she's cooking. Sometimes I think the only way she can reach you is through food.

I put on my light summer trousers, a sport shirt, and my favourite light shoes so well worn that the leather was split on top in several places.

'You can't go out like that,' my mother said. 'You've been on television. You've had your picture in the paper. Suppose someone sees you?'

Outside it was like walking in a hothouse. It had just gone seven. I walked by Anglesea Square. The row of poplars was still. But now and then their leaves caught a passing breeze. York and Clarence had all the houses bulldozed to the ground. And all that remained standing were the trees. And a signpost saying *Clarence Street*. Another said *York*.

On St Patrick — Percy the Barber was closed. The door boarded up. But from a window I could see the layers of the years on the walls. Haircuts 10 cents . . . minnows for sale . . . Ken Maynard at the Français . . . pictures of King Clancy . . . Albert Battleship Leduc . . . Howie Morenz . . .

By the river it was quiet. The water hardly moving. The sun was coming through a haze. Trees. White bridges. A silver church steeple on the opposite shore. It was like an Impressionist painting.

Then in Murray Street. The wooden houses, with the wooden verandahs, only on one side. As I came near Reinhardt Foods I began to hear the hacking. Then I saw the men. Their window was open. They were the same five men I saw before. By the thick wooden tables . . . with the knives . . . the choppers . . . attacking the meat from the bone. Hack, hack, hack. While the birds sang. The black squirrels moved quickly and stopped on the grass. And now and again a breeze set the small leaves of the poplars moving. Hack, hack, hack . . . Hack, hack, hack . . .

I would carry that sound with me long after I left.